GLITTERLAND

a spires story

ALEXIS HALL

sourcebooks
casablanca

Copyright © 2016, 2018, 2023 by Alexis Hall
Cover and internal design © 2023 by Sourcebooks
Cover design and Illustration by Elizabeth Turner Stokes

Published by Sourcebooks Casablanca, an imprint of Sourcebooks
P.O. Box 4410, Naperville, Illinois 60567-4410
(630) 961-3900
sourcebooks.com

Originally self-published in 2013 by Alexis Hall.

Cataloging in Publication Data is on file with the Library of Congress.

Printed and bound in the United States of America.
VP 10 9 8 7 6 5 4 3 2 1

To C—it's not the same without you.

FOREWORD

I've always wanted to be able to write a foreword for one of my books because, if nothing else, it implies the book has stuck around for a while. Except here I am, finally getting to write one, and I have no idea what to say.

Glitterland wasn't the first book I wrote but—by a commodius vicus of recirculation—it was the first that got published, which means it seems like the first in retrospect. And now it's nearly ten years old and that's really gratifying and really terrifying at the same time. Not least because it means I'm ten years older than I was when I started writing and I felt pretty old at the time.

Because I relentlessly second-guess myself, I can't quite tell the best tone to strike when talking about an early work. If I imply I've got better since, it suggests the book you've just paid money for isn't as good as another one you could have chosen to purchase. If I imply I haven't, then that suggests I've spent the past decade stagnating creatively. Although actually, I think "better" is a somewhat pointless term when you're talking about art in general (and, God, I find it difficult to refer to my own books as "art"). Ultimately, everything is a combination of contexts. I don't think I could write *Glitterland* today, but I couldn't have written the book I'm currently working on a decade ago and wouldn't be able to write it a decade from now either.

I kind of like that in a way, though. It means every book you write (or, for that matter, read) has its own place in time. I do, however, quietly think of *Glitterland* as the book that taught me how to write (inasmuch as you feel I can write—as always, I'm the person least qualified to judge that). From the absolute basics of how to plan a character arc and use dialogue tags to more up-in-the-air things like "how do you emotions". That last remains the most fascinating to me. One of the complaints often levelled at romance by, well, wankers is that it's a genre where nothing ever happens. And while that's manifestly untrue (romantic suspense is a thing, for a start) it also wouldn't be a bad thing even if it was. There's a power and a challenge and a complexity in both creating and reading stories that are almost entirely grounded in emotional journeys rather than in, say, who done a murder or who can blow up the most space aliens. Not that I don't like (and, indeed read, and occasionally write) murdery-alien-explodey books too. But I think what I found in *Glitterland* was a kind of freedom.

My agent likes to talk about authors having "core stories," which I think is her polite way of reassuring me that I'm not just being repetitive. Looking back, I think you can see a lot of my core stories in *Glitterland*. It's written in deep POV with an unsympathetic protagonist; it explores mental health; it focuses a lot on dialect and the complexities of the British class system; there's prominent cooking and board gaming scenes; and of course people do have a tendency to go on about Barthes. It also has quite an abrupt ending.

As does this foreword.

Alexis Hall

October 2022

Content Guidance

Glitterland includes sexual content, a character with bipolar depression, past hospitalisation due to a suicide attempt, talk of past suicide, suicidal ideation, discussion of self-harm, some self-directed ableist language, attempted on-page drug use, parental neglect, panic attacks, and outing of a character's mental health.

The whole seems to fall into a shape
As if I saw alike my work and self
And all that I was born to be and do,
A twilight-piece.

Robert Browning, "Andrea del Sarto"

We dress classy, we've got the nice handbags, we like our surgery, hair extensions, big eyelashes— we're very glitzy. It's the most important thing in the world, to look glamorous.

Amy Childs

1

NOW

My heart is beating so fast it's going to trip over itself and stop. ☆
Everything is hot and dark. I've been buried alive. I'm already dead.

I have just enough grip on reality to discard these notions, but it
doesn't quell my horror. My mouth is dry, strange and sour, my tongue
as thick as carpet. Alcohol-heavy breath drags itself out of my throat,
the scent of it churning my stomach. I'm pickled in sweat. And there's
an arm across my chest, a leg across my legs. I am manacled in flesh.

god, god, fuck, god, fuck

My body is far too loud. Blood roaring, heart thundering,
breath screaming, stomach raging, head pounding.

I'm going to have a full-blown panic attack.

The first in a long time. Except that's not much consolation.

Where am I? What have I...

out, fuck, have to get out

I twist away from the arm and the leg, rolling off a bare mattress onto bare floorboards. Maybe my first instinct was right. I
am dead and this is hell. The darkness scrapes against my eyes.
Where are the rest of my clothes?

And breathe, I need to breathe more. Or breathe less. Stop the light show in my head. My vision sheets red and black, like a roulette wheel spinning too fast, never stopping.

god, fuck, clothes

Scattered somewhere in the void. Trousers, shirt, waistcoat, jacket, a single sock. My fingers close over my phone. A cool, calming talisman.

Half-dressed, everything else bundled in my arms, I ease open the door, dark spilling into dark and, like Orpheus, I'm looking back. The shadows move across his face, but he doesn't stir. He sleeps the perfect, heedless sleep of children, drunkards, and fools.

My footsteps creak along a narrow hallway of peeling paintwork and I let myself out onto a wholly unfamiliar street.

NEXT

———

Breathe, just keep breathing. Keep breathing, and get away.

I stumbled down the pavement, the awfulness of this—this and everything—hanging off my shoulders like a rucksack full of rocks.

Still no idea where I was. Suburbia spiralling away in all directions. And, at the horizon, a haze of pale light where the distant sea met the distant sky. I fumbled for my phone. 3:41.

god, fuck, god

There was a single blip of battery left. I called Niall. He didn't answer. So I called again. And this time he did. I didn't wait for him to speak.

"I don't know where I am." My voice rang too high even in my own ears.

"Ash?" Niall sounded strange. "What do you mean? Where are you?"

"I just said. I don't know. I... I've been stupid. I need to get home."

I couldn't control my breathing. The most basic of human functions and even that was beyond me.

"Can't you call a cab?"

"Yes...no... I don't know. I don't know. I don't know the number. What if it doesn't come? I don't know." Anxieties were swimming around inside me like jellyfish, but I was usually better at not confessing them aloud.

It hadn't occurred to me to get a taxi, but even the idea of it seemed overwhelming in its magnitude. A quagmire of potential disaster that was utterly terrifying.

"Can you come and get me?" I asked.

Later I would see how pathetic it was, my desperate pleading, the weasel thread of manipulative weakness running through my words. Later, I would remember that calling for a taxi was an everyday event, not an ordeal beyond reckoning. Later, yes, later I would drown in shame and hate myself.

Niall's hollow sigh gusted over the line. "Oh God, Ash, can't you—"

"No, no, I can't. Please, I need to go home."

A pause. Then the inevitable, "Okay, okay, I'm coming. Can you at least find a street sign? Give me some idea where you are?"

Phone clutched in my sweat-slick hand, I ran haphazard along the houses. The curtains were shut as tight as eyes.

"Marlborough Street," I said. "Marlborough Street."

"All right. I'll be there. Just... I'll be there."

☆   I sat down on a wall to wait, irrational panic eventually giving way to a dull pounding weariness. There was a packet of cigarettes in my jacket pocket. I wasn't supposed to have cigarettes, but I was already so fucked that I lit one, grey smoke curling lazily into the grey night.

Don't drink, don't smoke, don't forget to take your medication, don't break your routine. Nobody had ever explicitly said, "Don't have casual sex with strange men in unfamiliar cities," but it was probably covered in the "Don't have any fun ever" clause. The truth was, casual sex was about the only sex I could stand these days. On my own terms, when I could control everything. And myself.

But tonight I'd broken all the rules and I was going to pay the price. I could feel it, the slow beat of water against the crumbling cliffs of my sanity. I was going to crash. I was going to crash so hard and deep it would feel as though there was nothing inside me but despair. The cigarette, at least, might hold it off until I got home.

I lost track of time, my nerves deadened with nicotine and my skin shivering with cold. But, eventually, Niall pulled up, and leaned across the seats to thrust open the passenger door.

"Come on," he said.

He was shirtless and tousled, a pattern of dark red bruise-kisses running from elbow to shoulder.

"I'm sorry." I stamped out my cigarette (how many had I smoked?) and climbed in.

He didn't reply, just shifted gears abruptly and drove off.

I rested my head against the window, watching the streets of Brighton blurring at the corners of my eyes. The motorway, when we came to it, was nothing but a streak of moving darkness.

Niall's fingers were tapping a tense rhythm against the steering wheel. He'd known me since university, back when I was different. We'd been friends, lovers, partners, and now this. Pilgrim and burden.

"I'm sorry," I tried again.

Silence filled up the car, mingling with the darkness.

"You can't keep doing this to me," Niall said, finally. "You're... it's...ruining my life."

"You seem to be doing a pretty good job of ruining your own." I turned away from the window. Touched a piece of shadow on his upper arm that might have been a mark. "I suppose you were with Max."

I'd never meant to hurt to Niall. It had just been inevitable ☆ that I would. In some ways, that only made it worse, as though I'd been careless with something precious. The truth was, sometimes I found it hard to even like him anymore. He'd seen me at my worst, but that only made me feel resentful and ashamed, as if the memories of a thousand mortifications were lurking behind his eyes like a swarm of silver fish.

"So what if I was?" he said.

"He's going to be married."

It had made a certain amount of sense that Niall and I would ☆ get together when they let me out of hospital after my first manic episode. He had made me feel something close to human again, and it had been easy enough for me to confuse gratitude with love. I didn't know what Niall had been looking for. Absolution, perhaps. Of course, he was still in love with Max. He always had been. I was supposed to have been his consolation prize, but I turned out to be a poor bargain.

"He can still change his mind." There was an ironic twist to Niall's mouth as he spoke, but I could tell he half believed it was a possibility.

"He's not going to change his mind. He wants to be with Amy."

"Filthy bisexuals," he muttered. Like all our jokes, it was an old one, and it had stopped being funny a long time ago. If it ever had been.

I tried to smile, but it felt like too much effort and my mouth refused to cooperate. Niall and Max had slept with each other intermittently at university as part of a general culture of everyone sleeping with everyone, but Max's liberality with his cock protected a heart that loved only cautiously.

"You need to stop waiting for him," I said.

"Fuck you."

"Right." There didn't seem much else I could say to that.

"If you love someone, then you fight for them." Niall's eyes were locked on the road.

"Or you let them go before you fuck up their life."

Niall laughed, sharp as knives. "That's *fucking* hilarious coming from you."

I closed my eyes for a moment, searching for the peace of a private darkness.

"You can't get through a night out without phoning me," he said.

I couldn't do this now, but a sour sense of injustice filled the back of my throat like vomit. "I didn't want to come."

"Can't you think about somebody else for half a fucking second? Max wanted you here."

"Ah, yes, Max. Always back to Max." Oh why had I said that? Was it always in me, this instinct towards cruelty? Or was just another thorn of madness. Either way, it was a weapon of the weak. And Niall knew it.

"So when you went completely batshit," he said, conversa- tionally. "And I visited you in the loony bin nearly every day. That was about Max, was it? And when I found you in the hallway unconscious and covered in blood. That was about Max? And all the times you've been too depressed to eat or leave the house and I've come to take care of you. That was about Max?" The needle on the speedometer was trembling. Eighty. Ninety. I didn't think Niall had even noticed. The engine thrummed heavy through the fresh silence.

"Every time I've stopped you hurting yourself. Max. Making sure you didn't get institutionalised again. Max. Picking up your medication for you when you can't. Max. Getting you to counselling. Max."

"God." I sounded as petulant as a child. "If I'm such a horrendous waste of your time, why do you bother?"

Once upon a time he might have said: Because I love you.

Once upon a time he might have said: Because I care about you.

"Because I feel guilty all the fucking time," he snapped. "And because on the last occasion I didn't *bother*, you tried to kill yourself."

The words echoed through my head. I tugged at my cuffs, pulling them down until they hung over the heels of my hand. One of the unadvertised advantages of bespoke tailoring. All my shirts were cut this way.

"That had nothing to do with you," I said quietly.

He didn't answer.

And now there really was nothing left to say.

The night ebbed slowly away, fading into a silver-grey London dawn. The rising sun gleamed dully from behind a sheet of heavy cloud, casting vague-shaped shadows across the sky as aimless as images from a magic lantern.

Niall dropped me off outside my flat and drove away like a man determined not to look back. I let myself inside and climbed the stairs. I'd always found something comforting in repetitive physical action. It provided an anchor point when all other certainties were uncertain. Except now I was sodden with exhaustion, weighed down by my own flesh and at the same time insubstantial, as though I would unravel into mist if I stopped concentrating on being alive.

I carefully fit my key to the lock, turned it, heard it click. Pushed open the door.

Stepped inside. Let the door swing closed behind me. The familiarity of walls.

Normal people didn't sit in their hallways. But I couldn't find the energy to go further. I lay down on the floor, stretched my fingers over the stripped wooden floorboards, rough and smooth, knots and whorls, the occasional deep gash like a scar. I was terrified of thinking. Terrified of memory. I wanted to cry, but I had long ago run out of tears.

In the past, we are drinking tea in my oak-panelled rooms, where the wisteria creeps beneath the arched windows, filling the air with scent.

In the past, Max and Niall are dancing at the centre of a sea of flesh beneath multicoloured lights.

In the past, I walk between green lawns, surrounded by golden stone.

In the past, I am brilliant and I am happy and my every tomorrow is madness.

In the past, words shimmer around me on silver threads and I pluck them like summer peaches.

In the past, the universe is a glitterball I hold in the palm of my hand. I am the axis of the world.

In the past, I am soaring, and falling, and breaking, and lost.

Then there are grey walls all around, a sullen haze of medication where minutes and months lose all their meaning.

Afterwards, I performed the halting ceremony of betterness in a crawl of grey days.

Somehow, I started writing again, laying words out like cutlery. Niall moved in. And then out again.

And now there was this. And yesterday.

2

YESTERDAY

It was Max's stag night, and I'd fully intended to get out of it. Because, when it came to letting my friends down, I had practice. Stratagems developed over year of missed weddings, skipped birthdays, and ducked parties. My usual technique involved accepting invitations with a convincing display of pleasure and gratitude, then demonstrating my commitment to attend by buying tickets, confirming bookings, and pretending to read all the emails (I didn't see this as a waste of time and money, so much as an investment in my future comfort), only to cancel— with great regret—at the very last minute. Everyone always understood. I gave them no other choice.

On this occasion, I'd executed it flawlessly, explaining to Niall by the coward's preferred medium of voice message about half an hour after I should have departed for Brighton that I didn't feel up to going out tonight. It wasn't even a lie. The only thing I'd misrepresented was the likelihood of me feeling up to doing anything ever again.

Unfortunately, Niall knew me too well. He turned up at the

flat, let himself in with the key he still had, and wouldn't take no for an answer. He called it a last hurrah. For who, or what, I wasn't sure. The people we used to be, perhaps.

And that was how, against my wishes and my better judgement, I ended up in Brighton. In a gay bar. At a stag party. Arranged for the groom by his best friend. Who was in love with him. And I thought I knew hell.

It was a Friday night, so the whole place was packed. Dancers had over-spilled the dance floor, their pressed-together bodies pulsating into all the empty spaces of the club, and the LEDs on the ceiling streamed overhead like a million multicoloured stars, falling and dying and shattering in fleeting, stained glass fragments on the bodies below. A twist of electric blue glinted on an upraised wrist. A smear of wild green across a throat. Cracks of pink and purple spilled with a glitter of perspiration down someone's bare chest. Synaesthetic chiaroscuro. An impossible entangling of space and skin, light and shadow.

They were playing the sort of deep, delirious electro-house I hadn't sought out in years. A thumping heartbeat of sex and sound, the drug to unite all drugs, the music of my mania. Even now, watching the grace of strangers from an endless distance, I felt a faint and faraway echo of something like pleasure, as though some long-lost, once-loved visitor was knocking on a door that no longer opened.

"Do I know you?" A voice from beside me broke through the music.

I didn't even turn. "No, I don't think so."

We had the VIP area upstairs, away from the crush, and in

easy reach of the cocktail bar. Niall had assembled us all here for drinks and drunken jokes, but by now, most of the party had dispersed into the crowd like waves lost in the sea. I was standing half in the shadows, my elbows folded on the railing, watching without interest what was happening below. I could just about make out Max and Niall dancing together and, in another corner, a couple of Max's merchant banker friends enthusiastically getting off.

"Are you sure? You look familiar. How do you know Max?"

Hints, it seemed, were not going to be taken any time soon. I cast a quick, grudging glance at my relentless interlocutor. Brown hair, brown eyes, a whimsical bracket to his wide mouth. Good arms. My type, once upon a time. And now? Nothing.

"We were at university together," I said.

"So was I." He sounded genuinely thrilled about it. "Oh, I'm Hugh, by the way, Hugh Hastings."

I performed a sort of half-arsed wave to discourage any handshaking and volunteered nothing further. Conversations were like fires; they tended to sputter out if you deprived them of air.

"Sorry, I didn't catch your name," he said.

"Ash. Winters."

"Wait," he cried, "I do remember! I read your book. What was it called? The smoke and the something?"

He gazed at me expectantly.

"*The Smoke Is Briars*."

"Yes! It was wonderful. I loved it. It was quite weird though, no offence. Is that what they call magic realism? Like that Spanish bloke." Columbian. Gabriel García Márquez—if that's who he meant—was Columbian. "Yes," I said, unable to care. "Just like that."

I felt unspeakably tired, but he was still talking, his interest flattening me like a cartoon steamroller.

"What else have you written? Won the Booker yet? Hah."

"I don't write anymore," I lied.

"Oh, no, really? But you were so talented. You should take it up again."

"I don't think so."

"Why not? It's not often that queer literature finds a mainstream audience. Your team needs you."

"I have nothing to say."

Hugh gave me the familiar blank, bewildered look that told me I'd finally succeeded in putting the conversation out of its misery.

"Want a drink?" he asked.

Alcohol played merry hell with my medication. "God, yes."

He grinned. "Actually, I've got something even better, if you like?"

I raised my eyebrows. "I hope that's not a pickup line."

He blushed. He was my age at least but he seemed centuries younger. "Well, we can if you like. I mean, I'd be up for it. But it's kind of one or the other."

As he opened his palm, I caught the flash of a familiar, chalky-white pill.

"I'll take that," I said.

Maybe he looked disappointed. I didn't give a damn.

"Catch you on the dance floor, then." He slipped me the E and wandered off.

Drugs were even worse for me than alcohol but, in some ways, so much better. What I held between my fingers was a little piece of happiness. Artificial, yes. Fleeting, yes. But then I wasn't sure there was any other kind. And beggars can't be choosers.

I was playing games with myself, putting up a show of resistance, as if I could take it or leave it. But the truth was, whatever the price, I would gladly pay it just to feel...better. Connected. Human. Alive. Anything at all.

A hand closed hard around my wrist.

"What the fuck are you doing?" demanded Niall. "Are you fucking insane?"

He was probably hurting me, but I was too far from myself for it to breach the numbness of my skin. "Well, yes. I have a note from my doctor."

"You can't fucking take drugs. You know what'll happen."

I flicked the tablet from one hand to the other, snatching it from the air before Niall could intercept. His body was behind mine, so it felt almost like it did when he used to hold me, his arms tight around me as if an embrace could make a difference. I half turned my head so I could look up at him.

"It's just this once." My voice was a wavering chord of desperation. "It'll be fine."

"No."

"It's not up to you."

His hand caught my other wrist. "I'm not going to let you hurt yourself."

"That's not up to you either."

But Niall pinned me and twisted my fingers open. For a moment, the little round tablet seemed to cling to my skin, as though it wanted me as much as I wanted it, and then it slipped and fell. It pinged off the railing and bounced away into the writhing crowd. Such a pathetic, bathetic tragedy, it should have been comical. Disappointment drowned me in a grey flood, bitter as ashes and sharp as briars.

Mission accomplished, Niall let me go so abruptly it felt as though he'd detached me from the entire world. I had a brief, intense sensation of falling and clutched for the sweaty brass of the railing.

"You're such a prick," I muttered, but it was the defiance of the defeated.

"So are you," he returned without any particular rancour.

For a moment or two, he stood next to me, resting against the railing. Broken rainbows skittered over the lightly curling hair of his forearms. His attention landed on Max, who was by the bar below us, laughing with one of his friends. His T-shirt clung to him, sweat defining the strong, beautiful planes of his back.

Amy made him happy. It was something Niall should easily have understood, but the heart rejects the lostness of things. And I was grieving, not for my friend, not for the past, but, selfishly, for a piece of fake white happiness. Well, I had to pick my battles. Once you've lost your mind, you're on a non-stop superhighway to dispossession of the self: trust, pride, control, dignity, respect, the right to fuck yourself up when it's the only thing you're capable of needing.

"I'm going to get a drink," I said.

"Ash."

"Are you going to stop me?"

Some scrap of emotion fluttered like a white flag across Niall's face. Then he shook his head.

Ten minutes and half a cocktail later, I was wankered in a completely disorientating, pleasureless way. All the physical effects of being drunk hit me like a train, but it was accompanied only by the escalating sense of foreboding that tends to signal incoming depression. I overpaid for a bottle of water and went slowly back to my railing. The dancers below blurred with the lights; the music seemed only distant noise.

All the counselling in the world couldn't teach me how to think rationally about my episodes, so I feared them. I feared them with a pure and primal instinct, like dreading the dark or flinching from fire. In all these years, this was all I'd learned: Depression simply is. It has no beginning and no end, no boundaries and no world outside itself. It is the first, the last, the only, the alpha and the omega. Memories of better times die upon its desolate shores. Voices drown in its seas. The mind becomes its own prisoner.

I pulled out my phone and checked the time. It was close to midnight, an entirely reasonable hour to slip away and fall apart in the safety of my own home. I leaned over the railing, looking for Niall, only to be arrested by a dazzle of silver through the haze of colour-shifting shadows, bright like clean water. It took me a moment to realise it was the light catching on the epaulettes of a man dancing just below me.

Fuck knew what I was doing staring at someone who thought sparkly epaulettes were any sort of fashion statement but, God help me, I was. Maybe it was the way he was dancing, eyes half closed, a half-smile on his lips, as though he honestly couldn't think of anything better to do in the world than wriggle his hips to music. To be fair, he wriggled them most effectively, showing off the lines of a spare and slender, lightly muscled body.

He was a ridiculous creature. A vulgar, glittering pirate of a man, all jewellery and fake tan, gold glinting in his ears, on his fingers and round his wrists. His dark hair gleamed with product and had been painstakingly teased into a quiff that defied taste, reason, and gravity. And yet I couldn't stop looking at him. It was horrifying but the truth was there, undeniable, like some faint sonic echo deep within my skin, the thin batsqueak of sexuality. I wanted him.

What remained of me these days was a muted thing, a patchwork of broken pieces. My loved ones had all slipped away from me, disappearing into their future happiness, and still I felt nothing. Niall had not been, by any means, my only lover since the institution. But that my hollow flesh should answer the brazen alarum of a man who was practically orange and wearing beneath his jacket a shirt that read "Sexy and I know it," could only have been the sick joke of a universe that despised me.

Suddenly he looked up at me and grinned. An absurd, wide, endless grin filled with artificially white teeth. And I forgot how to breathe. I expected him to go back to dancing, but instead he climbed onto one of the floor speakers beneath my balcony, pulling himself almost up to my eye level, like the world's most ill-suited Romeo in pursuit of the world's least convincing Juliet.

"I gotta say, babes," he said in a nasal Essex whine, "you're giving me sutcha bedroom look."

I stared down into his face, so close to mine. *Babes?* And, dear God, that accent.

"Well," I heard myself answer, "play your cards right and I might consent to do more than look."

"Omigod, you talk like the Queen."

I blinked. "Pardon?"

"Are you in parliament?"

I had the feeling I'd lost control of the conversation. "What? No. I'm a writer."

"Omigod, really?" He sounded both impressed and bewildered, as if I'd said I went fishing on the moon. "What do you write?"

I gave my standard answer. "Books."

He threw back his head and laughed, as if I'd been genuinely funny. "You donut. What's your name?"

"A.A. Winters."

"What, that's your name?"

"Yes," I said impatiently, "that's my name."

"That's what people call you?"

"Yes?"

"Like in bed, or whatever? They call you A.A. Winters?"

I met his eyes. "No, in bed they call me God."

He laughed again, the same uninhibited cackle. "Like it," he said, except he drew out the syllables until the two words were barely recognisable as themselves: *lie-kit*. "But, seriously, babes, what's your name? My nan told me not to go wif a geeza what won't tell you 'is name."

"You're going to...go with me?"

"I'm finking abaht it," he admitted, a trifle coyly for a man negotiating a one-night stand.

And I, of course, had never been coy. "Well, all right. I suppose you can call me Ash."

He told me his name but I didn't bother to remember it.

"Come on then, Essex," I said. "Get your coat. You've pulled."

His grin flashed through the gloom. "I'm already wearing it."

To my surprise, he reached up his hand, as though he expected me to jump the railing. "I'll go round," I said firmly.

"It's ahwight, babes, I'll catch you."

"I'm not going to throw myself off a VIP balcony on the off chance a complete stranger won't drop me."

"We could've been 'ome, the amanta time you've spent talking abaht it."

"Fine," I snapped. "Fine."

I leaned over the railing and took his hand. His nails were painted silver to match his epaulettes. This could only end badly. I scrambled gracelessly over the balcony and onto the speaker, which rocked under the impact of my landing and made me clutch at Essex like an utter fool. His laughter curled against my ear, the heat of his body enfolding me in an embrace. I shuddered. It was awful and lovely at the same time but before I could really begin to deal with the contradictions of my response, he had swung off the speaker and was pulling me down after him.

"There you go, babes. That was ahwight, wunit?"

I was beginning to think he had a vocabulary of about a hundred words, and fifty of them weren't English. I must have been beyond hammered to be thinking about sleeping with him. Of course, it was possible he didn't exist, but I doubted even the extremity of my psychosis could have conjured such a man.

He took my hand, actually took my hand, and led me outside.

I cast a glance over my shoulder, looking for Niall out of long habit. Putting aside the possibility Essex was a hallucination, there was always the serial killer option.

"I'm not really from arand 'ere," he volunteered. No shit. Brighton was the gay capital of England. No one here was from around here. Besides, with the spray tan and the accent, he might as well have been wearing a sticker that read *I'm from Essex, ask me how*. "I'm staying wif a mate."

He seemed to know where we were going, at least. We crossed the road and cut through a park, Brighton's pale Georgian buildings gleaming on all sides.

"You don't say a lot," he observed.

"I have nothing to say."

"Pity, you sahnd well nice." Oh, that glottal stop. Pih-e.

"You said I sounded like the Queen ten minutes ago."

"Yeah, but like"—a thoughtful pause—"sexy wif it."

"Thank you."

That should have been enough to quell any further exchanges but, somehow, he was still speaking. "I love talking, me. I'll talk to anyone. I'll even talk to myself. Oh no, that makes me sound like a right mental."

"It's fine." I chose not to share the fact I actually *was* a right mental.

"I just run on and on. It's 'ard to get me to shuh up, to be 'onest wif you."

"I'm sure I'll think of something."

He gave a melodramatic gasp. "Ah, you're so rude, babes."

It seemed, however, to have done the trick and, to my relief, we continued in silence. I didn't want to have to think about what I was doing and I resented his clumsy attempts to converse with me. We both knew how this worked. If I had to endure any more of his banal confidences, it would surely extinguish the faint flare of desire I (inexplicably) harboured for his body. It had been so long since I'd felt anything like it that I couldn't bear the thought of losing it. Like a piece of broken glass worn smooth by the tide, it was a bright trinket washed up onto my monochrome shores.

We'd been walking less than ten minutes and I had no idea where we were. But we seemed to be in the middle of the shopping district, which slightly reassured me on the murderer front, unless he wanted to off me behind Superdrug. My phone bleeped. It was Niall, of course, wanting to know if I was all right. I closed down the message and silenced my phone.

"That your mates?" asked Essex.

"It's not important."

"You should tell 'em where you're going. What if I'm like a axe murderer or summin?"

"Then," I shrugged, "you'll have axe murdered me before anybody has a chance to stop you."

"Oh, yeah, didn't fink of that." He brightened. "But they'd be able to tell the police who done it."

"I'll take my chances." That was the point at which I should have left it but, out of nowhere, some spirit of mischief (or masochism) seized me, and I added, "Besides, *I* could be the axe murderer."

"Omigod, I didn't fink of that eeva."

He stopped walking, chewing his lower lip as though he was wrestling with an intense, private dilemma. Or maybe it was just the effort of cogitation, I couldn't tell. Fuck, what had I done? He was going to change his mind, and where would that leave me? Alone, without even the smouldering ashes of this incomprehensible wanting.

"I'm not an axe murderer," I said, urgently.

"That's what you'd say if you was a axe murderer."

"But...but I'm not."

His raucous laugh exploded through the still night. "I didn't really fink you was, babes. And, anyway, where'd you get the axe this time of night?"

That...that...wanker. What was he trying to do to me? I glared at him and that only made him laugh harder, his teeth flashing and his jewellery jingling.

"Your face!" he said happily.

"Fuck you."

He gave another one of his theatrical gasps, eyes flying wide in a flurry of artificially lengthened lashes. Then he nudged me in the arm, as though he was inviting me to share the terrific joke at my own expense. I pulled away impatiently. Whereupon the most oblivious man in Brighton hustled after me, leaned in, and—of all things—kissed me on the cheek. It was so utterly unexpected that I didn't have time to avoid it, and then he sauntered off like nothing had happened. Leaving my skin to burn with the memory of his lips, as though he had branded me with his smile.

We kept walking. Around us the city glittered in shades of orange and silver, like a paste jewel in a tinfoil crown. The sky was a bruised swirl of blue and indigo, the air sharp-edged with salt. We passed a Waterstones advertising my forthcoming book. My gaze recoiled and landed, instead, on the street sign above: Dyke Road.

"I know I shouldn't," said Essex, as though he'd read my mind, "but it always makes me laff."

I didn't dignify that with an answer.

He prodded me in the arm. "You didn't say what books you wrote." He'd noticed? He'd remembered? Urgh.

"No, I didn't."

"What, is it like porn?"

"No," I snapped, "it is not porn!"

Oh, God help me, he was laughing again.

"I write, sort of...crime," I said, to shut him up.

"That's well sahnd. Like that geeza...wassisname...Derren Brown. Ah, wait no, 'e's on the telly. The uvver one. Dan Brown."

The last forlorn relic of my pride shattered on a street in Brighton. "Not like Dan Brown," I said.

"I read one of 'is coming back from Ibiza." Of course, he pronounced it *Ibeefa*. "I fought it was brilliant. To fink 'e made all that up in his 'ead."

"That's his job."

"Yeah, 'e's well good at it." Darian paused and then offered, a little sheepishly, "I'm trying to get into modlin, me."

I cast a sideways glance at his manicured beard, glossed lips, and painted eyes. "You do surprise me."

"Really?" he said, startled. "Cos it's the first fing people say to me: 'You should be a model, mate.' I reckon it's important to look nice. There's lots of fings you can't change, but if you make an effort wif 'ow you look, then you'll do ahwight, janarwhatamean?"

I did not, in fact, know what he meant, but I made a noncommittal noise in the hope it would discourage further insights into the human condition.

"Some people fink it's a bit shallow," he went on, profoundly undiscouraged, "but what I fink is that if you really like fink 'ard abaht it, then y'know...that's ahwight."

"Please stop talking."

"Sorry, babes, I do run on." Five seconds later: "D'you wanna see my catwalk walk?"

"Will you be quiet while you do it?"

"Course, babes."

He sashayed off, starlight catching at his epaulettes. My gaze slid down his spine in a caress as fervent as a sigh.

"Well, whadyafink?" He stopped a few feet away and spun round to face me.

My eyes—which had been riveted to his hips—flicked reluctantly back up. He smiled, a touch shyly, one side of his mouth quirking up a split second before the other.

"I'm honestly no judge, but I could watch you walk up and down all day."

"Awww, babes, that's proper sweet."

I stared at the ground, flustered.

"As a special reward, I'll show you my pose."

I looked up in time to see him draping himself over one of the industrial wheelie bins standing nearby. He arched his back, sending a ripple of motion through his body like energy down a Slinky. His jacket slipped from one shoulder to reveal the bare skin and sleek muscles of his upper arm.

My stomach twisted with pure and painful longing.

"You look very...very..." My lips were dry. "Sinuous."

"Lie-kit. Sin-u-ous."

"Well." God, I could barely speak. I swallowed lust. "It has the word sin in it."

He wriggled his hips. "And you, babes."

"And us for that matter."

He grinned. "I can totally tell you're a writer."

I couldn't have said what fresh madness possessed me at that moment, but I pulled my phone out of my pocket and aimed the camera at him. He came to life beneath its harsh, silver-flashing eye, his body twisting to the music of the shutter. He was shameless in his skin. Ridiculous. And beautiful. I watched the light as it slid down his bared throat.

My hands were shaking so hard I had to stop.

"Let's 'ave a look." Ambling back to me, he peered over my shoulder. He smelled sticky-sweet: cosmetics, cologne, and the faintest suggestion of sweat. "They're ahwight. Send 'em to me."

I didn't think it was worth reminding him I didn't actually know where to send them.

"The wheelie bin," I said, "is a particularly classy touch."

"I fought it was ahwight actually. Sorta urban. Not like Black urban. Just urban urban."

"I think you mean grunge."

"Oh, you're so clever, babes."

"Can we just go somewhere now and fuck? Without talking."

"Calm dahn." He grinned at me. "It's just rand the corner."

We went round the corner onto a residential street that rose steeply along one of Brighton's sudden, illogical hills. It was lined by prissy white-fronted cottages, the sort of self-consciously quaint dwellings that came with window boxes, balconettes, and jauntily painted shutters. It was not an auspicious location for a filthy, anonymous, homosexual liaison, and I entertained the horrifying thought that he might be taking me home to meet his nan before I remembered he'd said he was staying with friends. At last, we came to a huddled-over house with a wonky To Let sign and pile of bulging bin liners sitting outside it. Chez Essex.

"Ah, where's my key?" he muttered, trying unsuccessfully to insinuate a finger into the pocket of his skinny jeans.

Oh, for God's sake. Surely not. Having unearthed some fragment of wanting for this—for him—was I now going to be denied it?

He caught sight of the look on my face and started howling with laughter, staggering about on the pavement, almost doubled over with hilarity. Instead of putting all his clearly abundant energy into finding his fucking door key.

"It's ahwight, babes, it's ahwight," he said, gasping for breath and hooking the key from a string around his neck. "Fahnd it."

He battled with the door for a moment or two, finally bashing it open with his shoulder. I followed him into a narrow hallway, washed briefly and unprepossessingly orange from the street outside. A click signalled his attempt to turn on a light.

"D'you want summin?" he said. "Like a tea or some water or summin?"

"No, thank you."

He opened one of the doors leading from the entrance hall and flicked on the light inside. A bare bulb hung from a pockmarked ceiling, illuminating knobbly, mismatched furniture and a bare mattress pushed against the peeling wall. There was an open, mostly empty suitcase on the floor, but its contents had been arranged with surprising care about the room. Lined up on the desk was an extensive arrangement of male grooming products. And hanging in plastic covers on a metal rail was a collection of clothing, amongst which sparkly epaulettes represented the epitome of restrained elegance.

I turned the light off.

He turned it back on.

And I turned it off again. My body had too many secrets for me to share them with strangers. And there were too many questions I didn't like having to answer.

"Ahwight, babes," he said gently, for once getting a fucking clue.

The darkness came between us, sealing me safe inside my skin with the too-rapid rhythm of my heart. The thin curtains admitted only a faint glow from the street outside, enough to see the shape but not the certainty of things. Essex was just a shadow in the room, the shadow of a thing I wanted, which was itself a shadow of wanting. But it was unspeakably sweet to feel even that, and terrifying to know how quickly it would pass. A moment inscribed on water, a memory that would fade to grey. I was nothing but a ghost hunter, chasing the wraith of the man I used to be. A beachcomber of my own detritus.

I closed my eyes, adding dark to dark, and the wanting unfurled like the sails of a phantom ship. This could be my universe. This nowhere world, circumscribed by skin and breath, where nothing mattered but two bodies moving together. The past and the future rendered irrelevant by the beauty of the now, the sum of the self transmuted into a moment. Oh, was there ever a more seductive definition of madness? Behind my eyelids, I saw him dancing in spirals of coloured light, emerald, blue, and brilliant purple, enfolding him like the wings of an electric angel.

His hand brushed against my cheek. When had he moved close enough to touch me? I caught his wrist and pulled his hand roughly up so I could kiss his fingertips. I half imagined I could taste the silver on his nails, as sharp as glitter in my mouth. Maybe when he touched me, colour would spill from his hands like heat. I ran my tongue between his fingers and over the creases of his palm, drinking the pure, clean nothing of his skin. I came to his wrist, pushing against the sleeve of his jacket, my lips catching on the delicate, jutting bones beneath the base of his thumb. Against my opening mouth, his pulse thudded like a bass line. Heat swirled through me and I leaned against the wall, clutching his hand and dizzy.

I felt him move and turned my head to deflect his kiss so that it landed on the side of my jaw instead of my mouth. It shimmered there briefly like some iridescent, impossible butterfly. I dragged his hand to my hardening cock.

"I 'aven't even got my coat off," he said, but he still rubbed me through my trousers, clumsy friction that sent shivers of frantic pleasure racing through my body.

I made a strange, desperate sound, my nails sinking into his wrist. "Just...touch me." It came out somewhere between directive and supplication. But what did it matter? What did any of it matter? I'd never see him again. Nobody would ever know. All sense, all judgement, overthrown by an h-dropping, glottal-stopping glitter pirate, and I didn't have to care. And he could think whatever he wanted, as long as he kept his hand moving against my cock.

Suddenly, he caught my chin and turned me to face him.

"S'ahwight to kiss me," he said. "Essex ain't contagious." I didn't need to see him to hear the smile in his voice, rich as honey.

I had just enough time for a sound of protest before he kissed me. Oh God. It was beautiful, the softness of his beard and the rasp of the stubble that had gathered beneath his jaw. My mouth opened under his, inviting the flood of heat that followed, the sweet-slick entanglement of tongues and breath. I reached up to pull him closer, my hands sinking into his hair. Which was rather akin to sticking them into a swamp, he had so much product in it. My eyes snapped open at the damp crackle of gel beneath my fingers, my startled cry half smothered by the kiss.

"Careful, babes. A quiff like mine don't maintain itself."

The dim light gleamed on his cheekbones. Up close like this, it was distractingly easy to lose myself in the mysteries of his face. I shut my eyes and tried to find something to do with my sticky hands. But then he was kissing me again, driving me back against the wall. His arm was still pressed awkwardly between our bodies, my cock bumping arhythmically against his palm and against the wrist whose pristine, tender skin I had tasted.

I could feel his heart beating over mine, just as quick and hard.

"Your hands," I muttered into his mouth. "Touch me with your hands."

He made a soft sound I couldn't interpret and couldn't be bothered to think about, and his fingers fumbled at my trousers. I bit at his mouth in heedless impatience and then bit him again when he got his hand partially round me. Cool skin to burning, his palm as soft as falling snow, his grip exactly as hard as I needed, it was the sort of relief that becomes its own torture. And yet it was so unbearably exquisite that I had to pull away from his mouth. I pressed my face into his neck, shuddered and moaned. And when that wasn't enough, I dug my fingers into his biceps, hard enough that I felt the flesh yield even through his jacket.

It was a helpless free fall into pleasure. But he held me up, his other arm wound about my waist. And I let him, and I didn't care. I could have come like this, thrusting myself into his hand, my every breath sobbing out its ugly symphony into his oblivious skin. I lifted my head, eyes opening long enough to see the way his lashes cast shadows over his cheeks, his pale, kiss-swollen lips.

"Fuck me," I said, grabbing his wrist.

In the sudden stillness of our bodies, I realised the heat against my hip was the outline of his cock pressing against his jeans. It couldn't have been comfortable.

"Oh...err..." he said, unsteadily. "Yeah, ahwight."

Tearing at our clothes, we tumbled onto the mattress, sending it into a wild skid across the floor. Essex landed on me, cackling breathlessly like we were at the fairground. Irritating. But the pressure of his body against mine was bliss itself. He pushed himself to his knees and threw the jacket off his shoulders, followed by his T-shirt. I gazed up at the thick bands of shadow that streaked his torso as he moved. It was like looking at him through the bars of a prison cell and I suddenly regretted the lack of light. I reached up and stroked my hands over his shoulders, curving my palms about his shoulder blades. His skin was as smooth as the hidden interior of a shell and as supple as velvet as it flowed over the taut muscles of his back.

He made another of his soft, uncertain noises and then

clambered to his feet. In tantalising silhouette, I watched him yank off his boots and wriggle out of his jeans. I peeled off my jacket and waistcoat and threw them aside.

"You always wear all that?" he asked, tugging off my trousers and, with them, thankfully, my boxers—which I'd just remembered were silk, with a garish pattern of peacock feathers. They'd been a joke gift from Niall, back when we had jokes. A poor laundry ethic, and a conviction that nobody would see them, had been the only factors that had induced me to wear them tonight.

"Yes," I said, plucking at the buttons on my shirt. "All the time. Even in the bath."

He was laughing again, as his hands covered mine and finished the job for me. I didn't like being naked with strangers, which was awkward because I rather liked fucking them, but the darkness felt as cool and light as another layer of skin, keeping me safe from his eyes. I flung a leg over his hip and pulled him down on top of me. The naked heat of his body against mine was nothing short of rapturous. Sinuous had been entirely correct. He was a silken serpent of a man. Oh, God. Arching up, I rubbed myself against him with all the finesse of a rutting hog, sparks of light dancing across my vision.

"Wow." He breathed the word in the hushed voice most reserved for art galleries or churches. "You really wannit, babes."

"Yes," I said, not caring and clinging to him. "Yes. I really want it. Now fuck me."

"Lemme get summin."

Forgetting his earlier warning, I twisted my fingers through his hair, ruining whatever was left of his quiff. "It doesn't matter."

"Gotta be safe, babes."

I spread my legs under him and thrust my cock against his, making him gasp. "Don't let me go."

He kissed me. I don't know what he was aiming for but, in the gloom and the confused tangle of our bodies, it landed on my nose. "I won't," he whispered, dragging himself out of my arms. A pathetic noise clawed out my throat. "I'm just over 'ere."

I shivered, cold without him, newly lost.

I heard his feet scampering urgently across the room and then, from somewhere off to the right, there came the sort of sound a six-foot man might make falling over a pair of shoes. "Oh, no," he said. "What am I like?"

And then something very strange happened.

It was like a piece of me snapped into, or out of, alignment.

I laughed.

An awful, rusty noise that made me cover my mouth in shock.

"Shuh up!" protested Essex from somewhere on the floor, but it didn't seem as if he minded.

Except I couldn't seem to stop. I curled into a ball on the mattress, shaking and laughing.

"I said shuh up." He was back, his body curving round mine, his breath warm against my neck. "Or I won't."

"W-won't what?"

"What you said."

"Fuck me?"

"Yeah."

"You can say it, you know. You won't get arrested."

"My nan would 'ave a fit if I went on like that. It don't cost nuffin to be polite. Oh, no, I'm talking about my nan in like... when we're...like...y'know. That ain't right."

I twisted my upper body towards him and hooked an arm around his neck, pulling his mouth onto mine for a damp, ungainly kiss. "Essex," I said, against his mouth, "would you please, and grandmother permitting, be so very kind as to fuck me senseless?"

I felt his shuddery exhale against my lips. "Hunjed pahcent."

I flipped onto my stomach, and he covered me like sunlight in a rush of warm skin.

There was enough strength in his lean body for me to feel it as his weight pressed me down. The springs in the mattress dug into my chest. His lips ghosted over the tops of my shoulders, sprinkling pleasure as ephemeral as stardust over my skin, and I squirmed back against him, grinding my arse against his cock.

"God, fuck, do it."

He drew back a little. Then came the sound of tearing foil, the snap-snap of a bottle. Lubed fingers stroked me lightly and I thrust myself onto them. Not enough, not nearly enough.

"For fuck's sake," I snarled.

The flat of his hand between my shoulder blades shoved me back down.

"Don't wanna hurt you, babes."

"But—" At that moment, he twisted his fingers sharply inside me and whatever I had been intending to say was lost in a harsh gasp of pleasure. He withdrew and did it again, and this time I cried out in exquisite frustration. It was so close to what I wanted. My hands clenched and unclenched against the mattress. "Oh, God, Essex, please."

His fingers vanished, replaced by the head of his cock, pushing into me. He was careful, excruciatingly careful, but it had been long enough that even the stretch and burn of this slow penetration made me shudder and moan with the sweet intensity of violation. I lifted my hips to force him deeper.

"Yorite?" he muttered. Some drops of skin-warmed sweat landed on my spine. I felt each one as clearly as if it were a diamond.

I opened my mouth to tell him to get on with it and babbled instead. "Yes, fuck, yes, oh yes, fuck, please."

He eased himself out again and I sobbed out some more ecstatic nonsense, then lost even the power to do that when his returning thrust hit my prostate almost perfectly.

"Again."

And he did, in long, steady strokes, his hands curled about my hips to anchor me. Coloured lights splintered behind my eyes. For a few brief, blissful moments, all thought, all memory, dissolved like sugar in water. I was free. There was nothing but sweat and skin, hot harsh breath against my neck, a cock driving into me. Raw, undeserved pleasure stolen from a stranger in a dark room.

And then it was over. Like lightning from a clear sky. A

moment of glorious, shuddering oblivion, a pure glittering hope-fulness, and then the grim, inevitable return. To a puddle of cooling ejaculate trapped beneath my rapidly wilting cock and a man whose name I didn't care to remember labouring behind me. A wild disgust rolled through me. And a strange, inexpress-ible sorrow for the shining moment that is never more than a moment. Then Essex pulled me to him, his mouth open against the back of my neck, and came with a muffled, self-conscious murmur, his body streaming with sweat and shaking with strain.

We fell apart, Safetyboy Essex keeping a tight hold on the condom as he eased himself out of my body. I collapsed onto my back and threw an arm over my face as my breathing steadied. I wanted to move, to gather my clothes and get out of there, but neither my body nor my mind were quite cooperating. I heard Essex puttering about the room, presumably cleaning up. After a moment, the mattress squeaked, heralding his return. Something cool and damp tenderly enclosed my cock, and I jackknifed into a sitting position.

"What the fuck?"

"Wet wipe, babes."

"God, don't you have tissues like a normal person?"

"It's Olay. Wif aloe vera."

"Oh, well, in that case." I had to get out of here.

He scrunched up the wipe and flopped down next to me. "You totally trashed my 'air."

"Sorry."

"Are you always, y'know...like that?"

I opened my mouth and closed it again. There was a long silence. "No," I said, finally.

He gave an immense yawn. "That was proper special." Then he rolled right up close, tossed an arm and a leg over me, and fell almost immediately asleep.

I lay there in frozen horror, watching the pattern of shadows and cracks on the ceiling. This had all been a terrible mistake. And I had no idea where I was. How was I going to get away? What was going to happen? What had I done? What had made me think this would ever be all right? The image of my medication, sitting on the kitchen countertop, vivid to the tiniest detail of the prescription on the label, flashed across my mind. Fuck, oh fuck. My heart started racing. Anxiety shook itself like a wolf leaving its lair. I told myself it was psychosomatic. I was going to be fine. Yes, I'd broken all my routines, but at least I hadn't taken any drugs. Though I resented having to feel grateful to Niall for that. But how much had I drunk? Enough to dilute the carefully modulated biochemical sanity sloshing around inside me? Oh, God, was I going to go mad? How would I tell? When I found myself in hospital, that's how I'd know. Except, by then, I wouldn't believe it. *Please, please, I don't want to go back to hospital. I'd rather kill myself. Wait. No, I don't mean that. I don't mean that.*

Maybe I'd just feel shitty for a while. Crash in depression, rather than soar into mania. That would be okay, wouldn't it? I could endure it. I'd be strong. And it would be a fair price for that split second of physical happiness. My eyes burned as I bargained desperately and silently with a God I didn't believe in. Ah, the pitiful prayers of a rational man. If the mad can so be called.

I twisted under Essex's arm, and his deep, even breathing gusted over my skin. The unexpected warmth raised a prickle of goose bumps across my arm and shoulder. And, slowly, impossibly, my thoughts ceased their frantic churning. My heart rate dropped.

I...relaxed. My body felt heavy, sore but—in some distant way—satisfied. It was an unusual sensation. Anxiety and depression had conspired to render me a lifetime member of Insomniacs R Us. But, somehow, on a bare mattress, in a strange house, with a strange man sprawled over me, I was slipping into sleep.

Maybe it was going to be all right.

3
AFTER YESTERDAY

Days passed in a grey fog. I was becalmed. Without energy, without hope, with no sight of land. I could remember feeling better but I somehow couldn't believe in it. There was nothing but this.

Sometimes I managed to get out of bed. Sometimes I didn't.

Sometimes I slept. Sometimes I didn't.

Sometimes I thought about killing myself. The idea of it circled my head, shining and lovely like a tinsel halo. How beautiful it would be if everything could just stop. If I could stop. If I didn't have to feel like this. Yes, I thought about it and thought about it, but I was too exhausted, too depressed, to do anything about it. A paradox of such excruciating absurdity that I half-wished I believed in God. Then at least I'd know someone was laughing.

Sometimes I took out my phone and looked at grainy, flash-flooded photographs of a glittering man standing against a wheelie bin.

One day, in a fit of energetic self-loathing I didn't want to waste, I deleted them.

Sometimes the doorbell rang. I ignored it.

Sometimes my phone rang. I ignored it, too.

Sometimes it kept on ringing but the noise came from another country, a different life.

And then I got better.

I woke up one drizzly afternoon and, although I still felt like shit, it suddenly seemed possible to function. I got up, heated some Heinz tomato soup and, giddy with triumph, ate it.

There had been a subtle realignment of the spheres. The world was somehow a place I could endure again. If life was a grey corridor lined with doors, it was now within my power to open some of them.

Having experienced such unqualified success with the "eating some soup" door, I opened the "having a shower" door, followed by the "reading the newspaper" door. Not wanting to push my luck, I then went back to bed. The next morning found me stronger still, and I risked activities as dangerous as reading my email and checking my phone. I had seventeen messages, eleven of which were Niall apologising. The rest were, variously, my agent, Max, my mother, an automated reminder from British Gas, my agent again, and static on the line.

As a terrifying demonstration of the incestuous nature of my social circle, my agent was actually Amy Miller, Max's wife-to-be. To be fair, she had been my agent first.

 Apparently my latest book had been well received, which was to say that people who liked that sort of thing had liked it; people who didn't, hadn't. However, it would pay the bills, which was all that mattered.

I rang Amy, so she could congratulate me and I could congratulate her and to confirm my attendance at the proposed readings, signings, and interviews. And possibly the Edinburgh International Book Festival next year, an occasion I thoroughly despised. I always seemed to get stuck next to whoever was supposed to be the new Martin Amis. As if the old one wasn't bad enough.

"Also," said Amy, when that was all done with, "I'm having an awful dilemma and I need your advice."

"Oh?" I cradled the phone against my shoulder so I could dig my hands into my dressing gown pockets and wander aimlessly about the flat. "It must be exceptionally awful if you're asking me."

"Hah, yes. I don't know what to call myself."

"Amy Miller seems to be working for you."

"Yeah, I'm pretty fond of it and I intend to cling to it. But without going full-on Up the Patriarchy, I'd like to at least acknowledge the fact I'm getting married."

I felt amusement turn up the corners of my mouth very slightly. By accident or design, Amy always somehow managed to make me feel human. Perhaps it was she knew in abstract how low I could fall, but hadn't seen the worst of it. I didn't doubt she'd find a way to handle it, but it pleased me—yes, it pleased me—that she'd never had to. As if, incapable as I was of looking after myself, I could protect someone else. Or, maybe, sometimes I just liked to pretend to be normal. And Amy let me.

"Well," I said, "if you're making an informed, conscious decision to oppress yourself, it's probably a feminist statement."

"My thoughts exactly. But I can't be Amy Miller-Moreton-Smith. That's the worst name in the universe."

"That is, indeed, the worst name in the universe."

"So..." I could imagine her twisting a lock of hair idly round her finger. "I don't know what to do."

"Make Max change his name instead," I suggested.

"I already thought of that, but he says Max Miller sounds like a serial killer. And I don't want to be married to a serial killer."

"Also a music hall comedian." I hummed a bit of "Mary from the Dairy."

"You know some weird shit, my friend," she said. "And this isn't helping."

"Well, you could both change your names," I offered.

"Oooh, to something completely different?"

"Yes."

"Like...like Shufflebottom."

I coughed, remembering, out of nowhere, Dyke Street and a smirking glitter pirate. "Clutterbuck."

"Hiscock."

 "Gropebuttock."

"Oh, you've sold me," she said. "Amy and Max Miller-Gropebuttock."

"Glad to be of service."

"Speaking of service," she added, "I've got a dress fitting. Don't suppose you want to come with me?"

I really did not. "I'm not that kind of gay."

"Dammit. Can I do a part-exchange?"

"A homosexual is for life, not just for Christmas."

She laughed. "So, I'll see you a week on Thursday, okay? Sure you feel up to it? I can postpone?"

"No, I'm..." I had been about to say "all right," but for some reason my tongue tripped over the word. "...okay. Anyway, it's just a signing."

"Drink beforehand?"

"No, thanks."

"Great, let's meet at The Three Crowns at six."

I made an exasperated sound, not entirely devoid of affection. "What part of 'no' did you fail to understand?"

"The part where it means yes. See you soon, Ash. I'll bring pictures of my dress." She made an extravagant kissing sound into the phone and hung up.

The conversation left me feeling both better and faintly unsettled, although I couldn't work out precisely why. I put it down to the general restlessness that sometimes accompanied getting through a depressive period. When I was lost in the muck and mire of madness, it was as though nothing else existed. And, afterwards, it seemed incomprehensible that I had ever really thought like that. Self-recrimination inevitably followed.

The tapestry of my life was a ruin of unravelling threads. The brightest parts were a nonsensical madman's weaving. And now every day was a grey stitch, laid down with an outpatient's patience, one following the next following the next following the next, a story in lines, like a railway track to nowhere, telling absolutely nothing.

I'd wasted so much of my life. So many of my days, and all of my promise, all of my dreams, lost to hospitals, to depression, to wanting to die. This wasn't how it was supposed to be. *This is not who I am.*

Except, of course, it was. It was the only thing left to be.

I wandered the flat, opening curtains, plumping cushions, picking things up and putting them down again. Sitting distractedly on the arm of the sofa, I found myself going through the photos on my phone. I even plugged the thing into my computer to see if there was some sort of hidden recycle bin from which deleted objects could be restored. There wasn't.

4

A WEEK ON THURSDAY

I met Amy, as arranged, at The Three Crowns. It claimed to be a ☆
traditional English pub, which meant dark wood and warm beer.
Not that I would be drinking. Not after Brighton.

Stitch on, lunatic.

Amy was sitting at a table in the dingiest corner, sipping a
pint and reading on her iPad. Despite my terrible record for
showing up to things, she still hadn't given up on me. I couldn't
tell if that made her stubborn, foolish, or...nice.

"Hey you," she said, jumping up and hugging me. I gave her
an awkward squeeze. "Extravagant air kiss...mwah, darling...
mwah..."

This was another fossil of a joke. I couldn't remember where
it'd come from. I had a horrible feeling it might have been me.

Leaning in, I went through the motions. Mwah. Mwah. Sigh.

"And I bought you a drink. Full-fat Coke, not diet, on the
rocks, with lime not lemon."

"Thank you." I sat down, unbuttoning my coat and unwind-
ing my scarf.

"It's okay." She smiled at me. "You're a cheap date. It's one of the things I like about you."

"What about my swashbuckling charm and pretty face?"

"Went without saying, sweetie."

I took a sip of my Coke to hide a smile. Amy was the sort of woman who occasionally made me wish I weren't gay and clinically insane. She was pretty in what I thought was probably an Elizabeth Bennet sort of way: lively eyes, wicked smile.

"It's colder than Satan's arsecrack out there," she went on cheerfully. "Where's the bloody spring gone? How've you been?"

I hesitated, weighing fact and fiction, pride and friendship. "Well, truthfully, not entirely great. But I'm okay now."

"Yeah, I heard about Brighton."

Well, this was likely to be awkward. "Oh?" I adopted what I hoped was a neutral tone.

She nodded. "Max told me." There was a pause. "Everything."

"Oh."

Yes, this was definitely awkward, and there was only so much mileage I could get out of "oh."

She ruffled a hand through her pixie cut "I'm sorry, I don't want to dump shit on you. Shall we talk about how everyone loves the new Rik Glass instead?"

☆ "God, no." I recoiled in revulsion. "You know I hate talking about my books. Also, you can dump shit on me. Figurative shit, anyway."

"Are you sure?"

"I'll tell you straightaway if my mental health starts to buckle under the weight of your feelings."

"Don't be an arse." She rapped the table in a manner that suggested it was substituting for my head. "I didn't mean it like that. Even non-depressed people have a right not be whinged at."

"I'm consenting, meaningfully, to be a whinge recipient."

Maybe this was why I liked Amy. She was very good at making me feel like I might be salvageable. That I could be something other than a burden to someone. That I might be—as a stranger I would never see again had so sincerely believed—all right.

She folded her arms and took a deep breath. "Just remember you asked for this. But it's about Niall. Specifically about Niall trying to shag Max on the stag night, which I'm not okay with. Except I suppose that makes me some kind of evil straight girl stereotype."

"Excuse me." I gave her a sharp look. "Fidelity does not belong to heterosexuals. We queers can be boring and committed too."

"So Max told me when he proposed."

"Did he really?"

Now she was laughing at me. "Of course not. Though we did have the monogamy talk on a separate, less romantic occasion."

"And how did that go?"

"I'm neutral. He's pro. Niall apparently doesn't care." It was the closest to bitter I'd ever heard Amy sound. "Sorry. I know you all go way back and I don't want to come between that."

Something that, had I been a different person or lived a different life, might have been guilt stirred weakly inside me. If I'd thought about it for a second, I could have guessed how the stag might unfold. But, of course, I hadn't thought about it. I'd only thought about myself. "You could set up some kind of ... time-share," I said instead.

"Ash"—Amy was half-laughing again, but also faintly exasperated—"Max is a person. Not a listing on AirBnB. And if he wanted to be with Niall, he'd be with Niall."

Sometimes the simplest truths could be the most difficult. Although I suppose it depended which side of them you were on. "I know. I even think Niall knows that. On some level."

Amy's eyes narrowed. "Oh he does. Or he wouldn't have to guilt Max into bed. Well, not into bed. *Towards* bed."

She was quiet for a moment or two, her finger tracing a succession of fading abstracts in a puddle of spilled beer, while I tried to come up with something useful and/or comforting to say to her and failed on both counts. I couldn't tell if it was because the problem was complicated and insoluble, or if I was just hopeless. Some friend. Some lover. I couldn't even indulge in a one-night stand without having a panic attack. And here I was, still thinking about myself.

Finally, Amy looked up and sighed. "It just feels like whatever happens, someone is going to get hurt."

"That's just the way it is, sometimes."

We stared moodily into our drinks.

"Did happiness always used to be this complicated?" Amy asked after a bit.

I shrugged. "I have no idea. Happiness and I are barely on speaking terms these days."

Her eyes held mine for a moment. There was pity there,

which of course I hated, but also warmth. I waited for the clumsy platitude, but I had, as ever, underestimated Amy.

"Well. Let me show you some happiness." She slid her phone over the table. "Look. My wedding dress!"

"You curmudgeon." She glared at me in mock displeasure. "At least pretend to care."

I glared back. "I am not a curmudgeon."

"What are you then?"

"Optimistically challenged?"

"You're a curmudgeon," she insisted.

It was becoming difficult to dispute. With a show of reluctance, I reached out, took the phone, and looked at the photograph.

"Such a curmudgeon." She glared at me in mock displeasure.

With a show of reluctance, I reached out, took the phone, and looked at the photograph. A smiling woman in a white frock; seen one, you've seen them all. Except, no, it was different. It was Amy.

"You look pretty. And," I conceded, "happy."

"Not half as happy as the sales assistant standing next to me. You wouldn't believe what a wedding dress costs."

"No," I said firmly. "I wouldn't."

Rolling her eyes with—I thought—more amusement than exasperation, she pulled her phone out of my hands and stuffed it back in her pocket. "Anyway, what happened to you at the stag night? Max said you pulled."

"Oh...err..." I'd been about to relax into my non-wedding related conversational duties but now an absolutely scalding blush burst across my face. As far as I was concerned, what happened in Brighton stayed in Brighton. "I didn't think he'd seen. I barely spoke to him, actually. I'm shitty like that."

If Amy noticed my inept attempt to deflect the topic of conversation back to Max, she still let me get away with it. "He's more perceptive than he lets on. And he does care about you."

"I know he does." I hesitated, wondering how best to articulate something awkward. "It's just, Niall is sort of the lynchpin. He's the thing we have in common. Not that he's a thing. But Max is almost like a...a...friend-in-law. Or something."

She grinned at me over her pint of John Smith's. "Also, he's really scary."

"God, he is. Why are you marrying such a disgustingly perfect specimen of manhood?"

"I have really terrible taste. I should find some kind of broken, insecure, miserable weasel-type man with a tiny cock, right?"

I spread my hands. "Look no further. Um, except for the cock part. I'm phenomenally well-endowed."

Her smile vanished. "Ash," she said softly. My hands were resting on the tabletop, carefully placed so my cuffs didn't drag in any beer rings, and Amy covered them with hers. It was nice, for about half a second, and then it was too much, even from Amy, so I shook her off. "You're not broken. And everybody's insecure. Even Max, would you believe it?" She paused. "You do have a touch of the weasel though."

"I *what?*"

"I think it's that intent, curious, dark-eyed look you have. It's a bit musteline."

I gaped at her, speechless, and she burst out laughing. Her laugh was nothing like my glitter pirate's laugh, but the easy joy in it made my memories chime like bells. I felt a sudden, sharp pang of something almost like loss.

Before I had to wonder about it, my phone beeped a warning.

"Well." I finished the watery dregs of my Coke and stood. "You may give thanks that you're spared my withering and soul-destroying retort because I need to go."

Amy gave me the "Be seeing you" wave. "Best of luck. And try to have fun."

"Fun?" I gave a fastidious shudder. "Reading one of my own books? Why don't you put me down for a colonic irrigation at the same time?"

"See," she said. "Curmudgeon."

I tried to think of something equally devastating and undeniable. "Weaselist."

"You what?"

"Someone who holds prejudicial opinions against weasels."

"I think you'll find I was very flattering about weasels."

There was no way I was ever going to get the last word with Amy. It was literally her job. So I struggled into my coat, wound myself into my scarf, and headed out into the cold.

A couple of hours later, I'd had my photograph taken, been confused with Adam Foulds, had my photograph taken again, answered the usual questions about where I got my ideas ("it's complicated"), if I'd solved any actual crimes ("no"), and what advice

I'd give to an aspiring writer ("do something else"). I'd valiantly read some passages from *Through a Glass Darkly* and nobody had fallen asleep or thrown rotten vegetables, so I thought it was fair to say it had all gone off quite well. Retreating to a nearby table, I did my best to look approachable and happy-to-be-there while a wavering queue formed up in pursuit of my signature.

Of course, I wasn't happy-to-be-there. I was tired, drained, and inappropriately ungrateful. Sometimes it's beyond me to carry on a conversation with one person, and here I had a whole room looking at me expectantly. I knew I should have been glad for them, for these were the readers who kept me in pyjamas and tea bags. And I was. But I didn't see why I couldn't be glad quietly, at a safe distance, in the privacy of my own home. The truth was, somewhere down the line, between the hospitalisations and the drugs, I'd somehow lost the cornerstone of humanity: the ability to pretend, to counterfeit the basics of social interaction, to smile when you didn't feel like smiling, to seem like you cared about other people when you lacked the capacity to care about your-self. So that left me, graceless and wearied, pretending to pretend. An organ-grinder's brass monkey, capering to clockwork.

Another copy of my book appeared in front of me, dog-eared and well-read, which pleased me, just a little. I'd always found something slightly eerie about untouched books. Glass coffins, with the words sleeping inside.

"Who should I make it out to?" I asked, not quite managing to look up.

"Oh, I dunno," said a far too familiar voice, "'ow about maybe

'To the geeza what I slept wif and then done a runner on in the middle of the night, making 'im feel like a right slapper'?"

"That's quite lengthy," I said, after a very long moment. "I may have to adapt it a little."

"Whateva."

I wrote out my message, signed, closed the book, and pushed it back across the table.

"Right," said Essex. "Fanks."

His footsteps receded. I tried to think over the wild thundering of my heart.

Someone placed another book in front of me, newly purchased and pristine. My fingers trembled as I opened it.

"Who—" I began.

"Oh, I forgot." Dear God, Essex was back. "You left summin behind."

There was a flutter of turquoise silk, and my boxers with the peacock feather print landed right on top of the title page of *Through a Glass Darkly*. I jerked my head up just in time to see Essex flouncing off and the frozen expression of the tweed-jacketed gentleman standing in front of me.

"I'm terribly sorry," he said, after a moment, "but I only brought a copy of the book."

I put down my pen, picked up my boxers, folded them neatly, and tucked them into my inside breast pocket. Then I picked up the pen again.

"That's quite all right," I said, magnanimously. "Who should I make it out to?"

I escaped half an hour or so later without further incident. As I stepped onto Piccadilly, however, something made me look around. Sitting at the bus stop, bag at his feet, was Essex. He was wearing the same pointy-toed boots he'd had in Brighton and another pair of skinny jeans, a top that looked like knitted fishnet, and—presumably in deference to the occasion—a formal, fitted jacket with rhinestone-studded lapels. Metal bracelets and leather ties circled both wrists, his ears glinted with gold, and he had a sort of beaded crucifix hanging around his neck. He looked absurd and beautiful. And dejected. He was holding my book, open at the title page.

And I stared at him foolishly, unable to walk away. I wanted him. Still. Again. Just as much as I had when I'd seen him in Brighton. It was madness, and I knew madness, in all its many colours. I could just about justify indulging the impulse of a moment, but this was starting to look like a habit. What the fuck was wrong with me? Why, in all the vastness of the world, did a sparkly idiot from Essex make me feel alive?

I sat down beside him. He didn't look at me.

"'To a bloke I fucked—A.A. Winters,'" he read. "Nice. That's really nice. I don't fink you're a very nice person."

"I'm not," I said.

There was a long silence.

"So, am I some sorta minger or summin?"

I cast him a startled glance. "Uh, no. What? You're quite attractive."

"Bet you can't even remember my name. That right, Alasdair Ashley Winters?"

"How do you know—"

"Looked it up on Wikipedia, didn't I? Not in a like stalking way."

"For fuck's sake." I smoothed my cuffs in an effort to moderate my exasperation. "It was a one-night stand. You weren't expecting to take me home to meet Nana Essex, were you?"

"Leave my nan outta this." He wagged a finger at me, faded silver gleaming on the nail like a piece of fallen star. "Just cos it was a hook-up don't mean you go running out like you was on fire, janarwhatamean? That was bang aht of order."

I suddenly noticed that his eyes were blue. A pale, changeable blue that shifted in the light and with his mood, mapping a subtle, private spectrum from grey to green. I found them rather lovely, and it was terrifying.

"Well," I snapped, "I'm sorry I failed to display the appropriate casual sex etiquette, but what would have been the point of hanging around?"

"Dunno. Could've 'ad breakfast, could've done it again. But it's not abaht that."

"What is it about, then?"

He turned and caught me staring, and—like a fly in honey—I couldn't turn away.

"I fought you liked me," he said simply. "It's not like I wanted to marry you or nuffin, but I didn't fink you was gonna make me feel like a slapper."

I still couldn't break his gaze. I was dying in the sweetness of looking at him. His eyes. The laughing mouth that had kissed mine, and made me burn and shiver and *feel*. Chiselled wannabe-model features. The overly tended beard and lashings of fake tan that had somehow stopped being objectionable. It was official: I'd lost it.

"I don't like anyone," I said.

"What, nobody?"

"Yes, nobody."

"Omigod, babes." His eyes widened. "That's really...like...sad."

Fantastic. Pity from a man whose preferred skin tone was orange. I shrugged.

"I read your book," said Essex after a moment, waving it at me. "I fought it was good, actually. Not Dan Brown good. But I liked it."

"Thank you."

"I fought the title was well clever," he went on. "Cos like 'is name is Rik Glass and the book is called *Frew a Glass Darkly*. Like the Annie Lennox song."

Oh, good God. I put my head in my hands. "It's from the Bible, you arse."

"I 'aven't read it." He shot me an appraising look. "'Ave you?"

"Well, no," I flustered. "But it's a cultural consciousness thing."

"What's that abaht?"

"It's...kind of...the way people...know things about things, without really knowing...things...about them."

He poked me playfully in the arm. "That sahnds like rubbish, mate. So, how's it go? The full fing?"

I recited for him: "'For now we see through a glass, darkly, but then face to face: now I know in part; but then shall I know even as also I am known.'"

"That's well nice," he said, seeming pleased. "I dunno what it means. Cos you can't see frew a glass if it's dark, can you?"

"You're quite right, Essex. I shall complain to the editor."

"Isn't that like...God?"

"I suppose it must be."

"Don't fink 'e's in."

I put my hands in the air, miming shock. "What's a nice boy like you doing spouting blasphemies like that?"

"It's not being rude." He looked a bit affronted. "It's just what I fink, is all."

There was another awkward silence. It was a chilly evening, but warmth was creeping across my skin like the promise of summer. I felt weak and shivery with longing. So what if he was a habit? There was still no reason anyone would have to know. I stirred the dust of my pride: nothing. Fuck it then.

"So," I said, "I have...um...this antique rolltop writing desk. At my flat. Where I write. I wondered if you'd be, um, interested in...um..."

He played with one of the leather bracelets tied round his wrist. "What?"

"Fucking me over it."

He grinned gleefully. "I knew you liked me."

"I like fucking you. It's not the same thing."

"Whateva, babes."

That seemed close enough to a yes for me to take it as one. Something that might have been relief rolled through me, though why I felt relieved that a ridiculous glitter pirate from Essex had generously consented to fuck me over my writing desk, I had no idea.

"I got some conditions though."

So much for that. I sighed. "What conditions?"

"One," he said, holding up a finger to illustrate the point, "you're not allowed to make me feel like a prozzie."

"I wasn't proposing to pay you."

"Shuh up. Two"—up went the second finger—"you've gotta say my name."

I blinked. "While we're fucking?"

"Just like...in general."

"And if I agree, we can...?" An odd moment to turn self-conscious, but for some reason I couldn't quite manage to finish the sentence.

"Yeah." He gleamed a smile at me. "Ahwight."

There was a pause that grew into silence that grew into a great yawning chasm. Essex was regarding me with apparently endless patience and wicked amusement in his eyes.

I stared at my shoes.

"D'you need to phone a friend?" he asked, finally. I cleared my throat. "It's...not...it's just..."

"Yeah?"

"There's, well, a very slight hitch."

"Oh, yeah?"

I shot a look at him. "Are you doing this deliberately?"

He blinked slowly. Innocently. "Doing what, babes?"

"Oh, you fucker." I twisted my fingers together. "I can't remember your name, okay? Okay? I'm sorry."

He cackled. "Didn't fink so."

"You're enjoying this."

"Well, it's a good job I am, cos I reckon some people would be proper mugged off."

"Come on, I didn't think I'd ever see you again. There was no point." He just looked at me. "I've said I'm sorry. What more do you want me to do? Beg?"

"Mebbe later."

I choked on my own breath. Heat ran riot over my skin. Rather breathlessly, I said, "Good sir, may I please have the honour of your acquaintance?"

"Yeah, ahwight," he said. "My name's Darian Taylor." We shook hands solemnly.

Then he grinned. "And I'm gonna make sure you nevva forget it."

5

LATER

"Oh, fuck, yes, Darian. Fuck. Darian. Like that. Please. Darian, oh Darian."

One of my flailing hands caught my MacBook Air and knocked it onto the floor with an ominous-sounding crash.

"Oh no, babes. Is that gonna be awhight?"

"I don't care, just don't stop." I arched my back to better receive his cock, and he made one of his shy noises as I took him to the hilt.

He bent over me and planted a soft kiss on the back of my neck, against the strip of skin exposed near the collar of my shirt. "Gotta...say..." he managed breathlessly between thrusts, "I like it when you say my name. Sounds all posh. It's well nice."

"Shut up and fuck me. Darian."

He laughed, messing up the rhythm and making me buck and twist so impatiently that the antique inkwell Niall had bought me a couple of birthdays ago, and which I'd left languishing on top of the desk, tipped over. A tide of purple ink came rushing down the rolltop and drenched me.

"Erm, d'you want me to stop now?" asked Darian.

"Hell, no."

"You donut." He was laughing again, his body shaking against mine.

I growled at him to pay attention, but then he slithered a hand under my hips and wrapped it round my cock. Complaint lost, I gave a helpless, grateful moan, my palms slipping on ink and smooth wood, unable to find purchase. But he was there to hold me pinned between the twin pleasures of his hand and his cock. It was exactly the right sort of helpless. I writhed in pursuit of both, letting his body and all its lean strength drive away everything but desire and the frantic, undignified scramble after physical release.

Whatever the internal mechanism that moderated the human capacity for joy, mine had long been broken beyond repair. And I knew this was a poor substitute, a base shadow cast on the cave wall, a reflection in a tarnished mirror of ordinary things like happiness, love, and hope. But there were moments, fleeting moments, lost in the responses of my body to his, when it was almost enough. And, God, I wanted, I wanted. These crumbs of ☆ bliss.

My nails scratched at the desk, my breath a broken torrent. One of his hands drew back a curl of hair that, heavy with sweat, had fallen across my eyes.

"It's ahwight, babes."

I twisted my head to the side, feeling the discomfort in my neck and ink pooling beneath my cheek. "Kiss me."

"Course."

We grazed our mouths against each other in the barest of kisses. It was quite ridiculous. A bruising, graceless, haphazard business, a disorder of breath and a tangle of tongues, into which I drowned a soul-deep groan as I came.

And Essex—Darian—a few seconds after, shoving me hard against the desk, a hand on my shoulder and his mouth slack against mine.

Panting, I crumpled onto the floor, Darian sprawled out beside me. My shirt and waistcoat were a ruin of purple ink, my hands worse. My face felt wet, and when I wiped the inside of my wrist across it, I came away with a smeary indigo bracelet.

I turned my head and met Darian's wide eyes. "You look like you 'ad it off wif a Ribena or summin."

I stretched luxuriously. "It was worth it."

"That's the nicest fing you've evva said to me, babes."

"Fuck off."

He laughed.

I really needed a shower, but I didn't move. My little finger twitched across the space between us until it lay neatly alongside his hand.

"Is this you trying to cuddle wif me?"

I snatched my errant hand away. "No. What? No. Of course not."

"Come 'ere."

"I'll...I'll make you all purple."

He shoved an arm under my shoulders and pulled me over

until I landed in an inky splodge against his chest. It rose and fell under my cheek with the steady, endless cycle of his breath. Such a simple thing. And, in that moment, frighteningly beautiful.

"See," he said, tracing a purple spiral over the back of my hand, "this is why people normally get naked before 'aving sex."

"No chance," I growled.

"You did last time. It was well nice."

"This is this time. Now shut up and stop ruining my afterglow."

He was still and quiet for fully ten seconds. Then he tipped his head back and twisted it this way and that, looking at my study. "'Ave you really read all them books?"

"No, I just like the way they look on the shelves."

"No, but seriously. 'Ave you?"

"Well...yes."

There was a pause. Then he said, "I reckon you've gotta be so clever."

"Yes, I am. Terribly."

"'Ow'd you find the time?"

"It just comes naturally."

"Ha-ha, no. The books."

"Oh, I don't know." I was suddenly tired, not just in the expected physical sense, and it soaked through me like rain. I was tired of talking, tired of thinking, tired of him, and tired of me. "I suppose I used to like reading."

He nodded, as if this was a perfectly reasonable answer. "So what else you into, then? I mean, except reading and writing, talking like the Queen, and dressing like my granddad?"

"I doubt your grandfather frequented Savile Row."

"Naw, mate, 'e nevva left Romford. No, but seriously, what are you into?"

"Well, between reading and writing and talking like the Queen, I don't have a lot of free time."

"No, but seriously," he said again.

It was becoming a plaintive refrain, but what was I supposed to say? That I enjoyed long walks on the beach and occasionally trying to kill myself?

"Tea," I said desperately. "I really like tea."

I cringed into him, hardly knowing what kind of response such an answer deserved.

"Aw, you're so right, babes," he said. "My nan loves a good brew."

Suddenly I could breathe again. "Will you stop comparing me to your grandparents? Or I'm going to think there's something peculiar in your continued interest in sleeping with me."

He laughed his heedless, happy idiot laugh. "That's summin else you can add to the list of fings you're into."

"What? Being like your grandparents?"

"No, you donut, being wif me. I nevva met anyone who gets into it like you do."

"Trying to make me blush?"

"No, I just like it, is all."

He squirmed suddenly, and I peered up into his face. "Are *you* blushing?"

"No. Well. Maybe. Fank God for fake-bake."

I thinned my lips to stop a strange little smile making its escape. "I should shower."

Peeling myself off him, I sat up My study was, to coin an expression, totally trashed. There was no way on earth I was getting purple ink out of the cream carpet.

"Want me to come wif you?" Darian flashed a wicked, white-toothed grin.

Yes. Oh yes.

I imagined his body, sleek as an otter and glittering with water droplets. The way the muscles of his back would shift like dappling sunlight as I fucked him.

Darian's eyes flicked, with no pretence at subtlety, to my cock. "Tharra yeah, then?"

And then I remembered: the sharp silver nothing of the knife as it glided down my forearm like a tall ship with a scarlet wake.

"Uh, no, it's fine."

"Ahwight, babes."

"Just, um, make yourself at home. I'll be right back."

6

AFTER

"Can I ask you a question, babes?"

Showered, dressed, and only mildly purple, I stepped into the living room to find Darian sprawled out on my sofa like he belonged on it. Did the man have no understanding of the delicate ritual of casual sex? He should have left by now. More disquieting still was the discovery that I was not entirely horrified he had chosen to stay.

"You just have."

I perched, as though I were the interloper here, on the arm of my own sofa. But it gave me a fine view of Darian, stretched out beside me like a veritable invitation to debauchery. His toenails twinkled silver.

"Ha-ha, anuvver question."

"If you must."

"Do you know your plants are all like...dead?"

I looked around. As a certified loon, I was always being given plants, and Darian was right: they were all dead. Very dead.

I coughed. "Oh, yes, I'm the Green Reaper. I bring plants here to make them suffer."

"You what?"

"Not really. I... I've been away." And I had. Just not physically.

"Aww, babes, that's well 'arsh. You should've got your mum to take care of 'em."

Wonderful. I was now obliged to come up with an explanation as to why I hadn't made suitable arrangements for the plants I didn't care about while I was away on the trip I hadn't taken.

"My parents live in Brockenhurst," I said, which, at least, was not a lie. "I could hardly ask my mother to drive two hours across the country to water my plants."

"What abaht your nan?"

"Both my grandmothers are dead."

He sat up at once, snaked along the sofa, and wound his arms around me. I was going to pull away, but it would have been undignified. And I liked being touched by him just a little too much to be sensible. "That's sad."

"My mother's mother killed herself before I was born, and my father's mother passed away when I was ten. Grandparents die. It's what they do. I'm over it."

He nuzzled into my shoulder. It was like owning a dog that wouldn't shut up. But there I was, not pushing him away. "Don't be like that, babes. It's not nice to talk abaht people dying like it don't mean nuffin."

"Sorry."

Sorry? God, what was he doing to me? He was pulling me to pieces, and he didn't even realise. I leaned against him, letting the warmth of his body lap at me like waves, letting him hold me as though any of this mattered, and we sat like that for a few

minutes, in my unintended sepulchre for forsaken plants and forsaken selves. Of course, it was too good to last.

"Got anuvver question."

"What now?"

"You 'aven't got no food eeva."

"Bollocks."

"No, seriously, look." He unwound us, took my hand, and
pulled me into the kitchen, flinging wide my fridge door.

I pointed at the jar of Branston Pickle. "That's food."

"That's a condiment, babes."

"It is not a condiment. It contains vegetables. Ergo, it's a
foodstuff."

"Anyfing what you put on anuvver fing is a condiment."

"Well, by that twisted logic, maybe." I started opening and shut-
ting cupboards pretty much at random. "Hah! What's that, eh? Eh?"

He peered. "Whas what?"

"This!"

I pulled out a half-used Merchant Gourmet packet from
behind a dusty colander. Darian took it from me and peered
inside, then flinched back like I'd handed him a box of alligator
faeces. "Ahh, it's dead as well, mate."

"They're not dead. They're porcini mushrooms. They're supposed to be like that."

"I nevva seen a flat mushroom. That ain't right."

"They're dried, you...you...donut."

He kissed me, and it tasted sweet, like his laughing.

I boiled the kettle and soaked the mushrooms. We ate them

with Branston Pickle, sitting on the kitchen floor, and Darian said they were well rank. He was right.

"I tried to read your uvver book," he said, when we'd given up on the possibility of food. "The one abaht the smoke being briars or whateva. But I couldn't get into it."

"Oh. Right."

My discouraging monosyllables failed to have the desired effect. "Well, it weren't abaht anyfing. It didn't 'ave a proper beginning or a middle or a end or anyfing. And I didn't know what was supposed to be 'appening now and what'd already 'appened and what wasn't 'appening at all. What's wif that?"

I shrugged. "In fiction, like life, there's only ever the now. And the boundary between the real and the unreal is simply a matter of perception."

Who knew that now better than I?

"That don't make sense, babes," said Darian Taylor, Literary Critic. "I fink you should stick to the other stuff. You're good at that."

I rolled my eyes. "Genre tat."

"What? Don't you like it?"

"Well, I suppose it's better than digging a hole."

"But don't you like it really," he persisted, "writing summin to make people 'appy?"

"I don't really care."

"Aww, babes. That's sad."

"For fuck's sake," I said wearily, "stop saying everything is sad. It isn't sad. It's just...the way it is. It's my job, not a divine mandate. It's not as though..."

I'd been about to say something...something...about human naïvety...and the fact we had no fundamental right to happiness... or something...but his hand moved over my thigh, fingers brushing my cock through my trousers, and my breath hitched and my thoughts scattered, and I did not mourn them. He pushed me back onto the kitchen floor, crawling over me like some mountain cat stalking its prey. Well, he was the same colour as one.

"You don't like nuffin abaht it?" He spread his knees on either side of me. "Nuffin at all?"

My hips bucked. "I just don't see the point of talking about it."

"I'm just interested or whateva. It's called 'aving a conversation."

He caressed my face, light as nothing, sending a strange pleasure, part anticipation, part frustration, rippling over my skin. I felt like a lake, and his hands were the moon.

"For fuck's sake," I growled, "touch me properly."

"But seriously." Words I was coming to dread. "You don't like nuffin?"

"Do we have to do this now? You realise this is blackmail, Essex."

"Darian."

"Still blackmail."

He grinned, reached for my cock again, and tightened his hand until my back arched. "Yeah."

I drew in a ragged breath. "If I tell you, will you stop asking questions and...and..."

"And what? I like it when you say fings, cos it sounds posh and filthy at the same time."

"Make me come."

"'Ow?"

"With your hand. On my cock."

His own gave an appreciative sort of jump. He smiled. "Yeah. Reckon you could read the phone book and make it dirty."

I ran my hands up the inside of his splayed, denim-coated thighs, wishing it was skin beneath my palms. "This is the news at ten," I whispered. "Politicians are predicting hard times ahead."

It was a pathetic attempt at humour, but he threw back his head and laughed. I stared at the strong, clean line of this throat. "Ahwight, then," he said, fingers curling over the head of my cock while I squirmed.

"All right, all right," I said. "I like...I like that I can make it neat, okay?"

He rewarded me with a long, languorous stroke. "What's that mean?"

I closed my eyes, trying to pretend I lived in a universe that contained only my cock and his hand. And lazy pleasure that spilled eternally in silver spirals. "Well, there's always...an answer. Everything always makes sense. And can be...can be fixed."

"Oh, yeah," he said. "I 'adn't fought of that. It's well deep."

"That's all detective fiction is," I said, while his hand moved in a sweet, tormenting rhythm and I twisted to meet it. "A control fantasy in a world where everything is meaningless."

"Lots of fings 'ave meaning, babes. And, sometimes, when you fink maybe they doesn't, it's just cos you aren't looking for the same sorta meaning."

"God help me, I'm being wanked off by Yoda."

"Ha-ha, wanking the way to the dark side is."

"Shut up. For the love of Jesus fucking Christ on a *moose*, shut up. I'm trying to get off here."

He fell on top of me, howling with laughter. And, somehow, in that ridiculous tangle, his hand moving awkwardly against my cock as he snuffled hysterically against my ear, and me yelling at him, my body shaking with frustration, amusement, pleasure, bewilderment, so much bewilderment, I did, in fact, get off.

AND AFTER

It was long past midnight by the time I convinced Darian that his proper place was in the guest room, not my bed, and that "because I don't do that" was the only explanation he was getting for the arrangement.

"What abaht Brighton then?" he asked, hovering on the threshold as if he believed this was a negotiation.

"An accident."

I ignored his big, wounded eyes and retired for the night.

But of course, I couldn't sleep. I found myself wondering what it would be like to have him here with me, the sleek warmth of his body curled protectively about mine.

My thoughts circled like vultures. Non-specific anxiety clawed at me. I felt too hot, too cold, too trapped, too lonely. Tired and cruelly awake.

The night was a vast plughole, an endless spinning of the self through ever-narrowing circles.

It had been (*don't say it, don't spoil it*) a good day. I tried to rationalise it as the result of physical satisfaction but, in other more abstract ways, I had, almost without noticing, been something close to...

Happy.

My heart stuttered.

There was little I feared more than happiness, that faithless whore who waited always between madness and emptiness. My moods, when they were not sodden with medication, could turn upon a tarnished penny; happiness was merely something else to lose.

Words and images drifted through my thoughts, catching at me like briars, fading into smoke.

This wasn't safe. My world was one of only broken images, like I was standing always on the threshold of a mirror, unable to tell the reflection from the real. The shining city and the blasted heath—the truth lay somewhere between, a thin grey line, slender as the edge of a knife.

And I'd known this mirage before. These shimmering moments. But they each had their price that must be paid. Looking back brought little comfort, only pain. The memory of light only made the present seem darker.

This would hurt on the other side. Because it always hurt on the other side.

I knew I should protect myself.

I wished I could sleep. I wished I could stop thinking.

But my mind has always been its own enemy.

7

MORNING

Somewhere in the greyness of dawn, I drifted into a dream-studded semblance of slumber, only to be woken a scant handful of hours later by the unfamiliar sounds of somebody moving around the flat. My first, drowsy thought was that a burglar was using my shower, and then I remembered.

Darian.

I buried down into the duvet and grimly attempted to force myself back to sleep in the hope he would have left by the time I woke up again. Unfortunately, the endeavour was not a success, and I was left with no choice but to get out of bed.

I knotted myself firmly into my dressing gown and padded into the kitchen, where Darian was eating a bowl of Weetabix and reading *Heat* magazine. He looked repulsively cheerful for someone on the wrong side of noon. His hair was a marvel of engineering, shaming even the quiff I had witnessed in Brighton. His jeans were very tight, as was his T-shirt, which was black and had the words "Show Love" written on it in silver, hard-to-read letters. His shoes were exceptionally pointy.

"Morning, babes," he said. "I 'ad to go to the corner shop cos you 'ad nuffin. And guess what?"

I blinked. "Uh...what?"

"Look in the sink."

I looked in the sink. There was a dead plant sitting in a sort of water bath.

"I fink we can save 'er. The rest 'ave 'ad it, though."

"Uh, great, well done."

"It's like a horror movie or summin, innit?"

"Pardon?"

"She's the only one to get out alive. Do you reckon she's like a plant cheerleader or summin?"

"I thought the cheerleader always died first?"

"Maybe, I dunno. I don't really like horror, to be 'onest wif you. Like you're watching and eeva you're not scared so what's the point, or you are scared and then you're like...scared, janarwhatamean?"

This was all a bit much first thing in the morning. "I think so," I said dubiously.

"Kettle's boiled, by the way." He pointed helpfully, in case I had somehow forgotten the location of my own damn kettle. "Milk in the fridge."

"Oh." Relief. "Tea."

I was just pouring myself a cup, when suddenly there was an excitable Darian behind me, nosing into my neck, while his hands swooped about my person.

"What are you wearing, babes?" His voice struck me as

unduly incredulous for a man with a huge pewter ankh hanging round his neck.

"Gentleman's sleeping attire."

He turned me away from my tea, a dangerous action if there ever was one. I opened my mouth to complain but then he stroked my purple silk lapels.

"That dressing gown, babes," he said, at last, "is love. And I nevva seen pinstriped pyjamas before."

"Are they, err, love?"

"I fink they're just a bit weird. I mean, what's this pocket for? Carrying your teddy bear?"

"I don't know, pockets are useful."

"But why'd you need three in a pair of pj's? Seriously, babes, you go to bed in more clovves than I wear going out."

"Are you quite done, Herr Lagerfeld?"

He kissed my nose. "You're so funny, babes. Fanks for letting me stay."

"Thanks for...getting me off."

He laughed. "Any time. So, like, I've got this meeting fing wif a modlin agency today and then it's back 'ome cos Nan's expecting me. Unless like maybe you wanted..."

"Yes."

I'd spoken before I'd even had time to frame the thought. And ten seconds later, he was phoning his grandmother to let her know he'd be staying another night in London. What had I done?

I sat down at the table, sipping my tea while Darian babbled happily into his phone. "Yeah, gonna crash wif a mate...No, you don't know 'im... No, 'e's not a axe murderer or anyfing... I can just tell... Yeah, yeah, that's a good fought. But if 'e was, right, 'e'd 'ave already axe murdered me. Yeah, he's nice... He's well posh. You should hear 'im..."

I had a terrible split-second-too-late premonition of what was about to happen. And, despite my frantic *fuck no, don't you dare* gesticulations, he shoved his phone at me, explaining cheerfully that I should "say 'ello to Nanny Dot."

My mouth fell open but no words came out. I gripped his phone in frozen terror as if he'd handed me a live grenade. He grinned encouragingly, and I shot him a betrayed look, which seemed to make no impression on him whatsoever.

"Good morning, Darian's grandmother," I said.

"Oooh, 'e's right," she said, "you do sound lovely. You can call me Dot."

"Thank you."

"What's your name, young man?"

"My friends call me Ash."

"That is nice. 'Ow are you, Ash? Is our Darian behaving 'imself?"

"I am quite well, thank you. And, yes, he's a model house guest." *I particularly enjoy the way he fucks me.* "He's welcome to stay, um, any time."

"You two be good."

"Yes. Yes, we will. It was very nice talking to you, Dot. Goodbye."

I passed the phone back to Darian, with great relief. He chatted a bit longer and then hung up.

"I think I hate you," I said.

He bounced over and kissed me until I was moaning into his mouth and clutching great handfuls of Show Love. Finally, he drew back.

"Maybe I don't hate you."

He grinned. "Ahwight, I'll be back later, but I'm not gonna eat more of 'em dead mushrooms."

"We can order in. When we're not fucking."

"Aww, babes, you gottit all planned out. You're so romantic."

"You're unbearable in the morning, you know that?"

He did not look remotely chastened. "I'll cook summin nice," he went on, and thrust what appeared to be a crumpled train ticket into my hands. "But you'll 'ave to pick some fings up for me."

"You need me to pick up the 15:19 from Basildon?"

"Turn it over, donut."

"This... this is a shopping list. Darian, I do not do shopping."

"What? Nevva?"

"Well, sometimes, on the internet. When it can't be avoided."

He propped his hips against the edge of my table. God, they looked good in those exceptionally clinging jeans. "'Ow abaht just this once?" he said, with what I'm sure he imagined to be a winning look.

"No."

He fluttered his lashes. He actually fluttered his lashes. "I'll make it up to you, babes."

"Oh, will you now?"

"Yeah."

"You know, for somebody who made such a fuss about being treated like a gentleman of the night, you're remarkably eager to use sex to get what you want."

"Ha-ha, gentleman of the night. Lie-kit! But who said anyfing abaht sex? That was your mind in the gutter, mate."

"We are all of us in the gutter, but some of us are enjoying ourselves down there."

"What?"

"Nothing. Do we have a deal?"

"That you go shopping and I do anyfing you want? That don't seem very fair."

"Well, I don't like going shopping."

He frowned. "You won't," he asked, in a small voice, "make me do anyfing embarrassing or anyfing, will you?"

"God, no! I promise."

He cheered almost instantly. "Ahwight, then." He tapped the train ticket I was still clutching. "So, you need to get everyfing on the list. And make a salad to go wif it."

"Wait—what? You didn't say anything about a salad."

"Later, babes."

8

PANIC

I dashed to the internet to see if any of the local supermarkets had a slot open for same-day delivery.

They didn't.

Shit. Fuck. Wank. I was going to have to leave the house. Interact with people.

Make a salad? I could cope *fine*, thank you, as long as I had time to prepare. As long as I knew where I was going, what I was doing, what would be expected of me, and how much energy it would take. I needed to plan. Assess the danger. Break the whole activity down into safe, manageable chunks so that the enormity and unpredictability of what lay ahead didn't overwhelm me.

Go shopping?

It was a minefield of potential disaster.

I stared at my phone and thought about calling Niall, despising the way normal things could make me feel so utterly helpless.

Self-pity. Such an attractive quality.

But it was miserably unfair. Whatever I did, no matter how

hard I tried to pretend otherwise, there was no respite from my limitations. I was my own cage. And I hated it. Hated myself.

I put the list down on the kitchen table and carefully scrutinised it. Carrots, garlic, mince. And that was only the beginning. Argh. So many *things* heedlessly demanded in Damian's careful, round writing. I would be shopping forever. Assuming I didn't have a nervous breakdown in Sainsbury's, which wasn't as remote a possibility as I would have liked.

I considered which scraps of my self-respect I could bear to sacrifice. Niall would help me. Even after everything. Because he always did. And I would inevitably resent him for it. At first, gratitude had felt like love and I'd welcomed it. Now it felt like swallowing razor blades. And today I couldn't even bring myself to ask. I wasn't sure if that was a good thing or a bad one. Pride, like happiness, was something a madman could ill afford.

Clearly, I was going to fail this very simple task. Which left me wondering how to present it to Essex. "Hi, Darian, sorry, but I'm afraid you're shagging a mental who occasionally lacks the confidence to leave his own house. Still fancy me now?" That was out of the question. Absolutely out of the question. The sex was reason enough on its own to avoid ruining everything. But somehow, like a fool, I'd come to like Darian's insistent questions and the way he spoke to me and looked at me. As if he thought I was fascinating and impressive. I'd felt the very opposite of those things for so long I could barely remember what it was like to think otherwise. And I couldn't lose it. Not yet, anyway. Not so soon.

So that would mean lying to his face. Which I was, I realised with only a minor internal wince at my own perfidy, perfectly prepared to do. I just had to make sure it was plausible.

Except.

He would be disappointed.

And I did not want him to be disappointed.

Oh, no. I couldn't afford to tangle myself up in other people's expectations and inevitable disappointment. It would be awful. An ever-expanding cycle of everyone feeling bad, like a bulimic serpent eating its own tail. I'd been through it with my parents, with Niall, with nearly everyone I've ever known. I'd fuck up and let them down, they'd feel sad, I'd feel sad, they'd feel sad for making me feel sad, and so on, and so on, and so on. As if I didn't bear enough frustration and regret on my own account, without also feeling guilty for hurting the people who loved me.

Once upon a time, I too dreamed different dreams. My horizon was bolder and grander and more beautiful than the threshold of my own fucking flat. And now I lived in a world so narrow and so colourless that getting out of bed in the morning was a victory. That not actively wanting to die was happiness.

Fuck it all, I was going shopping. I was going to buy carrots. And it was not going to be a big deal. That just left the salad problem.

I opened up Google and stared blankly at the search box. With nothing to lose, I typed in "how to make a very easy salad in order to impress a man you want to fuck." It was unhelpful. The first hit was complete tat, the second was a list of fourteen things every guy should (apparently) know how to cook, but none of them were a salad, and the third was an article on how to tell if a man was gay. I was moderately certain Darian was gay. Fucking me had been a fairly subtle clue, but I was onto him. It seemed I'd found the one thing that wasn't on the internet.

I rang Amy.

"I have to go shopping and make a salad."

"My God, call the police."

"No, but seriously." (When did I say "no, but seriously"?) "How the fuck do you make a salad?"

"Oh, I know this one!" she said. "You go to Marks and Spencer, and they have them there in little plastic tubs. You buy as many as you need, take them home, put them in a bowl, and shout *ta-daaa*."

That sounded almost doable except for the Marks and Spencer part. There was probably one nearby, because this was London, but it might involve the Tube. And I certainly wasn't up for that at short notice.

"I can maybe get to a Sainsbury's," I offered.

She thought about it a moment. "Then you're fucked."

"Right."

There was a pause.

"Ash," she asked, "did you ring me because I'm the only person with a vagina you know?"

"Um..."

"Because, you know you don't need a vagina to prepare a salad, right? In fact, I have it on good authority that there are salads prepared sans vaginas all the time."

"Can you stop saying vagina over and over again? It's scaring me."

"It serves you right for being sexist. Vagina."

Even in spite of Saladgate, I felt a smile threatening at the corner of my lips. "Isn't it just possible," I said, "that I rang you because you're a brilliantly clever and generous person (who happens to be a woman) who I knew would be able to help me in my hour of need?"

"No."

"You're probably right."

"But, you know," she said. "You should try Max. He's a kitchen ninja. He'd love to help."

I flinched a bit. "I'll work something out."

"No, I mean it. Ring Max. This is totally his speciality."

"Yes but..."

"Anyway, sweetheart, I have to dash. I'm late for a meeting. The next Martin Amis, you know how it is. Mwah."

Ring Max, she said. As if it were simple. As if I could just pick up the phone and talk to him. I couldn't remember the last time I'd seen him other than as part of a larger group, or the last time we'd had anything like a conversation. Perhaps we'd been closer at university, but I'd lost so much of that time due to an extravagant combination of recreational drugs, mania, and electroconvulsive therapy. A title for my autobiography, possibly. Or an epitaph. The ECT had sort of worked, but it had fucked my memory inside-out and upside-down. Nearly everything had come back, in time, but it had left my life a jigsaw. I had the pieces but I didn't know what the picture was supposed to be.

University and its immediate aftermath were little more than a sensory haze. A blur of gold and green, the scent of old books, the slide of a stranger's body against mine. Rushes of chemical rapture. The heat of a nightclub, a sweep of lights, like a peacock's tail, bodies and heartbeats and music. I was king of a glittering world, a splintering, falling, shattering world. But what of Max? What could I remember of Max?

Patrician good looks and a self-deprecating smile. Cricket whites for dreamy afternoons. Punting and a panama hat in the full golden gleam of summer. And, in winter, a wine-red scarf by an Italian designer so exclusive even I hadn't heard of him. I think Max used to let me bury my hands in it on cold days. My skin, at least, remembered the softness. Like a kiss from a ghost.

It's quite an accomplishment to out-privilege me, but Max, the youngest son of an American heiress and an English viscount, was the sort of person who had no right to exist outside of Sunday night costume dramas and the novels of Evelyn Waugh. If there was any justice in the world, he would be profoundly unlikeable (or at the very least ugly) but, somehow, he wasn't. Imagine, if you would, the sincerity of an American coupled with the self-irony of the English, wrapped in the body of a Greek God. The bisexuality, we must assume, was simply a gift from the universe.

Leaving university with an effortlessly acquired First, he went on to effortlessly found a culture consultancy firm, which had been effortlessly successful, even in the middle of the recession. I wasn't sure what he actually did. Extremely wealthy companies hired him to improve their corporate culture. This seemed to involve Max telling them to buy fruit for their employees and then they'd give him millions and millions of pounds.

It was no wonder I was so reluctant to parade my endless inadequacies in front of him. Not that he hadn't seen them all already. But there was something implacably blessed about Max. He was practically a mutant and his mutation was being better than you at everything.

I didn't even know he liked cooking. No surprise that he was apparently excellent at it.

I rang him. What else was I to do?

"Ash, hi!" He sounded genuinely thrilled. He usually did. Talking to Max could make you feel like the most important person in the whole world. It was a heady drug. And Niall's prescription of choice.

"So glad to hear from you," he rushed on. "It's been, like, forever. Excuse me a moment." The line crackled and I heard him talking to someone else. He seemed to be telling them where to put some fruit. I snuffled in private hilarity and tried to pass it off as a throat-clearing as he came back onto the line. "I'm here. How are you?"

"I'm all right"—(awhight)—"actually. How about you?"

"Going out of my tiny mind over the wedding. It's an absolute 'mare. My mother's family are outraged it can't be held in Buckingham Palace, my father's family hate my mother's family, Amy's family think we're all insane and want to go back to Yorkshire. And I'm petrified they're not going to allow their only daughter to marry me after all. But—" Amusement coloured his voice. "—other than that, everything's fabulous."

"Oh, it'll be fine," I said. "You're filthy rich. They'll probably just have you murdered on your wedding night."

"That's reassuring, ta. I read your latest by the way. Absolutely loved it. I totally didn't see the twist, because I'm an idiot, but when I thought back, it made perfect sense."

"I'm quite proud of the title," I heard myself saying, "because his name is Rik Glass, right, and the title is *Through a Glass Darkly*. Which is an Annie Lennox song. And also in the Bible."

There was a moment of silence, and then Max gave a snort of upper-class laughter.

"Anyway," I went on before I ran out of stupid things to say that could be generously interpreted as my dry, ironic wit, "I sort of need your help."

He didn't hesitate. "Of course, Ash. What can I do?"

Shit. How to start? "There's this... guy...who I'm...well...shagging, I guess."

"That's great!"

"Yes, I quite enjoy it. Anyway, I sort of...gah...it's complicated."

"Complicated?" I could almost hear him frowning, golden brows sliding into intent little Vs.

"Look," I said, quickly, "I need to make a salad. How do I do that?"

Max spluttered. "God," he said, "is that all? I was braced for absolute disaster. Married man, BNP supporter, closet-case, accountant. Not salad eater."

"Oh, fuck off. You know I don't cook. Now are you going to help or not?"

"Of course I'm going to help."

"It has to be an impressive salad," I explained. "A *really* impressive salad."

"Oh, I see, you need a 'let's do it on the kitchen table right now' salad."

"They have those?"

"Abso-fucking-lutely they do."

"Well," I said impatiently, "hit me up. But remember I'm a salad neophyte. I'm not faffing around with pans or any complicated shit like that."

"Damn, you're a difficult man to please."

I didn't quite know how to answer that.

"All right," he continued, "how about pear and Roquefort with a honey and ginger dressing?"

"That's a sex salad, is it? Because, to me, blue cheese does not scream passion. But," I added, with a play of reluctance, "I suppose I'll have to trust you."

"It's a salad. It doesn't need a safeword. I'll send you the details. Also, we should go for a coffee."

"Yes, we should." This was how all of our conversations ended, with vague intentions and abstract good wishes.

There was a pause.

"Ash," Max said, with a trace of hesitation I was unused to hearing in his voice, "why do you always give me the brush-off?"

"I said yes, didn't I?"

"In a 'never getting round to it' way. I mean, you don't have to. I can be your Long Distance Salad Guru. But I miss you."

I shuffled uncomfortably. I was half convinced the reason I'd managed to retain whatever good opinion Max had of me was through the judicious application of distance. "What if I'm shit company?" I said, as though it was a very self-deprecating joke.

"What if *I'm* shit company." He paused and then, half jesting, half sincere, added, "Am I shit company? Is that why you've been avoiding me?"

I sighed. "I'm a misanthropic, clinically anxious, bipolar lunatic. I avoid everybody."

"Lies. You see Amy all the time."

"I work with Amy."

"Oh, so that's why she's entitled to misanthropic, clinically anxious, bipolar lunatic action despite the fact that some of us, it could be argued, have prior claim and should, therefore, be first in the queue?"

"There's a queue?"

"Yes, it's me."

"Max I...I just don't...I'm just not..." I trailed off. What could I tell him? *I'm so much less than I used to be. Seeing you reminds me.*

"Fine," he said. "Fine. If it has to be professional, then so be it. I shall come and consult with you about improving your corporate culture. Over coffee."

I gave a helpless, unexpected laugh. "I've got enough fruit, thanks."

"I bet you don't. I actually bet you don't. I bet you don't have a single piece of fruit in your whole house."

"Darling, I am the fruit." And while he was chuckling, I went on hastily. "Anyway, I'd better see about this salad. Bye."

And I hung up on him, like the selfish coward I was.

A few minutes later, my phone bleeped. True to his word, Max had emailed me salad ingredients and instructions. It seemed just about within my capabilities. On a good day.

I could do this.

9

LATER

"Yorite, babes?" said Darian as I let him inside.

"Yes, I'm fine," I said with impressive nonchalance. "How'd it go?"

"Fink I did good. I fink they fought I was a bit Ibeefa party boy though."

"I don't think orange has quite the same play in the international marketplace."

He grinned, unabashed. "Leave it aht. Did you get everyfing?"

"Of course."

"Come 'ere."

He kissed the smug right off my lips, like a cat licking cream. And I let him, smiling against his mouth, leaning into him only a little, as if today had been nothing at all. As if everything had always been all right.

BEFORE

Don't panic, don't panic, breathe, it's fine, it's fine. God, have these places always been so bright? Is it hot in here? I was suffocating on light. Lost in a maze of wire and geometry. The aisles were radiating away from me, endless, white and bright and silver, like a three-dimensional crossword puzzle, white space and a black abyss, and nothing, and nothing, and nothing. People roaring past me like cars down a motorway, their eyes like headlights, glaring through me. Thundering away in a rush of feet and a swoosh of breath. Strangers, and the loudness of their living, battering me on all sides, the whole world, crashing too loud, too bright against me. Wire-crowned waves, scraping my skin, fingernails in my eyes. *Why can't I find anything? A fucking carrot, where are the fucking carrots?* Why was this simple thing impossible? *Breathe. It's fine. Breathe, fuck it, breathe. Fucking basic. Okay, just rest, it's fine, just stare at this row of olives, nobody is looking, nobody knows.* Heart racing like a rabbit. Half-dried sweat seared my palms. But nobody knew. That's all that mattered. My sweaty, fearful little world: population, me. The pit of my stomach, where terror gathered, a cold iron snake coiled around my heart. I think I hated everything. All my words were whirling away into animal panic, thick as mud. This wild awareness of too much that was its own dislocation. Its own separation. Reality was peeling like a grape. I think I could hear my synapses. *Where are the fucking carrots?*

AFTER

"So what is this culinary masterpiece?" I asked, following Darian into the kitchen.

"Well, Gregg," said Darian, "tonight Darian Taylor will be preparing a menu of 'is Nanny Dot's cottage pie wif...well...that's it, actually."

"What? Who the fuck is Gregg?"

"The one wif the dimples off *MasterChef*."

"I do not watch *MasterChef*."

"Aw, babes, you're missing out big time. It's amazin'. The stuff they make on there...amazin'. And there's this voice-over what's all like—" Darian dropped his voice into a low purr. "—'Barry has prepared a filo of poutine wif a glazed salmon jus, pan-seared girolles, celeriac mash, and a basil and honey cream glaze.' And, mate, I gotta say I don't know what they're on abaht 'alf the time but I feel like I really wanna know, janarwhatamean?"

"I do know that if you try to pan-sear my girolles, I'll be throwing you out."

He laughed. "But, yeah, you should totally watch it, babes. Just not the celebrity version cos that's rubbish cos they can't cook. And it's always like MC Hammer 'as made beans on toast and you're sitting at 'ome finking like, oi, I can do that, fank you very much."

"It's on my to-do list," I said. "Right after 'stick a fork in my eye.'"

Darian dumped a large, leather-bound book onto my kitchen table and started rummaging through the Sainsbury's bags I'd left on the counter because I hadn't been able to face unpacking them. The orange plastic had kept glaring at me like it was mocking me for having nearly succumbed to a panic attack in a supermarket. The too-fresh memory of those strip-lit, labyrinthine aisles seared my mind like acid.

"You wanna look?" said Darian over his shoulder.

I snapped back to the present, safe in my own flat. "Pardon?"

He gestured at the book. "It's my portfolio, innit. Wanna look?"

Not really. I wanted him to do his cooking so we could fuck, and I could forget, forget everything in fleeting, physical pleasure. "Do you want me to?"

"Course."

I suppressed a sigh, pulled his portfolio towards me, and flipped it open. Darian's face, starkly, shockingly beautiful in its artificial stillness, gleamed up at me. His hair was platinum blond, his eyes a deep and steady grey. The generous mouth was stripped of its mirth, though not its sensuality. It was Darian, but not Darian. Some quintessence of Darian, laid bare by the photographer's art. Loveliness refined like a sharpened blade.

He'd come to stand behind me as I stared.

"Whadyafink?"

I cleared my throat. "You...yes, you're certainly, photogenic."

"Ha-ha, you just take millions of 'em. Bound to be one or two what don't make you look a right minger."

I turned the pages—his profile, a smile, a couple of fashion shoots, followed by an advertisement for a local college with the slogan *Stand Out, Be Yourself*, which seemed to involve Darian jumping in the air, mostly naked, through a splash of multicoloured paint.

"I would certainly enrol," I said. The pose, the tension in his uplifted arms and outstretched legs, had brought into definition all the sleek muscles I had felt shaking against me while we fucked.

"I was scrubbing paint from places where it 'ad no right being for days after."

"Why would you do that?"

"I couldn't just leave it up there, babes. It's probably like toxic or summin."

"No, I mean..." I tapped the page. "Why this?"

He shrugged. "Cos it's the job."

"Yes, but it's not really a job, is it? It's more of a..." I felt the sudden stillness of his body and my voice trailed away.

"More of what?" he asked.

"An aspiration. A hobby. I don't know."

He gave me a look I couldn't quite read. A faint creasing of the brows, a certain turn of the lips. "I fink that's a bit aht of order," he said, finally. "Maybe it ain't a job to you, but I like it and I get paid, so I reckon that makes it a job to me."

"Yes, but what about the future? I mean, it's hardly a career, is it?" Oh fuck, I sounded like my mother. Not that she would ever say something like that to me. Everyone had loved her when she'd come to visit me in hospital. Every week, without fail. So delicate in her pearls and her tap-tapping heels, her voice as soft and resolute as water. For the last twenty-eight years, she had been unfailingly kind to her wayward, broken, disappointing son.

"I don't fink I want a career, babes," said Darian comfortably.

"Can you really see me in an office, being all, 'Awhight, Mark, photocopier's dahn again.' And, anyway," he added, "it ain't up to you."

"No, you're right."

There was a long silence.

"You gonna like say sorry or summin?" he asked. "Um, why?"

"For acting like I'm some sorta skiver."

"I'm sorry," I said, because it was easier than arguing about it. How had I allowed myself to get dragged into this? I didn't care what Darian did with his life. But my attempt at an apology sounded so ungracious even to me that I found myself adding: "You're clearly very good at what you do."

He looked mollified. "Fanks, babes." After a moment, he went on, "I'm not gonna let my nan starve or nuffin. I do uvver fings as well when I 'ave to, but I reckon I won't 'ave to if I get an agent in London. Already got one in Essex but I'm finking big, janarwhatamean?"

"It worked for David Gandy," I said, with a faint, insincere smile.

He laughed. "I said I was finking big, not like totally massif. I'm nevva gonna be a high fashion model or nuffin like that. I 'aven't got the body for it. But I fink if I try really 'ard, I'll do ahwight."

"I'm sure you will."

I turned the page. I flipped past a couple more fashion shoots. It was disconcerting to see Darian dressed to someone else's specifications. As if he had somehow become the reflection of a different image. One picture showed him crouching a little coyly on a cobbled street in his ubiquitous skinny jeans and a V-neck sweater-vest one shade bluer than his eyes. The sleeves of the undershirt were rolled up to his elbows, and he was wearing a bowtie that I presumed was meant to be quirky or otherwise ironic, a pair of red Vans, and a trilby. He looked adorably, if incongruously, preppy and I suddenly realised how well he had arranged his body to display the clothes he was wearing.

"My mate Chloe," he said proudly. "She's a designer. Got 'er own shop now and everyfing. She's well clever. Loves clovves. Don't fink geek-chic is really me, though."

"I do prefer you with your clothes off," I agreed.

He leaned forward and flipped over the final page. I drew in a sharp breath. "I fought I'd better do summin arty," he said. "Just in case or summin."

His portfolio ended on a couple of black and white nudes. I gazed, entranced, at the way the light shimmered on his naked skin, drawing the eye into the shadowy secrets of his flesh.

"You look like Rodin's *Danaïd*," I whispered, unable to resist tracing the curve of his spine with my fingertip.

"You what?"

"But a man, obviously," I added quickly.

He pulled out his phone and Googled. "I'm glad you said that, babes, cos I know I 'aven't got a six pack but I don't 'ave moobs neeva."

"It's the juxtaposition of submission and sensuality."

He gave a slightly self-conscious laugh. "You like it, yeah?"

"Yes. It's beautiful." The other photograph was slightly more conventional—Darian leaned back on his hands, one knee raised for the sake of modesty. It showed the lean, strong muscles of his thighs and arms, the ripple of his abdomen, the vulnerability of his exposed throat. "They both are."

"You're staring at 'em like you stared at me in Brighton," he said. "Don't go making me jell of me, babes. My head'll esplode."

I was jealous of the camera. The one-eyed monster that had ☆ pinned him in its possessing gaze.

"What were you thinking?" I asked.

"Lots of fings, babes. I was finking abaht 'ow to make it look right, cos it takes a lot of finking to picture summin when you can't see it prop'ly cos it's you. And I was finking 'ow, my back.'" He grinned down at me, his foolish pirate grin, and I was suddenly sure he was, if not lying, at least eluding me. Not that I had any right to complain about that. Lying was my last unsullied ☆ talent. Then Darian's hand slipped past mine, a swift, insubstantial brush of skin, as he detached the page and handed it to me. "Go on, you can 'ave it, babes," he said.

I stammered something along the lines that I couldn't possibly.

"But you like it," he said, shrugging. "And I like finking of you looking at me like that when I'm not arand."

"But, your portfolio."

"I got uvvers, babes. And I done more commercial stuff now anyway." I stole another glance at the—at *my*—photograph. The sick flood of jealousy was receding now. And, instead, I felt oddly moved by the notion that some stranger, looking with a stranger's eyes, had seen Darian as I did, had caught a moment of his beauty beyond the inadequacies and uncertainties of memory. "Besides," he added, "I fink you like me better like this. Not talking and wif my bum in the air."

He surprised a laugh out of me, the sound ricocheting off my kitchen walls like a bullet.

"You're right," I lied.

He cackled. "Slay-ted. Now come 'ere and say fank you properly."

I twisted round and kissed him. "Thank you. I'll treasure it."

Or try to. Until my next depression convinced me that everything I valued was worthless and I destroyed whatever I could that used to matter to me. I was the climber of a sheer cliff, dragging myself on bleeding hands towards a summit that I'd never reach and sometimes didn't want to reach. The things I cared about were the hooks I'd driven into the rock face. Depression snapped them, one by one, one by one. My only certainty was the fall. Perhaps I should have told him: don't trust me with anything precious. But I wanted what he had given me too much to be anything other than selfish.

Darian left me with his portfolio and went back to unpacking. "You gonna 'elp, babes?"

It took me a moment to shake myself free of sentimentality.

"Not in the slightest. I'm going to sit here, do *The Times* crossword, and occasionally divert myself by leering at your arse."

He tsked. And wriggled. And I had to hide a smile in my palm.

"Well, ahwight," he said. "You can get away wif it this once, cos you did all the shopping. But I'm gonna need some music."

I nodded towards the iPod dock, and he turned it on, filling the kitchen with one of Bach's cello suites. He hastily turned it off again. "Not what I 'ad in mind."

I glanced up from *The Times*. "Not to your taste?"

"Naw, it's not that, babes, it's just I don't wanna be crying on the floor when I'm trying to cook my nan's cottage pie. Are you like allergic to fun or summin?"

"Yes, I'm in a programme. I have my five year token."

He gave me a look I couldn't quite read, before swapping my iPod with his. A pounding remix of "F**kin' Perfect" burst out of the speakers.

"Aw, I love this choon." I couldn't help watching him as he Ibiza-ed it up all over my kitchen, one hand in the air, hips slithering about like a pair of snakes in a bag, as he hummed along, paying only passing tribute to the rhythm.

It was frankly...

Well.

It was just the slightest bit charming.

I put my head in my hands. "Come on, babes."

"Hell, no."

"Why not?"

"Too many reasons to articulate, but let's start with: I'm English, I have some self-respect left to me, and we're in my kitchen, not a heart-warming American sitcom where people do that sort of shit because they are quirky and free-spirited. Also, I need decent quantities of drugs and/or alcohol to even contemplate getting down with my bad self."

He shook his head. "I don't get it."

"What's to get? They make you feel good."

"I'm like..." He put his fingertips together, forming a little square.

"Seriously?"

"Don't reckon my nan would like it."

"Your nan isn't the one getting blatted."

He shrugged. "But when I'm dancing, it's like...it's like 'ow you are when you're—" A touch of colour gleamed beneath his tan. "—when you're wif me, but except wif the music. That feeling. Y'know."

"I think I'll stick to fucking. Since, at the very least, I'm not expected to perform *that* in a room full of strangers."

He laughed and turned back to cooking, body still moving a little in time to the music.

"So, what did you do today?" he asked, chopping away.

Well, Darian, I spent the morning fretting about going shopping, the early afternoon psyching myself up to go shopping, and the rest of the afternoon nearly having a humiliating panic attack in the middle of Sainsbury's. That left me just enough time to put myself back together and de-lunatic my flat for your arrival.

"Oh, this and that," I said aloud, which was sufficiently discouraging that even Darian didn't press it.

"Babes," he said in a bit, "what you buy three garlics for?"

"You said to buy three garlics."

Laughing. Again. "Three bits, you donut. You trying to catch a vampire or summin?"

"I'm trying," I said frostily, "to solve seven across."

"D'you wanna hand?"

I sighed to demonstrate I was put-upon before I read, "'Nose ☆ and eyes, from what we hear, often indicated by hands.' Five letters."

"'Aven't a clue," he said, at last. "That don't even make no sense."

"It's 'votes,'" I said, scribbling it in.

"You what?"

"Well, 'from what we hear' usually means sounds like. 'Nose and eyes,' sounds like 'noes and ayes,' you know, yes and no, and voting can be calculated by raising hands. So it's votes."

"Oh, yeah," he said, nodding. "Wait, what am I saying? I'd've nevva fought of that in like a million years. You're so clever, babes."

I cleared my throat. He'd said he thought I was clever before (I am clever—mad, but clever), but I don't know why it suddenly made me uncomfortable. "It's just about learning the tricks," I said, awkwardly. "Once you know how they're put together, you can solve them. It's got very little to do with being clever. Want to try another?"

"Yeah, ahwight."

"How about this, five down. 'Honestly? No, otherwise.' Two, three, three."

"I don't like it when they're more than one word, I fink that's cheating."

"They're only small words. It's probably a phrase, something a bit colloquial."

"No idea, babes. Don't even know 'ow to start, to be 'onest wif you."

"Well 'otherwise' usually means you need to re-arrange some letters. So the keyword is 'honestly'—but, 'no' is telling you it means the opposite."

"I feel like my head's gonna fall off."

"It's 'on the sly.'"

"What?" He turned, wooden spatula in hand, and narrowed his eyes to shining blue-grey slivers. "Are you making this up?"

"No! 'On the sly'—it's an anagram of 'honestly,' meaning the opposite."

He shook his head, throwing mince into a frying pan full of browning vegetables. "Is this what you're into then? Messing abaht wif words and that?"

"It's just a habit really. Not much else to do—" I stopped in sudden horror. I'd been about to say 'in hospital.' Grey days, carefully ordering and disordering the meanings of things, putting down the letters one by one, like a bricklayer. "—at university."

"I couldn't wait to get done wif school, me. Three more years? Couldn't be doing wif that. I was like—" He performed a gesture I thought was meant to signify a sixteen- year-old Darian telling the British Education System to talk to the hand. "—no fanks."

I had no conscious memory of putting the crossword down. But, somehow, I had. I was just sitting there foolishly, talking to

Darian while he performed his haphazard alchemy at the stove. There had been nothing like this in my kitchen, and for that matter my life, since Niall, and possibly not even then. I think he'd resented cooking as much as I did, but if he hadn't provided food, then we would not have eaten.

I propped my chin on my hand. "Oxford was the best time of my life. I was eighteen and full of hope. I was going to change the fucking world."

"Wif doing crosswords and eating beans outta the tin?" Darian had his back to me, preoccupied with a pan of boiling potatoes, but somehow I knew he was grinning.

"I never ate beans out of the tin! I was in my prime."

"Yeah, cos now you're all crusty and past it and like, 'I remember when all this was grass, where's my shopping trolley on little wheels.' What are you, like twenny-five?"

"I'm twenty-eight."

"Man, your life is over." He swept over with a block of cheese, a plate, and a grater and plonked them down in front of me. "'Ere, might as well make yourself useful."

I drew back. "Oh no, I do not do manual labour."

"Babes, manual labour is like pulling a plough or stacking shelves down the Costcos. That's grating cheese."

I sighed and picked up the grater without further protest. "How much?"

"What?" He blinked at me.

"How much cheese do you want grated?"

"All of it, duh." He flitted off to drain his potatoes. "So, what else you do at university? Or was it all crosswords and Scrabble parties, wif the beans served under 'em silver dome fings?"

"Actually, I was my college Scrabble champion."

"Really?" He gave me an impressed look over his shoulder. "Is that cos you're all good wif words and stuff?"

I grated doggedly. It was totally manual labour. And since when did I say "totally"? "On the contrary, it's because I'm quite good at maths. Scrabble isn't a game about letters, it's a game about numbers. There's no poetry in it at all. If you're looking to make beautiful words, you're looking to lose."

"Well what wif it being a game, maybe I'd be looking to 'ave fun or summin crazy like that?"

He came back, took the grater from my inept hands, and finished the job himself in about two vigorous seconds. I somehow managed not to comment.

"Crazy," I agreed. Out of nowhere, I wanted to kiss his wrists, like I had in Brighton.

He mixed the cheese—all of the cheese, enough for a heart attack—into the mash and began layering it onto a baking dish full of mince and vegetables. Finally, he gave the whole thing a vigorous scattering of salt and pepper, and bunged it into the oven.

"Oh no." He gave himself a little smack on the forehead. "Forgot to take the leaf fing out, didn't I? What am I like? Just don't eat it by accident, ahwight? It tastes well rank."

"I think I can just about manage not to eat a bay leaf."

"It's easy done, babes. Specially if you're distracted."

I raised my brows at him. "Why, what are you going to be doing to me while I'm eating?"

He·gave one of his little gasps. "You're so rude."

At first I'd thought his shocked reactions were a form of flirtation—some sort of heavy-handed Essex irony—but now I wasn't so sure. Innocence was not a word for the twenty-first century. Nor did it seem the natural quality of so glittering a creature. I thought about asking him, but I stopped myself. He wasn't here to satisfy my idle curiosities. And it held its own fascinations: a man who talked like an innocent and fucked like a sybarite.

Later, he served up his Nanny Dot's cottage pie, and I presented my salad. "Babes." He peered into the bowl. "What's all this?"

"It's pear and Roquefort," I said, with an airy wave.

"I was maybe finking some lettuce and tomatoes. This is proper *MasterChef*."

Truthfully, it didn't go. Not even a little bit. The cottage pie was about as wholesome and straightforward as you could get. It was food for winter evenings and happy days. And the salad was rich, complicated, a little bit sweet, a little bit sharp, and seemed to be trying way too hard to be impressive. We'd both served each other a metaphor.

Fan-bloody-tastic. If Darian noticed I couldn't have served a less suitable salad if I'd tried, he didn't mention it. He just said he liked it and pronounced himself well stuffed at the end of the meal. Since he'd done the cooking, it seemed good manners to handle the washing up, which I did by bundling everything into the dishwasher and leaving it to thrash away in its own time.

I felt a sudden, anxious flutter of uncertainty. What was I supposed to be doing with Darian now? I needed to transition this cosy domesticity back to the safety of fucking—not all that advisable after a heavy meal. Mainly I just felt like sprawling on the sofa and...relaxing. What was wrong with me? Maybe he'd put sedatives in the cottage pie.

We drifted back to the living room, silence bumping along awkwardly beside us. In an ideal world, I would have been able to retire for brandy and cigars, and then come back when I was ready to fuck him. Dinner had just about exhausted my capacity for conversation, and besides, what else could we possibly have to say to one another? Physical desire was about as much as I was capable of mustering for anyone, and even that was transient, a thing of fading moments.

Darian bounced onto my sofa and, once again, I was reduced to perching in my own bloody home. I just didn't want either of us to get too comfortable. "Come on, babes." He grabbed me by my jacket and pulled me down. I landed half on top of him, half between his long, long legs. Which he then proceed to wrap lazily around me.

"You're creasing my suit."

He just grinned.

I tried to think of something to say, came up utterly blank, and then panicked. When had something as basic as talking to someone turned into an impossible task? If I survived tonight, perhaps I could take up spinning straw into gold.

But I should have known I could count on Darian. "So what else you like?" he asked incorrigibly.

The answer *you*, which served as both evasion and flirtation, rose to the tip of my tongue, but I didn't say it. What did I like? My pursuits were solitary to the point of solipsism and essentially performed the function of marking time. They were the things I did in the spaces between depression. Like Vladimir and Estragon passing bowler hats around. And about as meaningful. My entire life subsumed into the act of waiting: waiting to be ill, then waiting to be better, the one consuming the other.

Desperation consumed me. "How about a game of Scrabble?"

"Aww, babes, I would, but you'll 'ave me. I'll be like sitting there spelling, I dunno, *cat* and *jug* and you'll be like getting *hypoallergenic* on a triple word score."

"Hypoallergenic? Good God."

"It's on moisturiser, innit?" His fingers played idly along the back of my hand, sending little ripples of sensation across my skin. I shook him off and tugged down my cuffs.

"Of course it is. But, um..." I dug deep into my past as someone who was fun to be with. "We can play Nabble instead."

"What's that, then?"

"Well, it's the opposite of Scrabble."

"I fink maybe rugby is the opposite of Scrabble."

I tilted my head so I could bestow upon him my most lascivious look. "Well, you're very welcome to come scrum with me."

"Wish I 'adn't eaten all that cottage pie now. Let's do...wassit...

Nabble. And I don't mind losing, really. Cos you're sexy when you're being clever."

"Oh. Um."

"You blushing?"

"No. So, Nabble. Basically you can only play words that aren't in the dictionary."

"You what? God, they teach weird stuff at university."

I took the opportunity to haul myself out of the ridiculous sprawl in which he'd trapped me. "It's really simple. Any made-up word counts, assuming you have the letters, and somewhere to place them, and you can make a case for what the word means. But if it's not convincing, then it gets disqualified. So you couldn't have, um, f-s-k-s-w-z for example, as it blatantly doesn't mean anything. But you could have, I don't know, *dwelkin*."

"What's a dwelkin then?"

"I think it's probably a loosely knitted garment, a bit like a poncho, but made of yak hair."

He considered it. "Yeah," he said finally, "I can see that. I reckon there was probably like a trend a coupla summers back, but it nevva caught on proper cos they was naff."

 So I dug out my dusty—very dusty—Scrabble set and we sat on my living room floor, playing Nabble. Eventually I stretched out on my side, propping myself up with an elbow, nudging the letters around lazily with the fingertips of one hand. Darian, however, sat solemnly cross-legged, frowning over the board, a single lock of hair shaken loose from its gel, hanging in front of his eyes. A banal setting for a glitter pirate but it did not dull him. The sight of him stirred a wanting that was starting to feel familiar, though it was less frantic tonight. It was a warm, steady thing, like a heartbeat.

He was uncertain at first but soon he was nabbling like an old hand. First came *glink* ("that like look what happens when two people are fancying each other from across the dance floor"), then *gloffle* ("like when you put too much toffee in your mouf at once"), then *mooshes* ("ankle boots made out of crocodile levva wif pompoms hanging on 'em, big in New Zealand"), *rapazzled* ("off your head, obvs"), and *quimpet* ("like when hair extensions get all weird up at the top like what 'appened to Britney"). And then, somehow, I got silly and offered up *svlenky* to describe the motion of his hips while dancing, to which he responded with *flinkling*, which was apparently what my brow did when I was coming up with something sarcastic to say. From there we moved through a few variations too ridiculous to be recorded, I foolishly formulated *glimstruck* as a representation of how it felt to be around him, and then we graduated to kissing, still fully clothed like a pair of teenagers, on the wreckage of the Scrabble board.

He crashed over me like a wave and I was drowning. He shone so brightly and I was burning. Touched, by his hands and his body and his unintended mercies, I needed my distance back. Difficult, though, when my skin sang at his closeness and I blazed with wanting. I wanted to put my lips against his neck. I wanted to lick the sweat from where it would gather like glitter in the secret hollows of his flesh. I wanted him naked in my arms, like

I'd had him in Brighton, but with not even darkness between us this time. I wanted to give him pleasure. Lavish him in it. Bedeck him with it, like pirate gold. Weave him a crown of all my lost dreams. I wanted to kneel at his feet and suck his cock. I wanted him on his back, so I could look into his eyes while I fucked him.

"I want to watch you make yourself come," I said against his ear, breathless and terrified.

His head came up. "Err...what?"

"I want to watch—"

"No, I gottit," he said quickly. "I sorta meant why?"

Because I need you to stop touching me. Because I want to touch you. "Because I want to. And you did say you'd do what I said."

"Yeah, but it's embarrassing."

"Why?"

I felt uncertainty in the small movements of his body on mine. "Well, it's private, innit? And no point when I got you right 'ere, babes." I felt him smiling as he kissed my neck. "More fun wif two."

"I bet you look hot."

"Naww, I probably look well naff."

I slithered a hand beneath his T-shirt, my palm seeking out the delicate ridges of his muscles, learning the hidden landscape of his skin. "Haven't you ever wanted to watch someone else?"

"Um, I 'aven't really fought abaht it."

"Don't you think it might be hot?"

"I dunno," he said dubiously.

He tried again to kiss me but I kept talking, my voice ringing distantly in my ears, like I was giving a sex lecture to a vast and empty room. "Well, there's always an extent to which the erotic intersects with our notions of the forbidden and the repressed. Often the things that seem the most outrageous to our sensibilities are the ones that carry the most powerful erotic charge."

"You fink way too much abaht everyfing, babes."

I made a clumsy attempt to right my clothes, pulling my jacket onto my shoulders again and tucking my shirt back into my trousers. "Please."

There was a pause.

"You...uh...you really want me to like...wif myself? Wif you watching? Wif all your clovves on?"

I nodded. Fuck knew what my face was broadcasting.

"Well, ahwight," he said, at last. "But if it goes weird I'm stopping."

I nodded again.

And, after a moment, he peeled off his T-shirt, baring an expanse of smooth, dark golden skin to my gaze. I suddenly realised it was the first time I'd really had the opportunity to look at him, but it was not like looking at a stranger. As though my fingertips had unconsciously sought the knowing of him in secret touches, and read him like fragments of braille. He was quite lovely somehow, all sleek lines and subtle definition. He was also perhaps the most groomed man I'd ever seen in real life, though the fake tan couldn't hide the freckles that gathered across the tops of his shoulders and dusted his arms.

"Ahwight?" he said, looking awkward. I must have been staring.

"Oh, yes."

He gave a slightly shy smile.

He wriggled out of his jeans, not without difficulty, making me wonder how he'd ever managed to get into them, and finally out of his boxers. He took his uninspired cock in a half-hearted grip.

"You look gorgeous," I said.

"I feel like a right plum."

"You're beautiful." I meant it. I meant it so utterly I was choking on the beauty of him. I looked at him, as though it could be like touching, as though eyes could be pilgrims.

"Um, fank you," he said after a moment, hand moving lazily upon his hardening cock.

"You must know. You're a model, for God's sake."

He swallowed. "Yeah, but, y'know."

"What?" On impulse, I put my hand on his hand, aligning my fingers over his, feeling the heat of his cock against my skin, through his skin. His breath hitched, colour gilding the tops of his wide, angular cheekbones.

"It's just faking," he mumbled, eyes fluttering like he was falling into a dream, or waking from one. "Could be well busted underneaf."

"Bollocks. Now stop making excuses and get wanking."

He tipped back his head and laughed. He was fully erect now, hot and heavy beneath our tangled hands, so I left him to it. I put my back to the sofa, folded my trembling fingers about an upraised knee and watched, pouring myself into his every breath and his every motion, from the steady stroking of his hand to the involuntary flutter of his darkened lashes over his pleasure-closing eyes. I saw the slow kindling of desire through his body, like a match put to the corner of a piece of a newspaper. I saw the tightening of the long, lean muscles of his calves. The slight curling of his exquisitely manicured toes. The eager darkening of his cock and the glisten of pre-come that gathered on the head. The delicate feathering of his serratus anterior as he lifted an arm above his head. I saw the sinewy invitation of his hips as he twisted a little and—

"What on earth is that?" I asked.

His hand stilled. His lips clung to each other a moment before parting in speech. "What?"

"There's a man's name written on your body."

"Oh yeah, nuffin to be jell abaht, babes. It's only my ex."

"I'm not jell. Err, jealous." I tilted my head to better decipher a piece of ornate calligraphy. It appeared to read, somewhat bathetically for the amount of artistry that had gone into it, *Gary.* "It's just," I went on, "you have somebody's name indelibly inscribed on your flesh."

He pushed himself onto his elbows, abandoning his cock completely. "D'you want to be talking abaht my ex or watching me do myself? Cos I reckon it's either-or, babes. 'E's like a mate now and it'd be proper cringe."

There was something wrong with me. Well, there were lots of things wrong with me. But for some reason I seemed to be still asking about *Gary.* "I just don't understand why you would do something like that. And for someone you're not even dating anymore."

"'E was my first boyfriend. We was in love. Togevver for like monfs."

"Wow, months. And this led you to brand yourself?"

"I fink it's nice."

"I...have no idea what to say to that."

"Well, the people you love are always gonna be wif you. Like—" He tapped his chest. "—in your heart or whateva. So what's the difference?"

"One of them is symbolic and the other is the word 'Gary' literally written on your arse."

"No, it ain't." He paused. "It's next to my arse."

"Not the point."

"Can't believing we're 'avin' this convo wif me sitting 'ere wif my bits hanging out. I just fink, sometimes it's nice to 'ave stuff outside insteada inside."

"I'm a lifetime subscriber to the private repression programme."

"I just fink you're jell."

"Jesus wept, I'm not jealous."

He ignored me and, to my surprise, wrapped a hand round his cock again. I rather thought I'd killed the mood with my ridiculous questions, but apparently stupidity was one of his turn-ons.

"Like it when you look at me like that."

I didn't know how I was looking at him, only that I was and I couldn't look away. His hand moved harder and faster, in time with his quickening breath, drawing my attention back to his cock. My own gave an unhappy, neglected throb. God, I wanted to touch him. His mouth curved into a mischievous smile, his eyes a deep, lust-hazy blue. "I fink you're like protesting too much." He stroked the fingers of his spare hand over the pristine skin of his other hip. "You wanna see 'Ash' written 'ere? Or, y'know, 'A.A. Winters,' cos you're all proper."

"Just shut up and wank." The unsteadiness of my voice betrayed me. He'd only been teasing, but, in some twisted way, it was absolutely true. I would have written myself into his skin if only I could, like a prisoner marking the walls of his cell, just to prove I was still alive and that I did not drift, untouching and untouched, through a universe of empty spaces and fading stars.

"Y'know," he said, a few seconds later, "don't you fink it's sort of like a waste?"

"Hmm?"

"Like...y'know...this." He briefly indicated his cock. "Wouldn't you rather...?"

"Fuck?"

"Yeah."

Yes. "No."

"I fink," he said, after another moment, "maybe you do."

There was a heavy scent of arousal in the air, skin and sweat, with a sticky chemical undertone of hair product and cologne.

"Is that so?"

"Yeah." Another pause. "What would 'appen if I like...tried summin?"

I swallowed, staring at the movement of his hand as though mesmerised by the gliding skin. "I would protest most vociferously," I said quietly. "And accuse you of reneging on our deal."

He stopped. And pushed me down onto the carpet, pinning me beneath his naked body, his hands briefly forming sweet, warm shackles about my upper arms. I could feel his heart thudding against my back and I made a tormented, needy noise, utterly self-betrayed. I wished I could be naked with him, but it was too complicated, too revealing. I'd settle for this.

"What's reneging?" he whispered.

"Ch-cheating."

I twisted, pushing my hips up to meet him, burying my face in my forearms, the sleeves of my jacket cold, synthetic and wrong against my skin.

"This you protesting?" he asked, running a hand over my arse and down the slope of my back while I trembled.

"Yes, oh God, Darian."

"Just like checking...it ain't really, right?"

I turned my head and snarled at him, "Fucking fuck me, for fuck's sake."

"For a posho," he said, scrabbling with the buttons on my trousers and yanking them down, "you 'aven't got no class."

10

TOMORROW

The next morning, once again, found Darian repulsively chirpy, eating Weetabix and pawing his way through the newly delivered copy of *The Guardian*. Or rather the film and showbiz supplement.

"Morning, babes." He looked up with a dazzling grin. "You do like the papers wif lots of words in 'em."

. I gave him a dour, it's-too-early-for-anything-especially-you look. "And what is the use of a book, thought Darian, without pictures or conversations."

"Clever bloke, that Darian. And I know I didn't do good at school or nuffin, but I 'ave read *Alice in Wonderland*." He hesitated a moment, before adding a bit sheepishly, "And I seen the movie."

"Congratulations."

"Yeah, I got culture, me." I went to make a cup of tea while he burbled on. "When I was kid, we 'ad these books what my mum used to 'ave, wif these red leather covers and gold lettering on 'em. I fought they was like proper qualidee, y'know. We 'ad like *Robin Hood* and *Alice in Wonderland* and *The Lion, and the Witch and the Whajamacallit.* I used to read 'em all the time and fink abaht my mum reading 'em when she was my age."

I made a bland noise, to indicate I was listening but only because I had no other choice.

"Sorry, babes," he said. "I do run on. But speaking of culture and whateva, I was wondering..."

"Hmm?"

"I was like wondering..."

"What?"

"I'm like doing some modlin at Essex Fashion Week, cos—"

☆   I could not quite contain a spurt of laughter. "Essex Fashion Week? Do all the models go down the catwalk in white stilettos?"

He gave me a slightly wounded look. "Mate, that's well aht of order. It's being, I dunno, racist or summin. You're being racist against Essex."

Racist against Essex, indeed. I bit back the scornful response such a statement deserved. "I suppose you have a point," I said, instead. "It is, after all, unacceptable to make judgements about other people based on the colour of their skin—even if that colour happens to be orange."

"What's wrong wif you? That's me you're mugging off."

"I was joking."

"Was you?" said Darian, putting down his spoon with a clink, and regarding me with rather cool grey eyes. "Cos it sahnded like you wasn't."

I sat down at the table. "Just forget it. Go on, tell me about Essex Fashion Week. Or your happy childhood memories. Or whatever else you want. I'm listening."

He frowned, opened his mouth, and shut it again. Then frowned some more. "Yeah, ahwight," he said finally, though still with a wary expression. "It's sorta like Paris or London or Milan or whateva. Only like in Essex."

"You do know there's a bit of a difference in scale there, right?"

"It's a big fing, babes."

"Whatever you say."

He took a deep breath. "Do you maybe wanna come?"

I blinked. "To Essex Fashion Week?"

"Well, it's only a day, really."

"Wait. The Great International Essex Fashion Week is really only Essex Fashion *Day*?"

"Can you like stop being a bellend? Do you wanna come?"

"No."

There was a long silence. "Right," said Darian.

I took a sip of tea, relief banishing the stinging needles of anxiety that were darting up and down my arms, easing the tension that had settled on my shoulders. That had gone about as well as it ever did, and there was no further danger of false expectation. Or false hope.

"Why not?" asked Darian, sudden and swift as a blade.

"Pardon?"

"Why don't you wanna go wif me?"

"Because I can't imagine anything more excruciatingly dull."

"Right," he said again. And then, coaxingly: "Aww, babes, it'll be a right laff. There'll be like celebrities there and everyfing. You can meet all my mates, and my nan. And you'll see me do my fing." His eyes caught mine. "You like looking at me doing my fing." He leaned over the table and put his fingertips playfully against my lips, making me flinch back. "I fink you like it lots."

Even I didn't have the balls to try to deny that one. "Well, you're moderately pleasing to look at."

"Tharra yes?"

Go to Essex? To a fashion show? Throw myself among strangers and hope for the best? This wasn't a book signing or an interview or a carefully orchestrated social occasion. It was the utter unknown. How could I prepare for that? How could I make it safe when my ability to perform for the world came and went as randomly and unreliably as an ashamed lover?

And, someday, it would all come crashing down. And the world would see me for what I was. And then I wouldn't even have these pieces of pride to live for.

But maybe it would be fine. Maybe I would deride myself for ever having let terror paralyse me over something so trivial.

But maybe it wouldn't. Maybe the damn event would loom over me like the shadow of a waiting hydra until I could barely get out of bed for dreading it. Maybe it would be nothing but a grim struggle, a quiet dying like an animal caught in a trap of spiked smiles and metal words.

"I c-can't."

"Why not?" asked Darian, as if the answer could be simple.

"I mean, I don't want to." God, what was wrong with me? Why couldn't I just tell him I was...*mentally ill*. But the words were stuck, sharp edged, in my throat. The truth was, I'd rather be a dick than a lunatic. I'd rather be hated than pitied. "It's not my...err...thing."

"'Ow d'you know what's your fing 'til you've tried it?"

"I don't have to stick a tarantula up my arse to know I wouldn't enjoy it."

"This'd be better than that, babes."

"Wow, you're really selling it."

There was another silence, and I thought perhaps this would be the end of the matter.

"So." Darian drummed his fingers on the table. "You like sleeping wif me but you don't like being wif me?"

"I'm not tattoo material, Darian."

"Yeah, I got that, mate. But, y'know there's like a...fingy...a spectrum between marrying someone and just using 'em."

"We all use each other," I said, "and it's not necessarily a bad thing. At least nobody is lying."

"That ain't true. I don't."

I gave him an arch look. "But you're so very useable."

He eyed me steadily. "Ahwight," he said at last. "Your call, babes. I'll send the tickets and you can bring your mates or what-ever. Or you can throw 'em in the bin. I mean, the tickets. Not your mates." He got to his feet.

"Where are you going?"

"Home. Got stuff to do, got a shoot tomorrow."

"Oh, right. Yes, of course." I suddenly realised I'd probably never see him again.

And I felt a little dazed. "Are you...will I..."

"Yeah?"

"...see you again?" I finished pathetically, knotting my dressing gown cord round my fingers.

"Course." I looked up. His smile flashed. "At Essex Fashion Week."

My heart twisted like somebody was trying to wring it out. I did my best impression of a charming smile, lifting what I hoped might be a provocative eyebrow.

"One for the road?"

"I gotta get going."

He was already halfway out of the kitchen, but I went after him, caught him by his arms, and spun him against the door-frame, leaning up to kiss him hard and urgently. Just once more. Then I'd let him go. "What about a quickie then?"

"Uh, babes..." He laughed, a little awkwardly against my mouth.

I wound myself around him. *Don't go.* Pressed a hand between his legs. *Not yet.* "Uh," he said again, the heat of his mouth spilling into my mine, as sweet as wine in summer. "I'll miss my train."

"Fuck the train." I tried to smile. Tried to make desperation attractive. "Fuck me instead."

He untangled me. "I gotta go."

And he did.

Alone, resoundingly alone, I slumped onto my kitchen floor. Now who felt like a prozzie? I told myself to try to find it funny. Because it was, wasn't it? In some grotesque, mortifying way.

But my thoughts only echoed, bringing back nothing but themselves.

11
ANOTHER DAY

A tatty brown envelope, with an Essex postmark and my address incorrectly spelled, lay on my doormat. I stared at my newly cleaned, very white whiteboard, trying to muster the energy to plot my next book. I'd squandered most of last year on something that was supposed to be a companion piece to *The Smoke Is Briars*, excavating what was left of my soul in pursuit of something worthwhile. But what was left of my soul had sucked, and now I was behind schedule on the next Rik Glass, with no ideas and no interest. Oh, what was the point? It wasn't even as though I needed the money. I owned the flat and a depressive's expenses were close to negligible. But if I didn't write, then I would literally do, and be, nothing. A complete waste of a life.

ANOTHER NIGHT

Half past three, sleepless, and wanking without satisfaction to the memory of the taste of lip gloss.

ANOTHER DAY

Glass Ceiling? Glass Half Empty? Stained Glass? Broken Glass? Sea of Glass?

Smooth as Glass? Shattered Glass? Rose-Tinted Glass? Glass Houses?

ANOTHER DAY

What in God's name had possessed me to think "Glass" would be a sensible name for my detective?

Then I remembered: I'd only intended to write one book about him. Not six. I should kill the bastard off.

ANOTHER NIGHT

Scrabbling around in the dark, fingers shoved inside myself, altogether a poor substitute.

ANOTHER DAY

Egelkraut Splettstößer. And I could call the book whatever I damn well pleased.

Assuming I was willing to write about the adventures of a fifty-year-old German housewife.

Fuck you, Rik Glass.

ANOTHER DAY

Rik Glass had run out of cigarettes and discovered a corpse in the middle of his living room.

ANOTHER DAY

Shot Glass? Breaking Glass? Glasshopper? Cracked Glass? Under Glass? Raise Your Glass? Ground Glass? Glasswork? Glass Blower? Maybe not. Fibre Glass? Wine Glass? Hour Glass? Glassolalia? Fuck it.

ANOTHER NIGHT

4:07 was the worst time. The world had stopped moving around me. I was a prisoner of time. Memory tore at me like vultures. Why couldn't I sleep?

ANOTHER DAY

It was not a good day. Not only had Rik Glass run out of cigarettes, but there was a dead body in his living room.

ANOTHER DAY

Homicide detective Rik Glass smelled burning flesh and knew— Damn it.

ANOTHER NIGHT

Darian. How could you miss something you've never really had?

ANOTHER DAY

Best-selling crime novelist A.A. Winters sat at his desk unable to write and thought perhaps he would never have a good day again.

ANOTHER DAY

Afternoon was dripping into evening. Sleeping and waking had blurred into a grey haze. There was a packet of Weetabix on my kitchen table, the gaudy yellow box burning my heavy eyes.

I didn't even like Weetabix, but I couldn't find the motivation to throw it away.

My routines were crumbling around me. I could feel depression gathering like shadows in the corners of the room.

In short, I was fucking up.

I put my head in my hands. Realised they were shaking. Folded my fingers together tightly until they stopped.

There was a tatty brown envelope, with an Essex postmark and my address incorrectly spelled, propped against the empty fruit bowl.

ANOTHER NIGHT

In the buttery half-light of a spring dawn, I sat cross-legged on the floor where we had fucked atop my Scrabble board and opened Darian's envelope. It contained, as I had known it would, two glossy, complimentary tickets to Essex Fashion Week (Day).

There was no note. But on the inside flap of the envelope there was the shining pale pink imprint of his lips.

I rested my chin on my palm to smother something that felt like it could become a smile.

Then I rang Niall.

His voice, when he finally answered, rasped with sleep and alarm. "Are you all right?"

"Yes, I'm fine, I just wondered if you wanted to come to Essex Fashion Week with me."

"Jesus Christ, Ash...it's half past five. Have you taken your medication?"

"Yes, not insane at the moment, thanks. It's next week."

"Uh. What is?"

"Essex Fashion Week. Except it isn't really a week, it's only a day."

Niall groaned. I could picture him running a hand through his sleep-tousled hair and falling back against his pillows with a despairing flump. He was even worse in the morning than me. It had led to grim and silent breakfasts. "I have to be up in forty-five minutes."

"Will you come with me?"

"What? Where?" he asked. "I have a meeting this morning. It's important."

Perhaps I shouldn't have rung him so early. But my determination might have faltered if I'd waited. I certainly couldn't imagine making a decision like this at any other time. It had to be wrung out of me when I was weak, foolish, and impulsive. To say nothing of lonely, miserable, and half delirious with lack of sleep. "To Essex," I said, as patiently as I could. "Not today. Next Monday."

"Why do you want to go to Essex?"

An unanswerable question. "Essex Fashion Week."

There was a silence. "Is this a dream? Why the hell do you want to go to Essex Fashion Week?"

Because there's a man I can't stop thinking about. Because I feel terrible and I want him. "Research," I said.

"Research?"

"Y-yes."

"You're setting the next Rik Glass in Essex?"

"Uh, yes. It's going to be called..." I waited for inspiration to strike me from nowhere. And, unbelievably, it did. "...*The Glass of Fashion.*"

"Oh, that's quite good."

"Yes," I said dazedly. "Yes, it is."

"All right, then. I'll take a day off and pick you up next Monday."

I let the phone slip from my hand. In less than a minute, I'd somehow lost control of everything. I'd not only committed myself to attending a fashion show, but I'd claimed to be writing a book about it too. And the pretend book I would never have dreamed of writing even had a fucking title.

No plot, of course.

But it had a title.

I went upstairs to my study and wiped my latest attempt at a decent outline off the board. It was, in all honesty, no loss. I stared at the white horizon, wondering who to kill. A brilliant but hated designer? An innocent young model? An embittered has-been? A prestigious guest? A resentful journalist?

I felt a little dizzy, as though I were standing on the edge of a cliff. But I wasn't afraid. The vanishing point of the mind's eye, the locus of the gyre, was whispering to me across imagined waves. It would have been, at that moment, effortless to step onto the breath of the wind and be borne away like a falcon. But it was only mania tugging on the kite string of my consciousness. Glittering promises that were nothing but ashes. Falling, not flying.

I scribbled some notes while the ideas were fresh and, finally, crawled into bed. I had no expectation of rest. But I slept, deep and dreamless, and awoke safely on the ground. No cliffs or quagmires.

12
ESSEX FASHION WEEK

Essex Fashion Week was being held at a golf and country club near Chigwell, the sort of place that self-identified as a manor despite having been built in the 1990s. We eased into a gravel-lined car park not far from the main building, which was an inoffensive white square topped by a triangular roof that seemed to want to suggest chalet. Pale green countryside, most of which was golf course, surrounded us on all sides. So far, so chocolate box.

"Ye gods," said Niall, as a bevy of heavily bronzed women in tiny dresses tottered past on skyscraper wedges. "We're a pair of pale-skinned brunets in Essex. I think they're going to burn us like at the end of *The Wicker Man*."

I nodded. "Or you'll be whisked off to Room 101 and threatened with an immediate spray tanning."

"And I'll say: 'Do it to Ash, do it to Ash!'"

"But," I said, in a brainwashed monotone, "I love Essex."

Niall chuckled, the spring sunlight picked out a gleam of gold in his dark hair, and I suddenly remembered, not so much with my mind but with a rush of unexpected feeling, why we'd once been friends.

We made our way towards the main entrance, following the crowds into which we absolutely did not blend. I tried to ignore the stares. I think people were trying to work out whether we were celebrities or not.

"Follow the orange brick road," I whispered to Niall.

"I don't think we're in Kansas anymore," he whispered back.

Inside, a champagne reception was in full swing. Not wanting to jeopardise my equilibrium or start an argument with Niall, I virtuously declined my free drink. We were in a fairly generic function room, most of which was taken up by a catwalk in the middle and a lavish VIP area. There was a lot of activity over there, the click and flash of cameras filling the air like a chorus of clockwork crickets. Essex seemed to really love its reality TV stars and talent show contestants.

We wandered over to the exhibition rooms, where there were a number of booths belonging to local boutiques, fashion brands, and salons. If I'd ever wanted hair extensions, now was clearly the time.

Niall, on his third glass of champagne, had relaxed enough to charm a very blond, very gay seventeen-year-old and buy a T-shirt which read "Live Young, Die Fast." He took off his shirt and put it on immediately (much to the appreciation of the seventeen-year-old).

"I can't tell whether it's ironic, a mistake, or absolute genius," said Niall. "But I think I love it."

"It's well reem," avowed the seventeen-year-old, nodding ☆ sagely.

Just then came a cry of "Oh. My. God. Babes." And I turned just in time to receive an armful of Darian. "I didn't fink you was coming."

"Neither did I," I said, when he stopped kissing me long enough to allow me to answer.

"Aww, babes, you've made me so 'appy."

"That's like so beautiful," said the seventeen-year-old.

"Research," said Niall. "I see."

I blushed so hard, it was almost painful. As though I were about to spontaneously combust. "Um, yes. Darian, this is my friend Niall. Niall, this is my...my...Darian."

"Pleasure to meet you, Darian," said Niall coldly.

Darian flashed one of his bright white grins. "Fanks, mate, glad you could make it."

Niall glanced between us.

Darian tugged on my hand. "Come on, babes, you gotta meet everyone." He wriggled. "Omigod, still can't believe you came."

I cast a helpless glance in Niall's direction. He shook his head and followed as Darian pulled me into one of the side rooms. It was full of people. Golden-legged women in bright dresses. And athletic-looking men in very shiny, very pointy shoes. Oh, God.

"Ahwight, you lot," Darian called out. "This is Ash what I was telling you abaht. And 'is mate, Niall. They've come all the way dahn from London."

We were surrounded. Names flew shrieking past me like fighter planes. Most of the women, at least, seemed to be called Lauren.

"This is Gary," babbled Darian.

I shook hands with a man who basically looked like the Platonic ideal of David Beckham. God. No wonder Darian had his name tattooed on his hip. If I'd slept with someone like Gary, I'd want the world to know it too.

"And this is my nan."

I bent down on instinct to receive a brief hug from a tiny old woman wearing a lot of purple.

"And this is my girl Chloe."

I exchanged double-cheek kisses with Jessica Rabbit, bouncing awkwardly against her truly spectacular cleavage.

"She's like my best mate in the world," explained Darian. "If I 'ad a sister, she'd be my sister."

"So it's not incest or nuffin like that," she agreed placidly.

Incest? What the fuck?

"You're sleeping together?" The words tore out of me before I could stop them.

She giggled. "That'd be silly, Darian's gay."

I glanced hastily at Niall. His expression was unreadable.

"But you just said," I went on carefully, "it wasn't like incest."

"I just meant we're like so close in this deep like...what do you call it...like being on the same wavelength all the time... psy-psy-psychotic?"

"Psychic, babes," offered Darian.

"Yeah, yeah, not psychotic. That's like wanting to kill people... Oh no, I didn't mean that." She laughed. It was peculiarly charming, though it had no right to be. "It's just we've got this bond, right, so it would be sort of like incest if we was really related."

"Right," I said, as it seemed the safest possible answer.

"They did practically grow up together," said Nanny Dot. "She was always popping round 'ere and he was always over there."

"I fink I told you Chlo's got 'er own boutique," added Darian proudly. "And these," he gestured to indicate the clothes that surrounded us, "are all 'er designs. Me 'n' Gary and some of the ghels are gonna be modlin 'em later."

"Congratulations," I said.

Chloe smiled, showing teeth as white and straight as Darian's. "I love clovves, so it's like hunjed pahcent dream come true."

Gary put a perfect hand gently on her shoulder. "You totes deserve it, Chlo. You worked well 'ard for this. You should get me to do your PR for you. I'm finking like qualidee geezas on the door wif their shirts off."

"I'm not sure that's right, honey," she said.

"You leave it to me, ghel," said Gary, enthusiasm undiminished by outright rejection. "There ain't nuffin that don't need qualidee geezas."

The man had a point.

"Maybe you should do it, then," said Darian mischievously.

"Naw, naw, I'm gonna be organising it, aren't I? Someone 'as to check the geezas. Make sure they look ahwight. I mean, bloke comes in, nice face, so you get 'im out there. Turns out 'e's a right chubber. Can't 'ave that."

Chloe turned to me. "You should come see the shop, honey."

"I don't really need a sequinned minidress, thanks," I said.

"I do men, too."

"She ain't lying," said one of the Laurens, to great hilarity.

"It's just down Brentwood," Chloe continued, when the laughter had died away. "It's called Bedazzled. I fought it'd be like... Vajazzled except, y'know, *be* dazzled. I fought it was, y'know."

"Um, you know," I said, "you know bedazzled is a real word, right?" She blinked, her lashes beating like the wings of a hummingbird. "Is it?"

"'Pardon my mistaking eyes, that have been so bedazzled with the sun, that everything I look on seemeth green.'"

There was a long silence.

"Shakespeare," I said.

"Oh, honey," breathed Chloe. "That's so clever of you to know that. Darian, babes, he's so clever."

"Well," I said, "you invented it independently of Shakespeare, so that technically puts you on par with him."

She shook her head, tossing a chaotic spill of wine-dark curls over her shoulders. "You're so sweet, honey, but I wouldn't get bedazzled like you said cos I always wear sunglasses."

Beside me, Niall burst into hysterical laughter.

Thankfully, at that moment, we had to go and take our seats because the show was starting.

"I want an explanation," whispered Niall, as people began drifting slowly back to the main function room, carrying us along like flotsam.

"I wasn't completely lying," I lied. "I am thinking of setting the next book here."

"Not completely lying," he snarled. "Fuck you. All you do, all you've ever done, is lie to me. And what about Daryl, or whatever his name is? I suppose you're researching his cock?"

"It's Darian. And I...I like him."

Niall snorted. "How can you like him? Even putting aside the fact you've spent the last five years telling me you're incapable of liking anyone, he makes Winnie-the-Pooh look like Kasparov."

"Well, I wasn't intending to play chess with him."

"No shit. It's pathetic, Ash. Even for you. The depressive and the idiot."

I flinched, glancing around in case someone had overheard. "Can you keep your voice down, please? I don't want everyone to know, okay?"

There was a pause. "You mean you haven't told him?"

"N-no."

Niall shook his head. "You and your fucking lies."

And then the lights dimmed and the show started. It consisted, for the most part, of a succession of big-haired, highly glossed, occasionally orange models strutting up and down in a variety of figure-revealing outfits. The designers and the dresses soon blurred into an interchangeable rainbow, and my mind drifted, idle as smoke rings on a Sunday afternoon. I thought of Darian. Even here, where everything was bright and brash and fake, he glittered like something real.

It was terrifying to want something as much as I wanted him.

It was far too precarious and far too dangerous to imbue anything, or anyone, with that sort of power. Not when I couldn't trust myself. All it did was make him into something else I would lose, destroy, or have taken away.

But, in truth, I would have told a thousand lies to have him, and a thousand more to keep him.

As Niall had discovered a long time ago, the ability to make me happy was its own curse.

"Oh, thank God," he said, when the lights came up and the applause died away. "I was starting to lose the will to live."

"I'm afraid there's more later." I flicked through the booklet. "And we still haven't seen Chloe's collection."

He peered over my shoulder and groaned. "Well, at least it wraps up with designer underwear. I'm not very interested in clothes, but I'm quite interested in watching muscular young men walk up and down in tight pants."

"That's our national sport, darling."

He grinned. Perhaps I'd been forgiven. Again.

"I'm—"

But before he could finish, Darian came bounding over. It was all I could do to repress my stupid smile.

"Babes." He hunkered down in front my chair. "I gotta massif favour."

"Believe me, this is already a massive favour."

"Yeah, I know. But the fing is, right, one of Chloe's models 'as gone down wif leprosy..."

"Wait," interrupted Niall. "Leprosy?"

"That's what Chlo said. That fing wif your throat where you can't talk."

"That's laryngitis."

"Oh, yeah. What's she like? Anyway, babes, do you fink maybe you could come and stand in or summin?" He looked up at me with huge, beseeching eyes. "Please, babes."

"Holy fuck, no."

"It's not a big deal or nuffin."

"It *is* a big deal. Darian, I could never do something like that. I'm sorry."

Respected Crime Novelist Has Nervous Breakdown in Essex. On Catwalk. While Orange.

"You just 'ave to walk up and down," he said reassuringly. "You're well sexy, babes, I promise. You look more like a proper fashion model than I do."

Flattering but very much not the point. I shook my head. "I can't. It's... I just can't."

"He said no." That was Niall. I should have been grateful, but, somehow, I wasn't. It was an unwanted reminder of my own frailty and everything I should have been able to do but couldn't.

Heedlessly, I gripped Darian's hand. "I'm so sorry." I stared into his upturned, hopeful face. "Please don't ask me to do this. I really can't."

He grinned and squeezed my hand. "It's ahwight, babes. Just fought I'd give it a go."

I squeezed back. "You don't...you don't mind?"

"Course not. Still love you, babes."

"Pardon?" But he'd bounced away.

"Don't get your hopes up," said Niall dryly. "That's just the way they talk around here. They love everything. Especially hair spray. Shall we get going?"

"What? You want to leave?"

"I thought you would."

"But..." I cast a slightly hopeless glance in the direction Darian had gone.

Niall made an impatient sound. "This is fucking ridiculous. I don't know what's going on with you and Darian—"

"It's the sex," I drawled. "It's fantastic."

He continued as if I hadn't spoken. "But you need to get over it, right now. Before someone gets hurt. Before you hurt yourself."

"What's that supposed to mean?"

"You're ill, Ash. You're not capable of living a normal life. You know it. I know it. But do you think it's something Darian is going to understand or accept? You haven't even told him you're bipolar, for God's sake."

"It hasn't been a problem with him," I said faintly.

"Oh, come on, you're giving him false expectations. Have you seen the way he looks at you? He's going to want things from you that you just can't give him. Like today. Like now. You're lying to him and lying to yourself. You're building a house of cards and it's going to come crashing down. I can't keep saving you."

"I seem to be quite busy with all this lying and building you have me doing," I snapped. "And, for the record, I've never wanted you to save me."

"Without me you'd be dead or in an institution."

I stood up, and then blurted out: "Well, maybe false expectations are better than no expectations."

Niall shrugged. "Let's not have this argument. Let's go home."

"Fuck you," I said.

And ran after Darian.

He'd long since been swallowed by the crowd, so, after some aimless shoving, I made for Chloe's booth. She was surrounded by people in various states of undress and looked about as stressed as someone with that much Botox could look, but she still had a smile for me.

"Darian..." I panted, "...he said you needed help."

"Oh, honey, are you sure? He didn't fink it would be your fing."

"It's not, but...I'll..." I felt suddenly sick on the magnitude of it all. "...try. Though if you come near me with spray tan, I will end you."

She giggled. "Ahwight, honey. You're literally saving my life 'ere." She kissed me chastely. She smelled sweet and sticky, and her lips tasted faintly of strawberries. In some strange way, it reminded me of Darian and gave me courage.

She dived into her rails of clothing and returned a few moments later with her arms full of dark fabric.

"Try this, honey."

I clutched and looked round anxiously for somewhere to change that wasn't in full view of Essex.

Chloe nudged me into a sheltered corner and pulled some of the racks in front of me. "There you go." She smiled and left me to it.

Oh God. Oh God.

Just don't think about it.

I shed my bespoke suit and stuffed it into a Tesco's carrier bag I found lying on the floor (oh, how the mighty have fallen), and then slithered into a pair of artfully distressed waxed denim jeans that fit so tightly they came perilously close to being leggings. There was no way my wallet wouldn't ruin the line, so I dug out my Oyster card and my door key and slid them into the back pocket as though I were a sixteen-year-old on the pull.

Oh God. Oh God.

I hadn't worn anything like this since...well. Before hospital at least.

And then I shook out the top, which turned out to be a very low-cut V-neck in Jersey cotton, also distressed, with ripped sleeves and a pattern of holes and tears about the neckline and across the front.

I clutched it to my naked chest like an assaulted Victorian virgin.

"Chloe," I whispered. "Chloe. I can't wear this."

"Course you can, honey. What's the problem?"

Before I could stop her, she swept behind the racks and—in sheer fright—I dropped the T-shirt.

"Fuck." I scrabbled after it, an operation rendered both difficult and intimately painful by the jeans. And then Chloe gently caught my wrist, and I froze.

The pad of her index finger traced the long, jagged scar that ran up my forearm. I normally wouldn't have allowed anyone to do that, but it was as if she held me bewitched with the warmth of her painted eyes.

"Oh, honey," she said softly. "You was really going for it."

I shuddered, then nodded.

She let me go, leaving the rest untouched. I think I was relieved. The ruined skin on my arms burned and shivered like a waking monster.

The next moment, she was all business again, casting an appraising look over the rest of me.

"You look lovely," she said. "It really suits you, that look."

"Scarred and shirtless?"

"But," she continued, ignoring me, "you'll need a belt wif those." She pointed helpfully in the direction of my hips. "Put the top on and I'll get you like a coat or summin. And some boots."

She was back in what felt like seconds, with a studded belt and some heeled, snakeskin-patterned boots that I was still dazed enough to put on without protest.

"I was going to 'ave Darian modlin this wif nuffin else." She smirked and passed me what appeared to be a loose-knit octopus.

Good lord, a dwelkin.

"Wait, just this?" I said. "It's a cardigan."

She gave a horrified shriek. Suicide and self-harm were something this girl could take in her stride. But cardigans were beyond the pale. "It's not a cardigan," she squeaked. "Well. It is a cardigan but it's like...a real glamour cardigan, janarwhatamean?"

"I think, my dear, that's what they call an oxymoron."

"A what?"

"A contradiction in terms."

"Well, they 'aven't seen my cardigans, 'ave they? Put it on."

I stuck my arms through the sleeves. It was basically a cross between a cardigan and a shawl, with waterfall lapels at the front and a pair of asymmetric tails at the back that flowed down past my knees. There was also a sort of scarf, which turned out to be very long and growing like a set of tentacles from the collar.

"I feel like I'm in hentai," I muttered as I got tangled up.

"What's that, honey?"

"Nothing."

She caught up the two ends of the scarf and wound them about my neck and shoulders, letting them fall loosely where they would. It should have been an ill-intentioned object, except the wool was incredibly soft. Maybe I was losing it in my old age, but I think I genuinely liked it.

Also, Chloe was right. The thought of Darian wearing nothing but this was pleasing in the extreme.

She smiled proudly at me. "See. It's like a cardigan but like not a cardigan. Like sexy but snuggly."

"Well I'm neither sexy nor snuggly."

She giggled. "That's not what Darian says."

I blushed.

"You aren't going to tell him, are you?" I said.

"Tell 'im what?"

"About my...about..." I gestured to my arms. "I just don't want him to know."

She gave one of her slow, contemplative blinks. "Do you fink just cos 'e's 'appy 'e ain't nevva 'ad summin bad 'appen to him?" Before I could I answer, she went on, "Now, honey, I know you said no to spray tan and I'm like totes respecting that, but 'ow do you feel about bronzer?"

About ten minutes later, I was bronzed, glossed, quiffed, lash-curled, and guy-linered. What the fuck had I done? I stared at a stranger's reflection in the mirror. To be fair, it wasn't awful. It just wasn't me.

But then again, I haven't really recognised myself for a very long time.

I drew in a few slow, steadying breaths. All I had to do was keep breathing, walk a few meters down a catwalk, and come back again.

Maybe I could do this. Maybe I could.

I nearly laughed aloud at how easy it seemed just then. The stranger's eyes shone.

"Ohmigod, babes." Darian's reflection appeared next to mine and I spun quickly away. He was wearing ripped jeans, a white shirt split to the navel, and a slim-fitting blue velvet jacket. "You look well nice." His eyes travelled up and down my body, making me hot and self-conscious and thrilled all at once. "Well nice. Like...like Sandy at the end of *Grease*."

My mouth fell open. "Did you really just compare me to Olivia Newton-John?"

"I just meant like going from, y'know, prim to all sexed up."

"I feel...weird."

"You look amazin'. Amazin'."

He pulled me against him, hands snaking under the glamour cardigan to make the acquaintance of my arse.

Chloe gave a warning screech. "Don't smudge 'im!"

He grinned, tilting his head because, in my heels, I was just a little bit taller than he was. "You're giving me chills, babes."

"Is that so? Are they multiplying?"

"Hunjed pahcent."

"You'd better shape up, then."

"You're like totally the one that I want. Fank you for doing this, babes. You didn't 'ave to, y'know."

"I...know. I just. I don't know. I just hope I don't fuck it up."

"What's to fuck up, babes? It's just walking down a room wif everybody finking they want to do you."

I gave a shaky, unconvincing laugh.

"I know it ain't you," he said, after a moment. "But it ain't nuffin to be scared of."

"Fear isn't rational."

He nodded. "We'll be cheering you on all the way."

I raised a brow. "And wanting to do me?"

"Always, babes. It don't matter what you're wearing."

Heedless of Chloe's warning, I kissed him. It was a claggy business.

When we unstuck our mouths, Darian was laughing. "I fink we just swapped lip gloss."

The next twenty minutes of my life rushed by like motorway traffic and I had no idea how I got through them. The only thing I could recall with any certainty was the heat of Darian's hand holding mine. Backstage at a fashion show, it turned out, was madness without method. Nothing but shouting and running, a tornado of light and chaos and shoes. It was impossible to understand what was happening, but somehow things came together. And the models, who had been dishevelled and borderline hysterical in the seconds before, glided onto the runway like swans.

Could I do this? I didn't think I could do this.

"I'm gonna be right back," said Darian. "Just gonna do my fing."

My hand clenched about his, my nails pressing pale, desperate smiles into his skin.

But I had to let him go. So I did.

Then Chloe was hustling me to one side. "This way," she whispered. "You can watch 'im."

Backstage, unsurprisingly, afforded a poor view. Through a dazzle of light, I watched Darian recede and then come back to me. His face, his body, the way he moved were all so composed that it wasn't until he stepped through the wings, grinning, that I quite believed in his return.

"See, babes," he said. "Nuffin to it. Serious face on. Giving it a bit of strut."

It was slightly too late to say that I didn't strut (I don't) or that I really didn't want to do this (I didn't). But when I stepped onto the catwalk, all of Darian's friends leapt to their feet and burst into wild cheering. Essex, obviously thinking something important was happening, did likewise. I doubt I was much of a model, but I walked, turned, and did not fall over, cresting a wave of entirely undeserved appreciation that continued even as I fled into the wings, where I landed, breathless but safe in Darian's arms.

Kissing him to a chorus of applause that flashed like fireworks behind my eyes.

From there came a haze of laughter and congratulations, Chloe's voice rising stridently across the noise: "Y'know what, honey, you can 'ave the glardigan. It's yours."

"G-glardigan?"

"Yeah, it's like glamour and cardigan, innit?"

Of course.

The day unravelled into evening, event into after-party, sweeping me along with it. A group who—Darian informed me— had been on *Ess Fakta* performed to great enthusiasm, and then a DJ took over. We tumbled round a table near the bar, Gary going to secure the first round.

The revelation that I didn't drink inspired a squeal of glee from Darian's friends.

"They're meant to be togevver!" cried one of the Laurens. "So romantic."

"I just don't sec why you 'ave to be blatted to 'ave it up," said Darian. "I am hunjed pahcent sober and hunjed pahcent *li-ving*."

Chloe shook out her mane, which caused a cascade reaction through the group, and suddenly everyone was checking their hair. "You are so right, honey."

He was. He was. Just then, I didn't need a drink to feel drunk.

Darian wound an arm round my waist and said quietly, "You gonna come dance wif me later?"

I put my lips to his ear. "I want to fuck you later."

He gave me one of his wide-eyed, shocked looks, but I knew

he was only teasing. Suddenly I felt a hand on my shoulder. I looked up, and there was Niall.

"I didn't fuck it up!" Even I could hear how absurdly giddy I sounded, too bright, too happy, as though, at any moment, I would swoop away on the wings of mania. I tried to care, but I couldn't. Darian and I would run hand in hand across the clouds together.

"Well. Congratulations." I caught the sourness of drink upon Niall's breath.

There was an awkward silence.

"He was so good, Niall," said Chloe valiantly. "You would have fought he was like a pafeshunal model or summin."

"I, um, I thought you'd left," I said.

He scowled. "As if I could. Someone has to take care of you."

"I can take care of myself," I muttered, with all the dignity of a teenager.

"Essex is well safe," said Gary, returning with a tray of drinks and passing them round. "Like there was this one time, right, when Darian fought he was being burgled." A ripple of amusement passed over the table and Darian put his face into his hands.

"You always 'ave to tell this story."

"Cos it's hilarious, that's why. So Darian 'ere was carrying on like a right ghel, totally freaking out, ringing me up, being all 'What should I do, what should I do, I fink there's somebody trying to get in through the patio doors.' And I was like 'Phone the police, you donut, what am I supposed to do abaht it?'"

Gary paused with the casual ease of an experienced raconteur, dropping down into a free chair, and extending both arms across the shoulders of his neighbours. "So there 'e goes, creeping down the stairs at three in the morning, wif me on the phone and armed wif an eyebrow pencil—"

"It was well sharp," put in Darian.

"And, y'know what, right? It's a duck aht there."

"Yeah, yeah," said Darian, "but it was obvs trying to burgle me. It was a bad duck."

"I think we should be going," interrupted Niall. "We need to get back to London."

"But I don't want to go," I said plaintively.

"It's ahwight," said Darian. "'E can stay wif me. Protect me from bad ducks, right, babes?"

I tucked my head against his shoulder. "See, he needs me."

"Aww, I do." Darian looked up at Niall and smiled. "We'll be ahwight. I'll take care of 'im."

Something flickered across Niall's face like a shadow. I sat upright, filled by a sudden, despairing premonition. It left me shivering, even in the warmth of the glardigan, and I flashed Niall a frantic look, as though, in a split-second, I could make him understand: *Please don't do this to me. Let me have this. Let me have this happiness.*

"You can't take care of him," Niall said flatly. "He's a type 1 bipolar depressive with clinical anxiety disorder. I don't think you even know what that means."

For a moment, Darian was silent. His was the only response that mattered, though I told myself it didn't. Watching him was like waiting for an axe to fall, but I could not look away.

"I do actually," he said, at last. "I saw a fing on the telly wif Stephen Fry."

Niall gave a harsh, barking laugh. "Oh, you saw a thing with Stephen Fry. Well, thank God for that, we're saved. Did you get that, Ash? You're going to be *fine*. He saw a thing with Stephen Fry. We're in the presence of a fucking expert here."

"I didn't say I was an expert in anyfing," said Darian slowly. "Just that I wasn't totally clueless."

"I remember reading somefing in a magazine," added Chloe, "abaht Robbie Williams. Doesn't 'e 'ave bipolar as well? It was somebody what used to be in *Take That* anyway."

"Was it Gary?" asked one of the Laurens.

Chloe shook her head. "Naw, he was the one what was struggling wif his weight. I fink it was Robbie."

Niall slammed his hand onto the tabletop, knocking over a couple of drinks and causing Darian's friends to jump to their feet screaming in fear for their minidresses. Only Darian didn't move.

"You don't have a fucking clue," Niall yelled, over the chaos. "And I'll tell you now, you can't fucking handle it." He threw his words down like swords. "What are you going to do when he won't get out of bed or take his medication? When he cuts words into his arms, drinks when he shouldn't, takes drugs when he shouldn't, or sleeps with strangers who are bad for him?"

Darian flinched.

"Or what about when he keeps you up all night because he can't sleep. Or has a panic attack out of nowhere. And, let's not forget: what about when he tries to kill himself, again? Or he has another manic episode and won't eat or sleep or stop talking, and thinks he's...what was it again, Ash? Oh yes, Thomas Mallory, and the second coming of Arthur Pendragon."

I stared at him, silent and stricken. I didn't dare look at anyone else. Least of all Darian.

"What abaht it?" said Darian, finally.

Niall shook his head. "You have no idea, do you? You have to live with it, or the threat of it, every single day. Do you really think *you* could cope with that?"

"I dunno." Darian shrugged. "Maybe it ain't abaht coping or not coping. Maybe it's just abaht wanting to be wif someone."

"You're so fucking naïve."

Darian stood up. He was taller than Niall and frowning. "I don't fink I am. I fink you just fink I am cos I don't talk or fink like you do." He paused. "I fink."

I couldn't stand it. Voices were swirling around me, talking about me but not to me.

"You can't help him, Darian. You can't make him better."

"I didn't say I was gonna."

"You can't make him happy either."

Darian shrugged. "I fink I got the right to try."

It was like being in hospital again. Reduced from the first person to the third. From subject to object. I was disappearing into other people's sentences. I wanted to speak, but I didn't dare. I didn't know how it would sound. Whether my voice would break. If I would be plausible. If I had the right to want anything at all. What use to the sane, after all, were the words of the mad?

13

THEN

I stood up, turned, and walked away, the lights blurring to smears in my eyes and Niall's castigations stinging my skin as though I'd carved them myself. Again. By the time I'd stepped outside, I was running into the night.

Because that's absolutely the way to prove your sanity.

I heard a voice calling my name, but I couldn't stop. I couldn't seem to breathe enough air.

And I felt paper-thin and utterly unreal. Shredded. All I wanted to do was put a barrier of distance between me and everything that had just happened.

If only I could also outrun myself.

Maybe it would not be so terrible, to disappear entirely, to drift away in fragments beneath the moon, like pieces of torn of lace.

To cease to be.

That was something I could never make Niall understand, though I don't know how hard I'd tried. I had never wanted death, merely cessation; unfortunately, sometimes, they seemed to be the same thing.

Niall had done nothing but tell the truth, though he had wielded it like a weapon. But it was hard to forgive him for it.

And Darian? Oh, I couldn't bear to think about Darian.

I had never felt quite so ugly, helpless, or naked. But it had been my own fault, for trying to pretend I was otherwise.

Was it cold? I thought it might be cold. It was certainly dark. But these considerations beat against me like my body was a window pane. I was visible, but unreachable. A prisoner of myself.

Where was I?

I had slowed to walking. A road ran by (though not to Camelot). Fields lay on either side.

Oh, fuck.

Lunatic Writer Lost in Essex.

Maybe I was going to be murdered. Torn apart by wolves. Maybe I'd starve to death under a hedgerow. What did a hedgerow even look like?

All right. These were not rational thoughts. That, at least, I recognised.

The important thing was not to panic.

Like a shark scenting blood in the water, anxiety rushed over me in a great, devouring wave.

No, really, Ash, don't panic.

I fumbled for my phone.

Of course. Of course. I'd left it with my four-thousand-pound suit.

So I had a panic attack. A full-on heart-pounding, breath-choking, sweat-pouring, absolutely mortifying panic attack that sent me sobbing and shuddering to my knees in the middle of nowhere.

Minutes, hours, years, eternities later, I put myself back together. Still alive.

Somehow.

Still breathing and still alive.

I had two choices: I could go back, or I could go on. Going back was simply not an option. And didn't they say all roads lead somewhere?

(Was this madness?)

I kept walking and, sure enough, in about five minutes I came to a roundabout and a sign pointing the way to Chigwell Station. Another five minutes, and the red circle with the blue line loomed out of the darkness like the word of God. I would never have imagined the Underground sign could have been such a wonderful sight.

I traced a route on the Tube map. Central line to Woodford. Central line to Bank. That was. That was *easy.*

For a brief, fleeting, blissful moment, I felt in control of my world. I felt normal. And fuck Niall.

14

BACK

Exhaustion set in after I'd changed trains, along with a heavy misery that seeped into me like winter drizzle. Darkness rattled past. But it was all right. That darkness was taking me home. I could pull it round me like a cloak. Occasionally I let myself think of Darian. It felt like poking at an open wound, but I couldn't seem to stop.

Niall was sitting on the steps outside my flat, staring bleakly into the middle distance.

"My god, Ash." He hauled himself up with the railing the moment he saw me approach. "I've been ringing and ringing. Are you okay? You look terrible."

"Get the fuck out of my way."

"How did you get home?"

"I took the train. Because sometimes, on very special occasions, I am almost a human being."

He came towards me and I pulled back, glaring. "Ash, I'm so sorry. I'm so sorry."

"I don't care. I never want to see you again."

"Ash." He spread his hands helplessly. "You have to understand. I never meant to hurt you. I was trying to protect you."

"I liked him."

He sank back down onto the steps and put his head in his hands, hair falling forward in front of his face. I watched him torturing himself and felt nothing. Not even satisfaction for what he'd done to me tonight.

"How can you like someone like that?" he asked finally. "You have nothing in common. What can you possibly have to talk about?"

"He made me feel good. And you fucked it up."

"If he meant that much to you," he said sharply, "you'd have told him yourself."

"Well, that's up to me, isn't it?" I threw the words back at him. "Maybe I liked looking into someone's eyes and seeing something other than pity, resentment, and guilt."

"If that's what you see in my eyes, it's because you put them there."

"Get the fuck off my steps."

But he didn't move. And I wanted to be inside, surrounded by walls I had chosen. "Why him?" he asked, grabbing for me as I tried to scramble past. "What does he give you that I couldn't?"

I shrugged. "For starters, he's not trying to prove to someone else what a saint he is for being with me."

Niall went white. "I...that's not true." And then, rather desperately, "I love you, Ash."

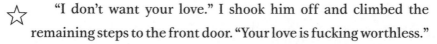
"I don't want your love." I shook him off and climbed the remaining steps to the front door. "Your love is fucking worthless."

"But I just wanted to make you happy." A note of pleading crept into his voice, and I ignored it. "Why wouldn't you let me? I always told myself it was you, not me, that you couldn't. That you were too broken. But...but now you've found someone who does make you happy, so it must have been me all along."

And then he started to cry, hoarse, gulping, undignified sobs that forced their way out of his throat as though they were choking him. I'd never seen him cry before. And tonight I didn't care.

"I just wanted to fix you," he said.

"This is who I am." I put my key to the lock. "I don't need fixing."

I let myself inside and went to bed.

I didn't know when Niall left.

15

MIDNIGHT

When the doorbell buzzed a couple of hours later, my instinct was to ignore it, but it kept on buzzing.

I dragged myself out of bed, pulled on a dressing gown, and went to growl into the speaker, "Will you leave me the fuck alone?"

"Bit 'arsh, babes." It was Darian's voice. "I got your suit and your phone."

I never wanted to see him again. To see disgust, or pity, or discomfort reflected on his face where there had been laughter, admiration, and lust.

But it was a bit late to pretend I wasn't in.

"Fine. I'll come down."

Darian was standing on the doorstep, looking unbelievably, unbearably shaggable, limned in silver moonlight and holding the carrier bag with my suit in it. "Yorite?" he said.

"Thank you for this. You shouldn't have gone to the trouble."

"Aww, babes, I'd be like so lost wifout my phone. I wouldn't know what to do wif myself."

"Right. Um. Yes. Thanks. Goodbye."

"You what?"

"Thank you for returning my things. Goodbye."

"I tried to come wif you before," he said quickly. "But you run fast for a skinny geeza and I couldn't find where you'd gone. Right numpty I'd've looked wandering arand in circles in Chigwell in the dark for hours and hours wif you being tucked up in bed."

An unexpected, unwarranted tingle of pleasure ran through me at his easy assumption that—even running into the night without a coat or mobile phone—I'd basically be fine. But then, he didn't know any better. He wouldn't. I'd done nothing but lie to him.

"You could have been set upon by a whole gang of ducks," I said.

"Aw, babes, don't joke abaht it. Ducks are roofless, I'm telling you. Now are you gonna let me in or what?"

"I had a panic attack," I blurted out.

"What?"

"I had a panic attack. On the way home."

"Aww, babes, are you ahwight now?"

"Yes."

"So can I come in?"

What was this? Kindness? Guilt? Naïvety, as Niall had said? "Did you want something?"

He gave a shy sort of smile. "Well, you said earlier abaht... y'know—" His eyes darted anxiously left and right as if he were about to try to sell me something that had fallen off the back of a van. "—doing it. I've come to collect. Cos you was well sexy today."

I couldn't imagine at what point I'd been even remotely sexy. Did he mean when I'd worn a cardigan? Or when Niall had spat out all my secrets? Or when I'd run away from them?

"I'm not up for a pity-fuck, Darian."

He blinked. "I don't pity you, babes. I fink you're doing ahwight, actually."

I made an odd sound. It had started as a laugh. "I'm really not."

"Not being rude or nuffin, but I fink what I want to fink abaht you is up to me, babes."

There was a long silence. How ridiculous, standing there barefoot in the entranceway to my flat, clinging to a Tesco's bag, and feeling...what? Something sweet and fragile. Far too fragile. "You...still want me?" I regretted the wretched words as soon as I'd uttered them. Insecurity was such an attractive trait.

"Yeah," he said and stepped inside.

I let him into the flat and flung the bag with my poor suit in it into a corner by the hatstand. We stood awkwardly in the hall, Darian hopping about on one leg like a demented flamingo as he pulled off his boots. I was being stupid. He'd been here before. We'd already slept together. That was the main—possibly only—reason I let people into my flat. Bright moments gleaned from the clumsy communion of anonymous skin. It was all Darian was ever supposed to be.

"Do you want something," I heard myself say. "Like a tea or some water or something?"

"Naw, babes, I'm good."

There was a hideously self-conscious silence.

"Bedroom through there," I said at last, pointing.

"Y'know, I always fought you 'ad a dead body in there or summin. Cos like you've nevva let me in."

"And you slept with me anyway?"

He grinned. "I guess I must've fought it was worth it."

"No dead body. I'm just...private."

He stepped inside. "It's like a library in 'ere." And then, "The bed is well massive, babes." And then, "Is this you? You look different."

"It's my graduation photo. I was very young." Nothing but a boy on the brink of madness.

"Do you still 'ave the robe fing?"

"Somewhere."

He gave me a hopeful, coquettish look.

"Don't even think about it. That's a very prestigious piece of academic dress."

I let him wander amongst the pieces of my life, picking things up and putting them down again, peering at photographs and pictures. The one he'd given me was still unframed, but I hadn't thought to take it down from where it was propped on one of my bookshelves. The sight of it made him grin.

"I knew you liked me, babes."

I rolled my eyes. "I just haven't found anywhere to put it yet."

"Yeah, yeah."

He reached up and ran his hand over the peacock feather

fan hanging on the wall, emerald green and turquoise spilling between his fingers, then winked at me. Cheeky bastard.

I scowled. "Those boxers were unfortunate. They're not my usual taste."

"You was like Cinderella, babes, running off, leaving only your pants behind."

"If you're my Prince Charming, I want a refund."

He laughed, picking up a feathered carnival mask and peering through its empty eyes. "Didn't fink you for a clutterer."

"Just in here."

"What's wif the fans and the masks and everyfing?"

I shrugged. "I like the beauty of artificial things."

"Oh my God, babes." He pointed at the wall. "What's this? No offence, but I fink that's the creepiest fing I've ever seen."

"It's quite all right, I didn't paint it."

He leaned forward in transfixed horror. "Why've you got a picture of a naked ghel and a skeleton?"

"I, err, I like the naked ghel...girl and the skeleton."

It was perhaps the first time I'd ever seen him lost for words.

"It's a Paul Delvaux," I added, trying to explain. "Just a print, obviously. The original's in the Tate Modern. He painted a lot of naked women in strange situations."

"Yeah, but why?"

"Um, exposure to waxworks at an impressionable age?"

"I dunno 'ow she's managed to doze off wif that skeleton staring right at 'er. And what's that uvver naked one supposed to be

doing? She looks like she's trying to get a taxi to take 'er 'ome
after living it a bit large."

I crossed the room and contemplated *Sleeping Venus*. "I can
honestly say I've never noticed that before."

"And what about them fellas at the back? What are they supposed to be? Dads at a disco?"

"I think maybe they're lamenting."

"They should be, dancing like that."

I put a hand across my mouth, but it was too late. I was laughing. There was nothing for it. I turned him round and kissed him,
clumsy with amusement, breath and warmth and mirth mingling
in the chalice of our pressed-together lips.

"Want me to get the light, babes?"

I shook my head and, before my courage could fail, yanked
off my dressing gown in the world's most impulsive and ineffec-
tive striptease.

Darian's eyes blurred to stormy grey. "Wow, babes, all this
time you didn't even 'ave your pj's under there. You should've
said. I wouldn't 'ave bovvered wif the paintings."

I spoke, once again, without thinking. "Sure you want me?"

His fingers climbed my ribs and then skated the ridged flesh
that marred my arms from elbow to shoulder, raising a trail of
goose bumps almost lost in the ruin.

"Course." He kissed me lightly. "You're so pale, babes. Fink I
must have some kind of fing for vampires or summin."

I laughed. Again. "Well at least I'm not an orange-utan."

"Ooh, that's aht of order."

"Going to make me sorry?"

He let out an unsteady breath. "Yeah."

I pushed him down onto the edge of the bed and knelt across his thighs. He cupped a hand at the back of my neck and pulled me into another kiss, sliding his tongue into my opening, moaning mouth. It was strange to be naked when he was not, slightly vulnerable, but, just then, it didn't trouble me. It brought with it a patchwork of sensation, the cool air and the heat from his body, the roughness of denim and the softness of velvet, all mingled with the pressure of his lips and hands, the places where his skin brushed against mine. My cock rose between us and he wrapped a hand round it, rolling his palm slow-hard-perfect across the head. I closed my eyes, gasping, and he did it again.

"What was I being sorry for?" I said.

"Dunno. But are you?"

"Oh yes," I murmured. "Very."

"Yeah?"

"Y-yes."

His other hand glided over my shoulder and slowly down my chest, nails scraping lightly over a nipple. I fell into him, hips driving my cock into the channel of his hand, as I shuddered, helplessly wanting. His breath curled across the top of my ear, and he made a sound of encouragement, pleasure, I wasn't sure.

"I 'aven't nevva," he whispered "...wif anyone like you."

I ground myself against him, my mouth pressed against the side of his neck, flooding with the taste of his skin, a touch of salt, the sour edge of his cologne, and the indefinable essence, spring water clear, that was Darian himself.

"You mean," I panted, "posh? Insane? Selfishly devoted to the pursuit of my own pleasure? What?"

"Like...free. And you're not selfish, babes. 'Aving a good time 'ere wif you doing that and being like that. It's well special."

But, after a moment, I caught him by the wrist, stilling us both. "Yorite?"

I tugged the lapels of his jacket. "Too many clothes."

He laughed. "And I should've said bossing me arand."

I tumbled off his lap and pulled him to his feet, remembering unexpectedly his body covering mine in a dark room in Brighton and how much I had wanted to see him. And then watching him in my living room, wanting to touch him. I'd turned away from both at the time, and the vulnerability of giving, like the thief I was.

Such a fragile thing, wanting to please someone else. Such endless scope for disappointment and failure. How much easier just to take.

"Yorite?" he said again. He put a hand under my chin and made me look at him, though I half pulled away, resisting.

"Yes, I just...want to touch you."

His mouth curved into its wide, generous smile. "It'd be a bit weird if you didn't, babes."

"In your world, maybe," I muttered, running a thumb over his chiselled model's cheekbones.

I unwrapped him slowly like it was Christmas and somebody had given me a shyly shivering glitter pirate, who made soft, uncertain purring noises beneath my mouth and fingers. Surely the best present I've ever had. I lingered over the smooth expanse of his skin, taut as silk over his sleek muscles, felt the beating of his heart, the rise and fall of his breath, and the heat that gathered like a benediction beneath my mouth. My fingers and lips became the enthralled cartographers of his flesh. My tongue traced the deep blue vein that ran like a river down his forearm, down to the branching tributaries that formed a delta at his wrist, and across the intricate paths that scored his palm. I'd done this in Brighton, at the time hardly knowing why, bewildered by my response to him, wanting everything and nothing at the same time.

I stroked the sinewy muscles of his upper arms and shoulders, tasted the deep hollows of his clavicles, the intersection of throat and collarbone, a secret, pendant-shaped plateau of skin ridged by ranges of bone. I slipped downwards, traversing the subtle planes and valleys of his body all the way to the neatly trimmed hair that formed a tantalising trail between the V of his obliques, leading from belly to perfectly groomed groin.

I dropped to my knees, and in the sudden, breathless silence, I actually heard him swallow. On a strange, entirely inexplicable whim, I turned my head and kissed the inside of his knee. I swept my hands up his thighs, the muscles flexing beneath my palms, the skin hot, and then I leaned forward and swirled my tongue over the straining head of his cock, sweeping up a drop or two of pre-come that had gathered there.

My glitter pirate made a noise that sounded a bit like "eeep."

I glanced up, heedless, smiling, generally idiotic. He wore

an expression of intense concentration, as though someone had asked him to do a really nasty piece of long division without the aid of calculator.

"Yorite?" I asked softly, in terrible Essex.

His hips moved infinitesimally. He opened his mouth. Said nothing. Then, "Y-yeah."

I curled a hand about his hip, over Gary actually, and the other at the base of his cock. And then I took him in my mouth.

Darian gave a hoarse cry that he tried to turn—unconvincingly—into a cough. One of his hands fluttered down to rest very lightly in my hair.

"Omigodbabes"—the words blurred into an incoherent whole—"I gotta sit down if you're gonna do that. I'll fall over."

I had to stop sucking his cock to laugh.

"Bed's behind you."

He flopped down as though he didn't have a single bone left in his body. Well. Maybe one.

I crawled forwards (dignity, what's that?), pushed his knees apart and pressed in close. Darian leaned back on his elbows, his chest rising and falling rapidly as he struggled to control his breathing.

"I've barely started," I said.

"OmigodI'mgonnadie."

I ran my tongue up the underside of his cock, teasing him.

"Do...do...that fing again."

"What thing?"

He made a tortured sound. "What you just did. Y'know."

"I might have forgotten." His hips bucked, his cock thudding against my lips, leaving a damp smear that I licked up gladly. He whined. Adorably. I gripped him again, circled his cock with my tongue and my lips, until he was arching off the bed, and then I took pity on him, opened my mouth and slid down on him until I met my own hand.

It had been, in all honesty, a while. And my gag reflex spasmed in protest. But it was worth it, entirely worth it, as Darian grabbed the nearest pillow and covered his face with it, muffling a blissed-out moan.

I prodded him in the knee until he re-emerged. And when he was back with the programme, I took my hand away, letting the last few inches of his cock sink into my mouth. I spread wide my arms in an absurd *Look ma, no hands* gesture that made him laugh and then gasp and then groan.

"You're well good at that, babes," he mumbled. "*Well* good. Like pafeshunal standard."

I spat him out, trailing saliva and choking with laughter, a few tears leaking from the corners of my eyes. "That is not a compliment."

He sat up, aghast. "Oh no, babes! I didn't like...mean...oh no! What am I like?"

"What I want to know," I said wickedly, "is where you acquired this knowledge of professional-standard oral sex."

"No, no, I 'aven't. I 'aven't! I didn't mean...it's just like...if somefing is proper good, right, you sometimes fink, wow, like, it's so good, you could get paid for doing it."

"Right. So you're saying I should jack in writing and become a rentboy?"

"What? No!" He paused, his eyes narrowing, and then he grinned. "Ah. Okay, okay. You got me. You was just messing abaht."

I pressed my face into his thigh, my shoulders shaking as I tried to stop laughing.

He cleared his throat. "I say," he said, in an outrageous RP accent, "suck me off at once. Rar."

I glared at him in outrage. "I do not sound like that! I've never said 'I say.' Or 'rar.'"

"Get on wif it, peasant."

I bit his leg, hard enough to make him gasp. And then drew his cock back into my mouth, so devoted to the act of pleasing him that I barely flinched when the head nudged the back of my throat. I drowned in the scent and the taste of him, pausing in my attentions to steal a glimpse at his face. His eyes were closed, the lashes casting crescent shadows over his cheeks, his mouth slightly open. He looked enraptured. And beautiful.

His eyes flicked open, catching me in an act that felt far more intimate than putting his cock in my mouth. He smiled. Stupid man. He touched me gently on the shoulder, twisted a lock of my hair around his finger, and I hollowed my cheeks and fucked him with my mouth. His hand tightened convulsively in my hair. The other groped for the pillow and dumped it back over his face. I reached up and pulled it away, tossing it over my shoulder. I heard it crash into something, but I didn't care enough to stop.

"Aw, babes," he muttered, twisting about like he was trying to stop himself thrusting.

He let me go, covering his eyes with the heels of his hands, elbows closing over his face like a theatre curtain. But I could still hear him, his frantic breath, and the strange, endearing hiccoughs of his swallowed moans.

In a while, when he was so close I could practically taste it, I sat back. "Like this? Or?"

"'Owever you wannit, babes. Long as it 'appens."

I looked up at him, sprawled all sweaty, desperate, and blissfully undone on my Egyptian cotton sheets.

"Can I fuck you?"

"Course."

I pushed him back and crawled over him, a glide of skin, smooth as glass and water, but so hot and real, taut and trembling with desire. His arms came around me and we were kissing, messy and urgent in a collision of mouths. I reached beyond him to the drawer of my bedside table, rummaging around blindly until I found a condom and some lube.

"You got some kinky stuff in there, babes," said Darian cheerfully, tucking a pillow under himself.

"Shut up or I'll use it on you."

He hooked a leg over my hip, and I pushed a slickened finger into him, followed by another, teasing the tight muscle to receptiveness. Darian's concentration face was back, a thin little line standing out between his brows.

"I won't hurt you." I pressed forward to drop another kiss on him.

His head was thrown back against my pillows. "You ain't."

I wrapped my free hand round his cock and gave it a reassuring stroke. He squeezed his eyes shut, teeth biting his lower lip.

"What's wrong?"

"Nuffin...just prob'ly look stupid."

"You look amazing."

That won a tiny smile.

"So hot. It's um..." What was it he said? "Well special."

The worst of it was, I meant every word. I put a hand beneath his leg and knelt between his thighs, ripping open the condom with my teeth, then rolling it on and lubing up one handed. A glance at his face confirmed he was trying not to laugh.

"Don't you dare."

"Such a pro, babes."

I positioned myself and breached him carefully, gritting my teeth against an urge to simply press forward and sheath myself inside him. "You really shouldn't mock people when they're about to stick their cock up your arse."

His breath hitched.

I stroked the underside of his thigh, inched a little further. His eyes had gone very wide. A few drops of sweat fell from my brow and mingled with the moisture that already glittered on his torso. I'd meant to torment him, just a little. Make him work for it. Beg me for it, perhaps. Or just moan in helpless abandon for me to take him. But then I glanced down and the sight of his body spread around mine utterly undid me. I gasped out his name, and a scattering of obscenities, and thrust myself into him, deep, then deeper, until our bodies met. A delirious rainbow of light unravelled behind my eyes, a herald of utter and heedless ecstasy.

I was afraid I might have hurt him with my lack of control, but Darian was stretched out beneath me, his head thrown back again to show the straining muscles of his neck, and the fingers of one hand were clinging to the intricate iron curlicues of my bedstead. Exquisite.

It was my last coherent thought.

All that was left was the tight heat of his body, his name to be whispered like a prayer, the taste of his mouth, the heavy scents of skin and sex and both of us together, the way his fingers tightened around the metal, his harsh gasps and broken cries, my hand on his cock, moving in the same rough rhythm as my thrusts. The impossible ouroboros of want and wanting, the twin pleasures of giving and taking, swirled together as richly as oils upon a canvas.

I forced my eyes open, fought my body's response and my instinct for selfishness. It was enough. A fingerhold on the precipice of desire, to stop me tumbling headlong into my own private rapture. A hard thrust, a twist of my hand on his cock, and the incantation of his name was all it finally took, his body shuddering under mine, his pleasure spilling over my fingers and onto his belly. I followed him mere moments later, collapsing into his waiting arms as I came in an intense, wrenching rush. Endless moments of nothing but joy and glittering pieces of madness. And, through the broken mirrors of bliss-closed eyes, glimpses of happiness in refracted rainbows. I clung to Darian, shattered, thoughtless, mindless, pleasure-wracked, safe.

I came back to myself, to my shaking, panting, sweating, aching body, and found it bearable. Peeling myself off Darian, I dispensed with the condom, and went for a towel on unsteady legs. Afterwards we lay together, and I kissed the faint freckles that scattered his shoulders in defiance of his spray tan.

"You're well good at that, babes," he said sleepily. "Specially wif your mouth. Like...wow."

I trailed my fingers over Gary. Take that, bitch.

"I'll put it on my CV," I murmured. "Excellent cocksucker."

"But I should really check it for you prop'ly, babes. As a favour or whatever."

"How noble you are."

"I'm well noble, me. Aw, y'know what?"

"Oh dear, what?"

"We should get the wavey fings what the judges 'ave on *Strictly*."

"I beg your pardon?"

"Y'know, the wavey fings wif the scores on 'em. Sev-VEN."

"I do not watch *Strictly Come Dancing*."

"God, babes, you don't watch *MasterChef*, you don't watch *Strictly*, no wonder you're bipolar depressed."

"Thank you, Doctor." I was silent a moment. "Wait a minute. Did you just say you would rate my blowjob as a seven? Get the fuck out of my bed."

He laughed and didn't move.

16
LATER

I woke in a panic, plastered to Darian's velvet-warm back, one arm draped across him, the other crooked awkwardly under the pillow, completely numb. I scrambled into a sitting position and pulled my knees up to my chest, trying to calm my body's anxieties and my mind's chaos. But it was no use. My heart raced. My thoughts whirled.

Darian slept on.

At least until I prodded him awake.

"Darian. Darian."

He rolled over, tousled and lovely, blinking dazedly in the half-light. "What's wrong, babes?"

I stared at him, for a moment utterly speechless at the magnitude of everything. "I'm going to make you so unhappy," I blurted out.

"What? When? Can't you like do it in the morning?"

"See," I said, somewhat hysterically. "I've already started. I'm waking you up in the middle of the night."

"S'okay," he mumbled, also sitting up. "I 'aven't got nuffin planned for tomorrow. Next shoot is next week, I fink."

"I can't do this." I wrapped my arms tightly around my knees and huddled at the top of the bed. "I can't be with someone. I ruin everything."

"But I like being wif you, babes. You're not gonna ruin nuffin."

"You don't understand." He touched my arm and I shook him off. "I know Stephen Fry has you up to speed, but I'm not charmingly quirky. I'm clinically insane. I've been in hospital. Involuntarily. Because I was too nuts to know I was nuts."

"We've all got flaws, babes."

I glared at him. "You're not taking me seriously."

"Well, you just said you was mental."

"Darian."

"Babes."

He wasn't getting it. I was a muddle of longing, frustration, and pain, my mind scattering like seabirds. "I'm not a fucking plural," I snapped.

"What?"

I pointed at myself. "Item: one babe."

"Ahwight," he said. "Mister A.A. Winters, Esquire."

I folded my hands across the tops of my knees and pressed my face into them. "Please don't laugh at me."

"No," he said, so gently it made me want to weep.

"You see," I mumbled. "This is what I'm like. Niall was right about me; everything he said was true. You'll end up hating me like he does. I don't want to do that to you."

"So, you don't 'ave to."

"I might not have a choice. And if you say we always have a choice, I'll kill you with a pillow."

There was a long silence. I sensed, rather than saw, Darian moving in the gloom. His smooth, naked shoulder brushed lightly against mine, sending a flare of response through the twisted labyrinth of my scars. I flinched. He kept making me feel things in ruined places.

"Look," he whispered. "I'm not clever like you, but I fink it's going to be ahwight. I'm wif you because I like being wif you and that's...y'know...ahwight. And when it ain't ahwight...then I won't be wif you. I'm not gonna let you treat me bad, babes."

"Oh great, so you're just going to walk out on the mentally ill guy when the going gets tough?"

"Babes, I'm confused. Are you sad cos you fink I'm going to be wif you or sad because you fink I'm not?"

"I don't know." All my doubts and all my fears were snarled up into a matted ball like hair fished out of the bathroom sink, and I couldn't tell which were real and which were baseless, how much I was protecting myself, or if I was—in my twisted, use-less way—trying to protect him. Some distant dead end in my mind was just about capable of recognising that I did not want a martyr to my depression, but I couldn't link my thoughts into a path that would take me there. I was a rat in the maze of my own thinking, and all the floors were electric, and all the exits were locked. "I don't know."

"We 'aven't 'ardly started," said Darian soothingly.

"But what if I go mad again? What if I get depressed?"

He shrugged. "You could get hit by a bus or summin tomorrow."

"Thanks, that's really consoling."

"I'm just saying."

I took in a deep, slow breath, willing myself to calm, to honesty, to courage. In short, all the things I didn't have. If he left now, it would be my choice. If he left later, it would be his, and I would be helpless. And hurt. "Darian, I tried to kill myself. Niall left me in the middle of a major depression, and I tried to kill myself." He was silent, so I went on. "He felt guilty and came back to apologise and found me."

"Must've been well 'ard for bof of you."

 "Yes, death is so very ugly. They don't tell you that. But it is."

I remembered little. I had already been sinking, sunk. And Niall's departure had been inevitable. Even welcomed, because he'd taken with him the last reason to keep struggling. Finally, the freedom to do something for me, only for me. My last and greatest gift: I could make it stop. I had lacked the foresight for pills. Or the courage to leap in front of a train or off a building. But, clutching a knife from the kitchen, I had felt—for the briefest of brief moments—a shining, perfect euphoria. Lost, of course, in the undignified mess that followed. And how could I forgive Niall? I hated him for every day that's hard to live.

I searched Darian's eyes for horror and condemnation, and found none. But then, I'd seen his portfolio. He was a model, the master of his face.

"That may well be you someday," I said.

He nodded slowly. "I guess I'll 'ave to see abaht it then."

"What the fuck is wrong with you? How can you care for me when I've always got one foot out the door?"

"I dunno. Look, babes, I know you fink I'm a bit shallow and I prob'ly am to be 'onest wif you, but I don't fink it's going to be easy, and I don't fink it's always gonna be awhight. But even if it ain't always awhight, that's awhight as well, cos sometimes fings just ain't, and that's 'ow they are. And I defo fink there ain't no point worrying abaht stuff that might nevva 'appen."

"Oh, God," I groaned. "Yoda's back."

"Yeah." His fingers whispered against the side of my face in the dark until I lifted my head. He tugged me into a kiss. The angle was awkward and his mouth tasted of sleep but I didn't care. I could have fallen into it, a sailor abandoning himself to the waves, just like in Brighton, but Darian wasn't a stranger anymore. I couldn't use him like that again, not when his kisses were full of promises he couldn't keep. Not with me.

I pulled away on a sigh of sheer physical need. "I'm a terrible risk to take with your happiness."

"I dunno," he said. "I mean, sadness is just a fing what 'appens. And sometimes people just 'ave to go, y'know." He shrugged. "I'm sorry fings was so bad, babes. But there ain't no point wishing you was different, cos then you wouldn't be you."

"No," I whispered. "I'd be better. I wish I'd met you before it all went wrong."

"I don't fink you would've liked me back then."

"Do you really believe I have to be the ruin of myself to like you?"

"Naw. I just fink it's what's now what matters. Anyway," he added, before I could respond to that piece of Hallmark wisdom with the contempt it deserved, "you gonna show me or what?"

"Show you what?"

His upper arm nudged against mine. "What you done."

There was a long silence. I was glaring at him, but he probably couldn't see it. I wondered if this was the instinctive, prurient curiosity that made people stare at car crashes. But, perhaps, just perhaps, I wanted to believe him. That, even if it wasn't all right, it would be all right. (What did that even mean? Was he some kind of idiot savant? Or just a man who genuinely didn't fear the pain of liking me?) But maybe the stark truth, written on my skin, would change his mind.

"Oh, for fuck's sake. Fine."

I uncoiled myself, leaned over, and flicked on the bedside lamp. Darian winced in the dazzle, blinking and rubbing his eyes like a child in a picture book.

I thrust out my arms, hands turned palm up, so he could see the long, white fishbone of scar and stitching that ran from my right wrist almost to the elbow, and its shorter, jagged sibling on the left. "Ugly enough for you? Or do you want the rest as well?"

He took my hands in his, holding me outstretched. Shudderingly exposed. "I don't fink it's ugly. It's just there."

"I hate that it's there."

"Why, babes?"

"Well, not even managing to kill yourself properly is a bit of competence nadir, don't you think?"

"I dunno, I reckon it's pretty 'ard. I mean, being alive is like a...whatjamcallit...like blinking, y'know, just summin you do wifout 'aving to fink about it."

I shook my head. "For most people, perhaps. For me it's a daily commitment I sometimes don't feel like making. But I hate that I tried. And I hate that I failed. This doesn't represent some beautiful moment in which I chose life. It's a fuckup, pure and simple. If it was up to me, I wouldn't be here."

His eyes held mine. In the circle of light from my lamp, they were greenish-blue, like looking at the sky when you're swimming underwater. "That true, babes?"

I opened my mouth to answer, but I couldn't meet all that sincerity, all that hope and generosity, with a lie that made things simple for me. "Sometimes," I said, finally. "But not always. It would have been so much easier, but then—" I swallowed. "—I suppose I would have lost some moments too."

It was strange—perhaps terrible—but somehow I found it easier to talk about wanting to die than wanting to live.

"They're not the moments I ever thought I'd want," I went on. "Sometimes I think they're very small. Like the crunch of autumn leaves. And the scent of Lapsang. And writing, maybe. And you, Darian."

He leaned over and kissed, not the scars, but the heel of my hand, as I had once, twice now, kissed him. "Aww, babes. I fink you're amazin'."

There was another long silence.

And then his fingers touched my upper arms, the meaningless non-pattern of scars and slashes. "What abaht this?"

"That's just old lunacy, from my first manic episode. I can't even remember doing it. They told me later that I thought there were lost words trapped in my skin and I was releasing them back into the world. Like a flock of phoenix." I tried to laugh, but nothing came out.

Darian's fingertips circled and swooped, trailing a feathery warmth across my skin, lighting up the lines on the madman's Etch A Sketch I'd made of my body. Scars or not, it felt the same. "What was the words?"

"I don't know. I can't read them. It's all senseless. It always was." He leaned in, and I shivered self-consciously beneath such close regard. "Trying to crack the Da Vinci Code?" I asked.

He laughed, looked up, and kissed me with such swift cunning I had no hope of evading it. "You're awhight, babes."

Oh, how I wished it were true. Instead I wound myself round him like poison ivy and clung. "Barthes said language is a skin. I'm sure he never meant it quite this literally."

"Who's Barfs?"

"Barthes. French literary critic. Gay. Perhaps overly fond of his mother. Prone to nervous breakdowns."

"You know such a lot of fings, babes."

I shrugged. "He used to be one of my heroes."

"You went off 'im? That's a bit 'arsh."

"He's dead." Safe in the gloom, I stretched up and put my lips shyly to the edge of his jaw. "He won't mind."

"But why?"

"He was hit by a laundry truck."

"Yeah, har-har. I meant why'd you go off him, you donut."

For a moment, I was silent, my head tucked against his shoulder, while I listened to the sounds of his body, magnified by the night. I could almost imagine I heard the brush of one eyelash against another, the rush of blood through veins and arteries, the cells of his body dying, dividing, and multiplying, like eggshells cracking. Finally I said, "Unhappy is the man who has need of heroes."

"I ain't being funny, babes, but now you're just being clever in a way that means you don't 'ave to answer the question."

I kissed him under the ear. "I'm sorry, Darian. I don't know what I like anymore. I don't know if what I think is what I think, if what I feel is what I feel, if any of it at all is me. If there is a me that isn't just a reflection of or a response to...mental illness."

"Course there is, babes."

"How will I know?"

"Cos you will. You'll know when summin's real."

I gave a laugh so harsh it hurt my throat. "I don't, though. That's the fucking problem. What part of 'insane' did you miss?"

The next thing I knew I was on my back, Darian stretched on top of me, his hips cradled by my hips, his legs pushing mine apart.

"I reckon you'll figure it aht."

He caught my unconvincingly protesting hands and bore them down against the pillows. His mouth nipped its way up my neck and then settled over mine. And he held me and kissed me until there was nothing else.

17
TOMORROWS

Slipped away sweetly in a haze of sex, one after another.

18

A MORNING

My phone was bleeping insistently and I was just as insistently ignoring it.

Eventually, Darian untangled himself and went to retrieve it.

"I'm starting to fink you gotta secret lover, babes."

He tossed my phone to me. I had accrued an extensive collection of emails and text messages. "Oh fuck. Oh, wanking fuck. I'm meant to be in Cambridge. There's a wedding tomorrow and a rehearsal dinner tonight." I rolled myself into sheets that smelled of both of us, pulled a pillow over my head, and whinged—in a rather muffled manner—about not wanting to go.

Unlike most of my social engagements, I hadn't made my usual internal commitment to avoid Max and Amy's wedding. There were some acts too low even for me. But somehow the reality of it had slipped away from me, along with everything but Darian, and I was left without resources.

Darian sat down on the edge of the bed and patted lightly at my shoulder. "Better get moving, babes."

"I don't want to. I feel panicky just thinking about it. It'll be awful. What if something goes wrong?"

He tugged at my cocoon. "It's just you being anxious or whateva. It's gonna be fine."

"Just anxious?" I repeated, as furiously as I could from beneath a pillow. "*Just anxious*. Fuck you. That's like saying, it's just a broken leg, start climbing that mountain."

"Sorry," he said with a distinct lack of repentance. "I just don't fink you should miss summin what's important to your mates."

"I've spent the last however many years letting my friends down. Believe me, they'll cope."

"Aww, that's sad."

I snarled at him.

"Sorry." A pause, and then, "You 'aven't let me down, babes."

"Give me time."

He slowly began to peel away my sheets, and I slowly stopped fighting him.

"But you did modlin and everyfing." He pulled off the pillow and put it back in its usual place. "What do you normally do when you 'ave to do somefing what you feel all anxious abaht?"

"I don't do it."

"That ain't true."

I sat up, sighing. "It's mostly true. I suppose I could take some diazepam, but I hate it. It makes me feel sub-human. I think Hamlet must have been on it."

"Don't fink they had that back in 'istory, babes."

"'O, that this too too solid flesh would melt.' It's exactly like that. And it's addictive, so if I'm not careful, I'll end up a clinically anxious, bipolar depressive with a drug problem." I waved a finger at him. "Oh, oh, and let's not forget its many many side effects. One of which is...depression."

He made a snuffling sound and hastily clapped a hand over his mouth.

"It's fine, laugh it up. It's funny, it's fucking ridiculous."

"But there ain't nuffin else?"

"Yes, Darian," I said with sharp-edged patience. "I really want to medicate my medication with medication."

"Suppose not," he said. "I remember finking you 'ad a lot of pills first time I stayed over."

I gaped at him. "Wait, you knew all along?"

"I knew you 'ad summin going on, but I wouldn't pry, babes. I fought you'd tell me when you wonnid."

"And you still slept with me? Wanted to be with me?"

He shrugged. "Course."

"You're a strange man, Darian Taylor."

"Takes one to know one, babes."

He made me smile. Just a little. And, in return, what could I give except ugly truths? "I don't want to take more pills than I have to. It's taken years to get this close to stable."

And, for the most part, it worked. Yes, depression dogged my footsteps and the promise of hypomania glittered sometimes on the horizon, but I hadn't been manic for a long time. I didn't know whether it was the ECT, the medication, the counselling, or the very fact of being appropriately diagnosed, but it wasn't something

I dared to question, in case I broke the spell. I wouldn't have called myself a superstitious man, but when it came to the intricacies of my biochemistry, the complexities of my illness, I was as helpless as a frightened child who prayed to a god called science.

"They've tried to fix the anxiety," I said, "but if you take this, you have to take that, or stop taking the other, and the whole bloody awful cycle begins again. They did find something that helped a bit. But I stopped taking it."

"Yeah?"

"Yes. The side effects...I...got fat, okay? And I know it's shallow, I know it's irresponsible, Niall's told me a thousand times, but, honestly, I'd rather be anxious than fat."

"I'm wif you, babes." Darian sounded suddenly about as serious as I'd ever heard him. "Also, right, if you fink abaht it, it's stupid to 'ave medication what's supposed to be for stopping people being depressed what also makes 'em fat. Cos that'd be well depressing."

I shook my head. What manner of idiocy would lead someone to put their vanity above their mental health? And what manner of idiot would support such a choice? But I couldn't help liking that he did. Accidental or not, it was the first flicker of understanding I'd ever received that I had the same right to be just as shallow and stupid as everyone else. That I did not have to be grateful to simply roll from day to day as a bloated, mindless zombie.

"Then," I said, "we're both shallow and deserve each other."

"Naw, naw, it's not abaht what you look like, it's abaht being happy wif 'ow you look. And if you ain't happy, then you ain't gonna look good whateva."

"Deep."

He gave me a look I couldn't quite read, frowning a little. "I know what I'm talking abaht, okay? I was a bit of a chubber when I was growing up. What wif being gay as well, it wasn't a mayja laugh."

Truthfully, I couldn't imagine him as ever being less than beautiful.

"And don't fink," he added, in a more playful tone, "this means I'm gonna let you get away wif not going to your mate's fing."

I gave a hollow groan. "But I could be consoling you for your minor childhood wounds. Healing you with my sweet, sweet loving."

"Shuh up. And stop...like...stalling. Cos getting married is important."

"Is there any way I could convince you it's an outdated, het-eronormative construct that has no place in a secular society?"

"I fink it's totes romantic."

"Oh, dear God." I dived back under the covers.

"Come on, babes," he said, tugging on a toe I'd accidentally left out in the cold. "It'll be ahwight. Want me to go wif you or summin?"

I stuck my head out. "Would you?"

"Course. I love weddings, me. I'd get to eat cake and meet all your mates."

Oh, fuck, I hadn't thought of that. Spending hours, and days, fucking and laughing with Darian in the privacy of my own home was one thing. Introducing him to all my Oxbridge friends as my... what? boyfriend? was quite another. Nobody would understand.

And I couldn't blame them—I hardly understood myself. People would smile, of course, but I would see the question behind the smile: has Ash finally completely lost it, has his self-esteem plummeted to such depths that he's trawling Essex for totty? And, anyway, surely it wouldn't be fair on Darian, having him stand around, being charmingly bewildered, while everyone talked over his head and laughed and speculated behind his back.

Laughed and speculated behind my back.

"Actually," I said hastily, "it probably wouldn't work out. You know what weddings are like. This has been meticulously planned for the last twelve centuries. Wars have been fought. If I showed up with an unplanned guest, I think it might cause the end of the world."

"It'll be fine, babes. I bet you anyfing there's like a dead uncle or somebody wifout their partner or summin."

"I don't think we should risk it."

"Well, call and ask. And if they're like no, I can send you off wif good foughts and good vibes and everyfing and go back home for a bit. Cos my nan probably finks you've got me tied up in the basement or summin."

"Note to self: move house, get basement."

He laughed. "You don't have to tie me up, babes. I'm like a volunteer."

"But if I had a basement, you'd look good tied up in it."

"You say the sweetest fings. Now get on wif ringing your mate."

"Uh..." I had been so distracted by the basement that I couldn't think of a single plausible excuse for why I didn't want him to come with me to the wedding. The truth—"I don't want my friends to think less of me than they do already, which they inevitably would if they saw me with you"—would have done the trick, of course, but came with the unfortunate side effect that I probably wouldn't be tying Darian to anything ever.

I hadn't entirely been lying about the wedding being an event from hell, so calling Amy seemed like it might be a sensible gamble. She would probably tell me that it wasn't possible to accommodate a random gentleman she'd never met before on the happiest day of her life, which would liberate me to go back to bed with the random gentleman in question.

Amy picked up after a couple of rings, greeting me with a slightly wary edge to her voice I'd never heard before. I put it down to general wedding-related stress.

"Um, yes, hi. Amy...I kind of wanted to...the thing is..."

My flow of awkward was interrupted by the buzz of voices over the line, and I lost track of my own stammering. Amy said something I couldn't make out, and things quieted down a bit. Then she spoke into the phone again. "Sorry, what was that?"

I tried again. "I'm sort of...there's a... I know it's really short notice, but..."

There was another interruption. "Just a minute," said Amy, and for a moment I thought she meant me, but then she was back. "What's the matter, Ash?"

Fuck. Shit. Wank. "Oh, um. Nothing's the matter. I just... there's a guy... I know the answer is probably no, but can I bring him to—"

"God, yes." She sounded so incredibly thrilled that it was only then that I realised she'd been expecting me to pull out. Abandon her on her wedding day. As I had wanted to do less than five minutes ago. And probably would have done, had it not been for Darian.

There was no denying it. No hiding it. I was a terrible, terrible person. Selfish. Cowardly. Worthless. My stomach churned, as though I were trying to flinch away from myself.

"Are you sure?" I said. "I mean, what about the seating plans? Won't it throw everything off? I mean, it's okay if—"

"Not at all. It's absolutely no problem. The seating plan is already buggered beyond belief, so he can come to the dinner tonight as well. One of Max's great-uncles passed away a couple of weeks ago. And Greg and Laura are getting divorced so they both decided not to come in case they met without a lawyer present. Although since Max knows about eighty lawyers, I don't know what they were worried about."

"Right," I said dazedly.

"I can't wait to meet your man. But now I have to go before this turns into a blood bath. See you later, and thank you, thank you, thank you, mwah, darling."

"Right," I said again. I looked into Darian's wide, hopeful eyes. "You can come."

He grinned. "We are gonna give it large, babes. Ohmigod, I need your help." He bounced, naked, off the bed, and started scrabbling around on the floor, emerging a few seconds later like an excitable retriever. "Do you fink *these* or *these*?"

The choice in question seemed to be silver-sequined Ugg boots or silver-sequined Converses.

"I honestly have no mechanism for forming an opinion," I said, after a moment.

"Fink it better be these." He waved the Converses. "Sparkle but subtle."

"I think subtle has long since left the building."

There was nothing for it. I had to get dressed. Thankfully it wasn't too much of a challenge, since Niall once unkindly suggested that I always looked like I was going to a wedding, anyway.

"Check you, babes." Darian crept up behind me and squeezed. He was wearing a jacket that looked as though it was made from the feathers of a bird of paradise—which, I suppose, passed for formal wear in his world.

"Let me guess," I said, "I look like I work in parliament."

"Oh, my God, babes, look at all these ties." Peering into my wardrobe, he gave a gasp and pulled out a silver twill Stefano Ricci tie, set with Swarovski crystals. I'd bought it because I was so fucking depressed I would have bought anything. "Wear this one."

I cringed. "With a navy suit, or indeed ever, absolutely not."

"But it's so bling, babes. It goes wif my shoes."

"That tie says one of two things. It either says, 'I'm a wanker,' or 'I'm mentally ill,' and, though I am both, I have no wish to broadcast it."

Somehow, between expressing my determination not to wear the tie and leaving the house, I ended up wearing the tie.

19

AFTERNOON

"I've nevva been to Cambridge." Darian bounced excitedly on the balls of his feet as we dropped my bags off in the room Amy had booked for me at her old college. "It's well nice."

"Bah. It's just like a smaller version of Oxford, where they cheat at Tiddlywinks and punt from the wrong end."

"You gonna show me rand?"

"No, we're going to stay here and fuck—I think we have time before dinner if we're quick about it."

"You're so romantic, babes."

We fell onto the single bed with such abandon that it went crashing into the wall, knocking a chunk out of the plasterwork. From the arched, wisteria-woven windows came a sudden shaft of sunlight, warmed gold by the surrounding sandstone, in which the dancing dust motes glittered like stars.

EVENING

The rehearsal dinner was being held in the fourteenth-century

Old Hall—though I was unsure why we needed to practice eating and having awkward conversation.

"Are we like 'aving dinner in a church?" whispered Darian, awestruck.

"It's just a college dining hall."

"What's wif the stained glass?"

"Most likely an eighteenth- or nineteenth-century addition."

He gave me a look. "I just fink it's proper weird."

At that point, we got swept along into the rest of the milling guests, escaping only from the hurricane of introductions, greetings, handshakes, and meaningless civilities when we finally washed up in front of Max and Amy and the rest of the wedding party.

Amy threw herself into my arms. "Ash, you came. I'm so happy!"

"Um, yes. And I brought, um, Darian."

Amy beamed at him. "Thank you for coming to the wedding of a total stranger. I hope it isn't completely awful."

"No way. I love a wedding, me. I fink it's proper nice, taking an oaf to be with someone for your whole life. I reckon most people wanna get done wif me after five minutes, janarwhatamean?"

"That's a blatant lie," said Amy staunchly. "You're lovely."

He gleamed under his tan, blushing. "Awww, fanks. 'Ow nice are you? Did you come 'ere? Like Cambridge?"

"Yes, this is my old college."

"You must be well clever."

"I'm well good at bullshitting." She grinned. "Why do you think I'm an agent?"

"What? Like a spy?"

"Err, no. A literary agent?"

"Oh, right. Ha-ha." He shuffled his feet.

Amy looked grave. "Of course, I have to say that, because otherwise I'd have to kill you."

Darian laughed, and a vague, unexpected warmth swept over me. Something I hadn't felt for a long time, something almost like pride, in Amy, in Darian, and a little bit for me. It seemed, just then, an impossible kindness that two such people could find something worth liking in all my sharp and scattered pieces. I turned into Darian's shoulder and smothered a smile there.

One of his arms slid round me as though it was the most natural thing in the world. "This place is well nice for a wedding." He nodded approvingly. "Well classy. But didn't you find it a bit like depressing when you was 'ere, cos everyfing is so old and like... I dunno...serious?"

"God, yes. We're only here because there was no fucking way I was getting married in Oxford, and Buckingham Palace wasn't available, so what can you do?"

He laughed. "I hope you're gonna be happy togevver."

Amy gestured to Max, who was caught up in what looked like a tense, familial negotiation. "Have you seen the guy I'm marrying? If I can't be happy with him, what chance is there?"

Darian followed her pointing finger. "He's qualidee. Hunjed pahcent," he agreed.

"I know, right. I mean the arse alone..."

"Totes."

"Are you two quite finished?" I said. "Or maybe you want to marry each other? I suppose I'll be able to bring myself to console Max. Taking one for the team."

Grinning, Darian snuggled me further into the crook of his arm. "He's getting jell."

"There, there, Ash." Amy smirked. "Your arse is quality, too."

I was about to make a severe retort when Max turned around, and the whole cycle of introductions had to start again.

"Well, bless my heart," exclaimed another voice, as incongruous within Cambridge's oak-panelled walls as Darian's. "What a perfectly charmin' homosexual."

My mouth fell open. Beside me, Darian's did the same. Max had never told me his mother was Scarlett O'Hara.

Even wearing a single string of pearls and a black dress of such breathtaking simplicity it would have made Holly Golightly seem crass, she looked as though there ought to have been at least six gentlemen callers dead at her feet. She must have been at least fifty, but time had not dared to touch her. Max's beauty was her beauty. His bone structure a bolder, more angular version of hers. His hair, the same precise shade of impossible, gleaming gold. At her side, he was making frantic, windmilling "I'm sorry, I'm sorry, I'm so sorry" gestures with his hands.

"Come here, you darlin' darlin' thing," she said, crooking a finger at my date.

Darian looked nervously over his shoulder, on the off chance she was referring to some other darlin' darlin' thing. And then, with the air of a man going to his execution, allowed her to claim his arm.

She smiled at him like a firing squad readying arms. "I have always believed a gentleman needs a lick of the devil in him."

I glanced at Max's father, who was wearing a tweed jacket with leather patches on the elbows and had a face like a three-day-old tea bag. At which point, taking advantage of my split-second distraction, Max's mother stole my glitter pirate, leaving me standing there, jilted like Suellen.

"I'm so sorry," said Max. "She's actually the worst person in the world."

Across the room, I caught sight of Darian, being whirled off through the guests. "I fink she's mental!" he mouthed urgently and without subtlety.

I hid a smile and went to get a drink.

And another.

And another.

Anything to keep me afloat in this sea.

Somehow I ended up on the edge of a group of people I vaguely recognised from university. The conversation—politics, literature, the state of the economy, what had happened to so-and-so—washed over me. Bored. I was so bored.

"Ash Winters," drawled a voice that sounded gratingly posh to my ears and yet seemed familiar, "we must stop meeting like this."

I gazed into a face I might once have found attractive. Brown eyes, brown hair, sharp, clever features, a thin blade of a mouth, whimsical and cruel.

"Quite," I said. Who the fuck was he?

"Hugh," he said, a smile concealing what was clearly irritation. "Hugh Hastings."

Nope. Not a clue. "Of course."

"We met in Brighton." He smiled again. "We went to the same college."

Oh, that Hugh. Right. The one I hadn't pulled at the stag party.

"You know, after you left with that—" He waved a hand as if Darian defied mere description. "—I remembered how I knew you."

"You did?" A vague sense of unease uncoiled like a serpent. It was just anxiety. Paranoia. Relax. Breathe.

"Yah, you were the one who had the complete psychotic break, right?"

Suddenly I was the centre of a circle of curious, glistening eyes. Somebody could have mentioned Robbie Williams, but there was nothing, just a hungry silence. I felt a shamed flush sear my cheeks. My head spun. My mouth filled up with the taste of bile.

"Yes," I said, with broken-glass calm. "Yes, that was me."

"Oh, you're that fellow." A different voice. "You poor bastard. Are you all right now?"

I'd had this nightmare before, but I'd always woken up. I smoothed my cuffs. "Yes. Yes, I'm fine."

Another voice? The same? It didn't matter. "What was it like?"

I was still smoothing my cuffs, and even I could see how it looked, a tic turned habit turned compulsion. *Stop smoothing your cuffs.* But I couldn't, I just couldn't. I couldn't even look at them. "What do you mean, what was it like?"

"Did they lock you up?"

"Was it like *One Flew Over the Cuckoo's Nest?*"

"How did you get out?"

Breathe, Ash, breathe. "I dug a tunnel into the sewer system from beneath a poster of Rita Hayworth."

There was a long silence as everyone tried to work out if the clinically insane were allowed to be sarcastic. It might have worked, too—I could have deflected them, and held them at bay instead of the other way round—but my breathing was too shallow, my voice too unsteady. It wasn't a joke anymore, it was another piece of derangement. I might as well have been standing there in white pyjamas.

(Another myth. They let you wear whatever you want, and you still dress like crap because nobody cares and neither do you.)

I swallowed. "I got better, so they let me out."

"Can they do that?" asked Hugh.

It took everything I had, but I risked a glance at him. Just then, I was not too proud to plead. *Don't do this to me.* He had liked me once. But his face reflected only the blank, uncomprehending confidence of the wholly unhurt, and a touch of private malice. It seemed that being slighted by a lunatic was not something easily forgiven.

"I thought," he said, "once you were in the system, it was impossible to get out again. I read a book by this American journalist who pretended to be batshit so he could expose what it's really like for mental patients but, of course, once he was admitted, he couldn't prove he wasn't meant to be there."

Murmurs rising like the sea to engulf me.

"I mean, I can kind of see why. If an insane person tells you they're sane, how are you supposed to tell it's not further evidence of their insanity? And that would be really dangerous, wouldn't it?"

I felt the weight of all those expectant stares.

"We do walk amongst you," I said, at last.

Pity. I was drowning in pity, as slick as oil.

I felt sick. Small and sick and utterly, utterly lost. I wanted—I needed—Somebody to save me. But how could you be rescued from yourself?

Hugh's voice pricked my skin like a thousand tiny needles. "And the orange chap in the feathers is your boyfriend now?"

Again, that stomach-churning surge of interest from the others. I could see what they saw: the madman and his fool. And now they would have us caper. Their scrutiny had been unpleasant enough when it touched upon my past, but now their eyes were burrowing into my present. A better man would have owned his truths. But, at the moment, the vulnerability of mere madness seemed nothing to the vulnerability of showing that I cared.

I managed to meet the stares and gave what I hoped was an insouciant smile. "I wouldn't go that far. He's more of a-a fuckee, really."

"A fuckee? Is that like a fuck buddy?"

"Yes, like a fuck buddy, but without the tiresome buddy requirement."

Someone chuckled. Finally, it wasn't pity. "So, sort of the late-night drive-through of sex. For when you get that craving for something cheap and filthy, like a Big Mac."

"Precisely," I said. "None of the hassle of a relationship and cheaper than a whore. And, now I think about it, cheaper than a Big Mac too."

I waited for the laugh that never came.

Nobody was looking at me, except Hugh. He put a hand to his lips, as if to conceal whatever lay beneath it. I thought, perhaps, a smile.

And then, I knew. I knew what I had done.

In that endless, awful second, I would have gladly destroyed the world, myself, and everyone in it, to avoid turning round. I'd plumbed the depths of my own shame and disappointment so many times it barely mattered anymore, but how could I face Darian? Knowing he had finally seen the truth of me?

He was standing behind me. Of course he was. His eyes had that shiny look of someone on the brink of tears. His mouth opened and closed a few times, before he said finally, "Mate, that's...that's bang aht of order." His voice broke on the final word. "I fought you liked me."

And then he turned and walked away.

Everyone was staring at me. I should have been running after Darian, apologising, throwing myself at his feet, even, but I was pinned by eyes, like a moth in a glass case. Besides, there was little value in the remorse of a creature like me. I was sorry, of course I was sorry, but it was the regret of the thief who got caught, not the regret of the truly penitent. The scene was already replaying in my head, and I could not imagine a version of events in which I did not sacrifice Darian to save myself a little humiliation. I was too weak, too selfish, and I simply did not deserve to apologise to him.

"Man, that was cold," whispered someone, in a voice that hovered on the brink of awe.

"Ouch," said Hugh. Spite glinted in his eyes. "Bit of a mismatch in expectations there, I fear."

I shrugged. "Plenty of cocks in the sea. Anybody got a cigarette?"

Blindly, I took the whole packet and a box of matches from Hugh and went into the quad. My hands were shaking so much that I could barely hold the flame to the tip of the first cigarette. But, finally, I lit up.

I smoked cigarette after cigarette, littering the flagstones at my feet with fag ends and burnt out matches, breathing smoky poison into the still night air. My eyes stung, moisture gathering at the corners. It must have been the cold. Or the cigarette ash.

"I don't understand." Niall stepped through the doorway. "Why would you go to all that trouble for him, and then do that?"

I gave a startled, sobbing hiccough, and dropped my last cigarette. I cursed, extinguished it with my foot, and tried surreptitiously to dash away my tears with the heel of a hand. I'd meant it when I'd told Niall that I never wanted to see him again, but right now I couldn't find the energy to argue about it. In some strange way, it was almost nice to see him. At least I wasn't alone in the dark, with nothing but an empty packet of cigarettes. "I don't know either."

"You should go after him."

I scraped out a mirthless laugh. "I don't know where he is and this isn't a fucking rom-com. I'm not going to catch up with him just as he's getting onto a plane, kiss him in front of a crowd of applauding strangers, and live happily ever after. Besides, what am I going to say to him? I'm just a manic depressive standing in front of a moron, asking him to love me?"

"Well, no," said Niall, "but you could say you're sorry for being a prick."

"Oh, fuck off, Jiminy Cricket."

He sat down on the step, hands folded loosely between his knees and, after a moment, I crumpled down next to him. This felt almost like being back at university except for the gulf of time that stood between the eighteen-year-old I used to be and what was left of him. Though perhaps, for Niall, nothing had changed at all. He was still longing for Max and stuck looking after me.

"I thought a lot about what you said," he said finally. "You were right about all of it. But I wasn't lying when I said I went out with you because I loved you. And that I still love you."

It had been so long that I'd been anything but an obligation to Niall that the words sounded almost like a foreign language.

"And that makes everything all right, does it?"

"It really doesn't. I'm so sorry, Ash. I lost sight of you. Not because of your illness but because of me." He stared at his interwoven fingers. "The truth is, I've spent half my life loving men who didn't want me. It's stupid, but there it is."

"God. We really do have first-world problems, don't we?"

Niall gave a soft sigh. "Yes, we do." He unlocked his fingers and laced them with mine. It wasn't until he touched me that I realised how cold I was. "Unfortunately, they still hurt."

I nestled my hand into his. It felt...nice. So nice that I had to say ungraciously, "What did I do to deserve the pep talk? Or can't you break the habit of trying to save me?"

But he only smiled. "I'm just pointing out that you've acted like a complete dick. Because that's what friends do."

I pressed my free hand to my heart. "Oh, stop. Before I cry."

"Wanker."

"But you wuv me."

"Don't push your luck."

Suddenly I blurted out, "I don't have his number. I don't even know where he lives."

"Facebook? Twitter?"

I realised I was digging my ragged nails into Niall's hand and forced myself to relax. "I don't know. I don't know. I didn't bother to ask. And, anyway, it doesn't matter. It's over."

"Look, I'm not trying to be your fairy godmother, and, for the life of me I can't understand it, but it seemed to me you really liked him."

"I didn't like him. He just made me feel good. It wasn't real. It was a biochemical blip."

Niall shrugged. "When you put it like that, so is everything. That doesn't make it worthless. Or any less real."

"Then we're all mad here," I muttered.

"We must be," he said, smiling a little, "or we wouldn't have come."

We sat for a while in silence. A round, fat moon, jaundiced by the lights of the city, floated in an ink-blue sky.

"We're probably missing the dinner," I said at last.

"It'll be fine. As long as we don't miss the real thing."

I stole a glance at Niall. His face was so familiar to me that I had long since ceased to pay it any attention. Once we had been friends, once we had been lovers. And now we were just two people who knew each other too well, who had—through care- lessness, not malice—hurt each other too much.

Finally, I said, "I know I never told you, but...I did care about you." There was a pause. "I mean, as much as I'm capable of it."

☆   "Wow." He looked thoughtful. "You are really bad at express- ing your feelings."

"Shuh...err, shut up. And," I swallowed. "I did want you. You're, um, not entirely unwantable. And I'm sorry if I ever made you feel...like. Not."

Niall made such a strange noise that I thought I might have made him cry. But, no, he was laughing. And, laughing, he dragged me into a hug.

"What the fuck are you doing?" I protested. "Let me go!"

Eventually, he did. He shook his head. "Not entirely unwant- able. Be still my beating heart."

"Oh, leave me alone." I stared at the flagstones between my feet. "There's...there's one more thing."

"My hooks are tentered."

I'd always been certain this would be an admission of weakness, that it would lessen me somehow, or that it was a truth so fragile that utterance would shatter it. But the words slipped out, as they had in my whispered confession to Darian some days that felt like a lifetime ago, effortless as honey.

"Thank you for, you know, everything. And I'm glad you came back that day." They did not break. I did not break. And I felt not mortified, but free.

Niall stared at me. And then began to cry.

"Will you stop it, you big nancy?" I patted him awkwardly between the shoulders. Typical, really, that I'd fucked and been fucked by this man six ways to Sunday and I didn't have a clue how to comfort him. "No wonder you can't get a boyfriend."

"I know you won't believe me," he said, sniffling, "but going out with you was okay. When we broke up, for ages afterwards, all I could think about was the bad stuff. But there was good too, wasn't there?"

"Yes. You saved my life at least twice, once literally." I took a deep breath. "You're kind of a muppet but I meant what I said."

"You mean all that deeply sentimental, mushy stuff about you maybe caring about me just a little bit?"

"Look, I need to stop having this heart-to-heart before I throw up. My heart gets claustrophobic."

He smiled in such a soggy way that I felt obliged to give him my pocket square. "I can't blow my nose into this." He held it up in the moonlight like it was a priceless *objet d'art*. I sensed he was mocking me, which was a vast improvement on crying. "It feels like sacrilege."

"Gucci will never know."

Niall snuffled into my handkerchief. And then tried to hand it back to me.

"You can keep it. Really."

"Well." He somehow contrived to smirk, even with a red nose and swollen eyes. "Little Timmy won't starve this winter."

"Fuck you. I'm clinically depressed. I'm allowed to buy nice things."

"You mean you're a vain git with too much money."

"That too."

There was another silence. It was oddly comfortable. I let my shoulder rest against his, just a little bit, and we leaned against each other.

Eventually, he asked, "So, it's definitely a no to the *Notting Hill* moment?"

I nodded. "Even putting aside what an almighty fool I'd look, he deserves better than me. All it needed was a crowing cock to end the scene."

Niall choked. "Did you just draw a direct comparison between you being a bit rude at a wedding and Peter's denial of Jesus Christ?"

"I...might have gone too far there."

"You think?"

"Well, I'm an atheist. They're both just characters in a book I haven't read."

"Stop trying to dodge the issue." He poked me in the leg. "Ash, I'm not trying to be your conscience or anything, but you can't just ditch Darian in the middle of Cambridge."

I hunched over my knees. "He's probably already gone."

"Then go check. Seriously, it's the least you can do."

"I can't face him, I can't. And, look"—my voice rose—"can you stop fucking judging me for five fucking seconds? It's practically our whole relationship."

Niall held his hands up in a gesture of surrender. "I'm sorry, okay, I'm sorry. I just think it's a shitty thing to do to someone."

"No shittier than what I've already done."

"Actually, I think it is. And you're better than that, Ash. I know you are."

"I'm not." I shook my head. "Maybe once, but not anymore. Deal with it or don't. But, if you're going to try to be my friend again, stop pretending I'm someone I'm not."

There was a long silence.

"That's fucking unfair, you know." I shrugged. "It's the way it is."

"Why are you trying to push me away? Was Darian not enough for one night?"

He was right, of course. Whatever the broken things we had scattered across the years, Niall knew me. And tonight I was wielding his kindness like a blade to my skin.

"Sorry," I muttered. "Wow. Progress."

"Fuck off."

He laughed. "So what now?"

"I don't know. Back to the dinner, I guess. And, after the

wedding, I might go home and watch *Notting Hill*. While crying manly tears and eating handful after handful of wasabi peas." The worst of it was, even I couldn't tell if I was joking.

"Want company?"

"No." My response was instinctive. But then I thought about it. "Actually. Yes. All right."

He grinned. "You know, you're shockingly sentimental, sometimes."

I shrugged. "All cynics are."

LATER

I stood on the Mathematical Bridge watching the moonlight curl over the dark waters of the Cam and tried not to think where Darian might be.

LATER

I walked cobbled streets, ankle-deep in shadows, trying to find the courage to return to our room, but there was only an emptiness, as unchanging as my tearless eyes.

LATER

I took a ludicrously expensive room in a hotel on Thompson's Lane. A lavish glass-walled box overlooking a gleaming toy city. Somewhere beneath the spires and gables, Darian Taylor was hating me.

I lay, fully dressed, on top of the bed and watched broken pieces of light skittering across the ceiling. I simply couldn't face his disappointment. The damage I knew I'd done. I'd ruined Darian, just like I'd ruined Niall. It was better this way, for both of us. Darian would get on with his life, and I would drag myself through the ashes of mine.

When Niall had left me, it had felt so inevitable. *I can't bear it*, he'd said. *I can't bear you.* I'd known for a long time how futile it was. He might as well have tried to love a parasite. I'd picked up the knife because I'd understood, at last, that there was no changing. No going back. And going on had seemed not only unbearable, but pointless. My whole life, an exercise in treading water simply not to drown.

And yet here I was, having made the same mistake all over again. I should have learned, even if I was incapable of anything else. But Darian had slipped past me somehow, like light through fractured glass. For some bright, fleeting moments, he had made me happy, and all I had done was hurt him.

LATER

Cambridge drenched in a bloody dawn. My world without Darian.

Sleep, of course, had proven elusive. Somehow, I had grown too accustomed to his body and the murmur of his breath.

I thought about going back to the room, but it was too late, and he would not have waited.

He would not have waited.

LATER

Darian had gone. There was nothing left in the room but my suitcase and the heavy perfume of the wisteria.

I sat down on the edge of the bed, which was still rumpled from our exertions yesterday. Suddenly I couldn't breathe.

But it was better this way.

His last gift would not be his reproach.

I could remember him laughing, sparkling, my dear, precious glitter pirate. And I could keep deluding myself that, for a little while at least, I'd been the man he'd believed I was, instead of the man I am.

Dizzy, a little sick, I staggered to the window. Yanked up the sash. I still couldn't catch my breath. Oh God, fuck, I was going to die and, for once, I didn't want to. I was choking on fucking wisteria. I braced myself against the casement and just about managed not to have a panic attack. I kept thinking I'd get used to them someday, but no. They thundered over me like a train, like a fucking train, every fucking time.

In the quadrangle below, the wedding guests wandered aimlessly back and forth. I should have been with them.

From a nearby window, open like mine, drifted the opening bars of "F**kin' Perfect."

I put my head in my hands and felt like crying.

20

AFTER

When Niall left, the silence of my flat felt like a funeral. I went into the kitchen to water the sole surviving plant, my attention drifting untethered between the grey-misted, grey-gravelled street below and the grey stream falling from my grey tap.

I closed my eyes. I was going to crash, wasn't I? And now I was drowning the sole surviving plant.

I stuck it on the rack to dry out. The water droplets clinging to the leaves glittered like tears. They thudded onto the draining board, heavy as a heartbeat.

It was barely evening, but I crawled into bed. Depression-stupefied, weary and hopeless, I should have slept.

But I was strangely restless. Slightly tearful. And troubled by wayward thoughts.

Depression was thoughtless, tearless, an animal's uncomprehending pain.

Some hours later, I realised.

I wasn't depressed. I was sad.

This little piece of hurt was all my own.

I lay there, in the dark, rolling the idea across my mind like a pearl.

SOMETIMES

I would wake in the middle of the night, or pause arrested in my day, because my skin would shiver with the memory of a touch.

As though it wanted to tell me something.

DAYS

The ideas unfurled across my whiteboard and, slowly at first, I wrote them down, letter by letter until I had sentences, paragraphs, chapters.

Amy said it felt different from the others. More about people than puzzles.

She said she liked it.

And I liked writing it, my every word a piece of broken mirror, showing me a glimpse of Darian.

SUMMER

One day, after meeting Max for coffee, I stumbled down a back alley in Soho to get away from the crowds, having formed the erroneous impression that this would constitute a shortcut rather than a descent into hell. Somewhere between Eros Movie

Rental, the French Pussy "Private Dancing" café, and a sex shop called The Whack Shack, I found myself staring at a small red door. It was edged in flaking gold and opened onto a narrow staircase leading who knew where. The reason I'd stopped at all was because the sign above the door read "Alice in Inkland."

I was not in the habit of wandering, at random, into mysterious buildings in Soho, and years spent trying to rationalise the ever-spinning fairground ride of my depression had left me with a deep wariness of impulsive behaviour. Impetuous to insane was too narrow a line, too easy a step. My first thought, as I hesitated (curious and curiouser) on the threshold of that odd little door, was that perhaps it didn't exist. There weren't any passersby so there was no way to subtly re-orientate myself by the road markers of other people's behaviour. But I did have my phone, and a cursory Google search confirmed that there was, indeed, a newly opened tattoo parlour in Soho called Alice in Inkland.

Which at least meant that I wasn't slipping heedlessly into mania.

I couldn't have explained why, but I went inside. At the top of the staircase was a tiny, red-painted room, the walls liberally plastered with posters, photographs, flyers, and glass-fronted frames containing what I presumed had to be tattoo...art? There was a counter against the far wall, carved with the words "Then fill up the glasses with treacle and ink." There was also nobody there.

Thank fuck.

I turned to leave.

"Can I help you?"

I turned, like a thief caught in the act. From a door I hadn't noticed, a woman I presumed to be the owner had emerged. She was, frankly, enormous. With hair as red as a poinsettia plant. She was wearing a sleeveless top that showed the tattoos that swirled, bright and savage, up her arms and across her shoulders.

I blinked, stammered, and gestured ineffectually with my hands.

"Riiiight. See, this is why I don't do walk-ins. Same reason I won't shag you if you're drunk."

"Um. Pardon? I'm not drunk. Not that I want to shag you. No offence. I'm just not into. Women. Um. Pardon?"

"I'm not something you regret in the morning."

"I'll be going." I indicated the door.

But her voice called me back. "What did you want, anyway?"

Darian. World peace. Actually, fuck world peace. Darian. "I think I...wanted a tattoo."

"I got that much from you walking into a tattoo parlour."

"Oh, right."

She folded her arms. "What did you have in mind, bozo?"

I felt heat surge to my cheeks. This was exactly why I didn't do impulsive. "I sort of wanted a name."

Her eyes made a lazily appraising journey from mine to my toes, and then back up again. "That sounds like a story."

"It's not a story. It's an epilogue."

"I'm an artist, not a stonemason." She made an illustrative gesture in my direction. "And that's a body, not a tombstone."

"All the same."

"Again: art, not therapy."

I arched a brow at her. "Art is therapy."

She was silent a moment. "What's your name?"

"A.A. Winters."

"What, the novelist?"

Too late now. "Yes."

"I dig your books. I enjoy a good mystery. But I don't know why you keep murdering everybody your detective likes."

"It's so I don't have to bother with character development. Are you going to do this, or not?"

She snorted like a particularly peeved Minotaur. "So you can laser me off when you have a change of heart?"

"I don't think my heart is changing any time soon."

"Hmm."

"Just out of curiosity," I said at last, "how do you make any money at this? For a tattoo artist, you seem pretty reluctant to do any tattooing."

"For a man claiming he wants a tattoo, you seem pretty reluctant to get a tattoo."

"Touché. But actually," I said, surprising myself, "I'm not." And it was true. I nearly laughed. At least there would be something on my arms that was the consequence of a rational choice. If whatever I felt for Darian could in any way be described as rational.

"Have you given any thought to a style? A look? Placement?"

"I honestly don't care." I was giddy with my own power. "Just don't put it in a big red heart and we're good."

She gave me a vicious glare, stomped round to her counter, pulled out a book, and slammed it down. "Look at my portfolio, mister. Look at it."

I looked.

"Do you see anything in there resembling a big red heart?"

"No."

I turned the pages. Her work was rather striking.

"Do you actually know anything about this at all?" she asked suddenly.

"No."

She flapped an impatient hand at me. "Did the internet pass you by? Oh, wait, I know, you're a time traveller. You're dressed like one."

"Yes, yes, I'm a Time Lord. Now, can I have a tattoo?"

"You should research shit before you jump right in. I could be any sort of unsanitary incompetent."

"I suspect—" I closed her book and passed it back across the counter. "—if you were an unsanitary incompetent, you'd be gleefully branding me right now."

There was a long silence.

I stooped to base manipulation. "Look, if you don't, I'll find an unsanitary incompetent."

She stared at me through narrowed eyes. "Okay. Come on through."

I followed her into the second room. In contrast to the first, I felt like I'd turned up unexpectedly at the dentist. Everything was very neat and precisely laid out. In one corner there was a sink area and an autoclave, in the other a bench laid with inks and equipment. I took the big padded chair in the middle. It reminded me weirdly of getting ECT.

"What's your name?" I heard myself ask.

"I go by Alice."

I suppose I should have guessed.

When she was done at the sink, she came and sat down next to me. "Not your arse then?" She lifted her brows wickedly.

"Forearm will do, thank you very much."

I peeled off my jacket, rolled up my sleeve, and turned my hand palm up.

"Want me to cover this up for you?" She tapped my scar.

In case of emergency, break skin?

"So I can look like someone who not only failed to kill himself, but then tried to hide failing to kill himself under a tattoo?"

"It could have been a really hardcore cat for all I care." She shrugged, her fingers assessing my skin for the inadequate canvas it was.

"Well, it wasn't."

We talked a little about colour, positioning, and size, and then she said, "You still haven't told me the name."

"Oh, right. It's..." Why was it so difficult to say aloud? "Darian."

"And how are you spelling that? Don't want a 'beautiful *tradgedy*' going on."

"With two a's. D-A-R-I-A-N."

"What's he like?" she asked.

"He made me happy."

"Wow, I feel like I know the guy. I can tell you're a writer. It was like seeing a word picture materialise before my very eyes." There was a pause. "Do you maybe want to try that again?"

It took me a long time, but, on this occasion, she didn't press me.

"He...he...he's a kind, ridiculous, beautiful glitter pirate. I don't know what else I can tell you. He makes me laugh. He makes me hopeful."

It was only after I'd spoken that I realised: present tense.

"I can work with that. I'll freehand for a bit, and if you like it, we'll go from there."

"All right."

She picked up a pen, put it to my arm, and a ribbon of ink unfurled across my skin.

"By the way," she said, "you didn't ask the question."

"What question?"

"The question everyone asks. Will it hurt."

"I don't care if it hurts."

THAT NIGHT

Across the moon-pale scar that marred my forearm, Darian danced in dark ink, the gracefully curving edges of his name unravelling into a spill of colour as joyful and haphazard as the promise of stars.

SOME DAY

Walking with Amy to a signing, we passed a trendy clothing chain, the sort of place that sold about twelve different types of jeans, and there was Darian. He'd been poured into one of the twelve types of jeans and was tugging playfully at a long, multicoloured scarf. Like most of his work, it was a careful piece of self-composition, but there was enough of my Darian, in the smile and in the eyes, that I had to look away.

"I banged a model," I said. "Check me."

But, somehow, the words didn't come out right and I just sounded sad.

SOME OTHER DAY

I was sitting by the bar, reading *100% Essex: Doing It the Essex Way* on my Kindle (for research), essentially on-call for the latest of Niall's inevitably disastrous dates. He was over by the window and had already run his hand through his hair three times—which either meant he was flirting or it was the signal for "Help, get me out of here." In retrospect, it had been a bad choice of signal. Next time I would suggest quacking like a duck if he wanted the date to end, which would send a clear message and come with the added benefit of not requiring my involvement.

"C-can I maybe buy you a drink?"

Without looking up, I quirked a finger in the direction of my Coke (full fat, not diet, with ice, and lime not lemon). "I've already got one."

"Oh. Yes." A nervous laugh. "I didn't really think that through."

Relenting, I put down my Kindle. "It's quite a context-dependent line."

"What would you suggest?" asked the Adonis at my side.

Dear God. Those eyes. That mouth. That body. Oh, that body. And he seemed to be talking to me. I waited for my libido to notice, but it lay there like a dead cat in a basket, and all the prodding in the world wouldn't rouse it.

This was officially fucking ridiculous.

And I couldn't keep staring at him, waiting for my cock to get with the programme. "How about..." I held out my sleeve, running a thumb lightly over the fabric. "What do you call this?"

"Um. A jacket? A sleeve? A really nice suit?"

"Steady on, we're not playing charades with auntie. The material."

"Oh, right. I'd say..." He touched it delicately with a forefinger. "Super 120 wool."

 "I like a man who knows his fabric, but the correct answer was...boyfriend material."

There was a not-quite-awkward silence.

"I think you ruined my delivery," I said. "Normally I'm beating them off with sticks after that one."

"I believe it," he replied, with just enough irony to almost make me smile. "David," added the divine creature, holding out a hand for me to shake.

"A.A. Win—Actually, call me Ash."

"What do you do, Ash?"

"I'm a writer, I supply terrible pickup lines to strange men in bars, and I'm a bipolar depressive."

"I'm a freelance web designer, and, err, I have OCD actually."

"What a relief we can't breed together."

He gave a startled laugh. "It's not so bad. It's not crippling or anything. Just really annoying for whoever I'm dating."

"I'm not looking for a relationship, David." Well, that was blunt. I winced. The man had barely said hello.

But he was, if anything, even more embarrassed than I was. He slapped a hand over his mouth. "Oh, shit. That sounded like I was coming on way too strong." He gave a lopsided smile, far too sheepish for a man who looked like a walking wet dream. One of his front teeth was slightly crooked. Before I'd met Darian, I would never have noticed. "Bunny-boiling comments aside," he said, "I'm not necessarily looking for a relationship either."

His eyes lingered on my mine, his smile curving suggestively.

I re-checked my libido for signs of life. There was nothing. I thought about going with him anyway.

But I didn't want to.

Fuck. Did this mean I'd grown as a person?

"I'm probably going to regret this for the rest of my life," I said, "because you are seriously the most gorgeous man who has ever failed to pull me, but...I don't think I'm looking for that either."

To his credit, he didn't drop me like a plastic carrier bag. "Just out of something?"

"I wasn't even in it."

"Oh, those are the worst kind." He slipped gracefully onto the barstool next to me, moved the menu into alignment with the beer mats, and then hastily disarranged them again.

"I can't even bring myself to rebound," I said, pretending I hadn't noticed. "I'm just sort of stuck."

"What happened?"

"Bloody hell, I've turned into one of those wounded men who sit around in bars and whinge on about their broken hearts to hotties they should be fucking."

"It's fine. Really. I think one chat-up per night, maybe per year, is about my limit."

So I told him. Or, at least, I started. But then Niall flopped down onto the other free seat and interrupted by yelling at me. "What the hell was that? Where was my rescue? He could have been psycho."

"Was he?"

"No, just another closeted stockbroker with submission fantasies."

"I thought you liked him." I shrugged. "You usually flick your hair about when you fancy someone."

"I do not!" He tried to lean casually past me so he could see David. Subtle, Niall, subtle. "So, what were you two talking about?"

I tried to sound casual. "Oh, nothing much."

"Nothing much? I know what that means. Can you please stop moping about Darian?"

I hung my head. "I can't help it, I'm sorry."

"For God's sake, why don't you just apologise?"

"Because...because...I can't. Because then it'll be over."

Niall pulled over my Coke and took a gulp. "It's already over. You're not with him, are you? And look at it this way: if he feels about you even a little bit of the way you feel about him, he'll understand. And if he doesn't, you owe the poor bastard an apology anyway. Because you were a shitbag."

"What did you do?" asked David, wide-eyed.

Before I could explain, Niall jumped in. "You know that bit in the Bible when they're all like, 'Hey Peter, do you know this Jesus bloke?' and he's like, 'Hell, no.' It was like that, but even worse."

"My word."

Niall abandoned even a pretence of subtlety, put his elbows on the bar, and peered around me. David gave him a little wave, and Niall sat back with a stunned expression on his face. He ran a hand through his hair.

"Shut up, both of you." It was hard to look stern in two different directions, but I think I managed it. "I make one slightly hyperbolic comparison and I never hear the end of it. By the way, Niall, David, David, Niall." Hmm. Payback time. "David's a web designer. Niall works for a charitable trust. He particularly enjoys blonds and people with issues, so..." I made a *you two should totally shag* gesture. And grinned as Niall went bright red.

"I can't believe you said that," he muttered. "You are just the worst friend ever."

David laughed. "We should probably get married. It'll make a great story to tell the grandkids."

"What?" Niall was still visibly flustered which I probably should not have been enjoying to the degree I was. "It was all going really well until my arse of a mate decided to throw me to the wolves and that stole your heart away?"

"Come on," I protested, "it was funny." But they weren't paying much attention to me.

"So, what kind of charity do you work for?" asked David.

"We're an independent educational equality think tank. We could, ah, do with a new website actually." Niall fiddled with the straw in my Coke glass. "Perhaps you could come and...maybe... do some consulting for us. We could discuss it, um, over dinner?"

I felt almost sorry for him. He'd gone the ashen colour of a man stuck in the middle of a dreadful line but unable to get out without finishing it.

"I'd love to take a look at your website." Perhaps David found ineptitude endearing. "And I'd love to go for dinner."

Niall grinned sappily. "Then it's a date."

"I thought you said it was a consultation."

"It's a date. For a consultation." He paused. "Oh fuck it. Fine. It's a date, all right? Come on a date with me. Save me from myself. I clearly need help." Belatedly, Niall seemed to remember I still existed. "Err, we're going to get some food. Do you want to come?"

"Do I want to be the third wheel on your consultative date consultation date? Now let me think about it. No." I gave Niall's arm a quick squeeze. "And, anyway, I'm washing my hair."

I left them to it.

NIGHT

Sleepless, staring at the ill-shapen lump of the glardigan hanging from the top of my wardrobe door, Niall's words echoing incessantly in my mind, Darian's camera-caught smile burning behind my eyes.

What was he doing? Did he ever think of me? Had he waited in Cambridge? Or longer than that? For the apology I was too ashamed to give. And then what? Had time and memory diminished me for him, taken the sting from my cruelty, the edge from my passion, until I was no longer a lover or a villain but some incidental character who had played a minor role in a life that told itself elsewhere? Was I nothing but the posh nutter who'd slept with him and then been pointlessly rude about it?

If that was true, why would he not fade for me? Was this to be my punishment? He would move on, forget me, and be happy, and I would live like this, trapped within my wasted days, while the world cast at my feet the bright reflections of his image like shells from the receding tide.

His still-unframed photograph was propped on my bookshelf, as it had been from the day he'd given it to me. I had tried to throw it away and, when that had failed, to put it away. But there it was.

Every day, I told myself it was better this way. I'd as good as saved him, and probably myself. Whatever we'd had, it'd been a thing with no future, because I have no future, merely a dreary present that Darian Taylor had briefly made brighter.

I wondered if he suffered in my absence, as I suffered in his. It seemed impossible. When my own happiness was a mystery to me, what hope did I have of being instrumental in someone else's? I had tried to make Niall happy once, but all I'd done was nearly destroy us both. And even if I went to

Darian, after all these months, bearing my too-little too-late apology like a cat with a dead sparrow, what else could I give him? Some pieces of truth. My stitched-together self. Once, he had thought he wanted me, and I had barely believed it then. Would he still?

How could I ask him? How could I be enough?

Then I remembered. Essex Fashion Week, my lies coming down around us like hail, and my gentle Darian claiming his right to be with me. Or, at least, the right to try. An unlikely champion, and Niall an unlikely dragon, but Darian had been the only one to ever take to the field for me. And when it had been my turn, I had simply fled like the coward I was.

All I'd had to say was *yes*.

Yes, he is my boyfriend.

Was it too late, now, to pick up my tattered colours and ride out in my tarnished armour?

It was easier, surely, to live uncertain, than with the shame and surety of rejection.

But didn't I, too, have a right to try?

I could tell him I had spoken out of selfishness and cowardice. I could tell him I was sorry. I could tell him he was the only thing in the world I wanted. I could cast myself at his feet, like the spoils of love and war, and ask nothing in return. And give him, at last, the choice I'd denied him in Cambridge: to have me, worthless as I was, or to reject me.

It was what he deserved, and I would have to find the strength to bear the answer.

Ignorance was a fool's shield. Living without knowing was almost as miserable as living without Darian.

Tomorrow, then, tomorrow I would go to Essex. And find the man who had not turned from the worst of me until I had cast him aside.

TOMORROW

I did not go to Essex.

EVENING

I picked up my graduation photo, the one Darian had thought so unlike me.

Looking into the unmoving, unblinking eyes of a boy with everything, and everything to lose, I realised I had become a stranger to myself. I had envied that boy, with all his hopes and dreams, his pride, his self-respect, and his glowing future. I had wanted to be him again and thought myself less than he was.

Perhaps I am.

But, though he was admirable and admired, nobody had ever looked at him with wide grey-green-blue eyes and said he was amazin'.

I could not be that scarless, fearless boy again. But, for a little while at least, I had been someone I could almost stand. Pieces of a better self, reflected in someone else's eyes.

The photograph crashed against the wall, shards of glass strewing the floor in malicious, twinkling diamonds.

NIGHT

Sleepless, of course, infinite scenarios scrolling behind my eyes like a cinema of self-destruction.

The problem with admitting the value of anything was the pain that followed its loss.

And I was still lying, the strata of my self-deceptions so deep and intricate, even I sometimes lacked the power to see through them.

The truth then, stark in the bleak hours after midnight. It would have been noble to cast myself at Darian's feet and ask for nothing in return. But I wanted everything.

Everything. Whether I deserved it or not.

Once, I'd lived a life full of wanting and, like anyone else, I'd taken it for granted.

But, in time, depression had flayed it from me, the wanting, the everyday hopes and dreams, and all the little desires. They became too dangerous to keep, too fragile to survive, and my bitter, barren soul could nurture no new ones. I'd kept only com-promises, the shadows of old passions, things I just about learned to preserve.

Today is a day in which I will not want to die.

Today is a day in which I will want to get out of bed.

My writing, my few remaining friends, the harsh, meaning-less sex I sought with strangers: these were safe to want, and I knew they would not be taken from me.

But a lover? I was so very afraid of Darian—the unsought

miracle—and almost relieved to have driven him away. Yet the wanting remained, like the memory of his hands on my skin.

I wanted Darian. With a pure, deep certainty, the first I had known for a very long time.

Through the darkness, came the sharp, sudden quickstepping of my pulse. But it was not fear alone I felt. It was something else, too rare and insubstantial a thing to bear its naming.

When I was young, the world had given me so much and everything had come so easily to me, that I'd hardly needed to try. And if I had ever struggled against my illness—if it had not already eroded me past the point of recognition—it was in a manner invisible even to myself. Through hospital days, my mother's voice, ringing sweetly: "Just try a little, darling, can't you try?" I hadn't even fought to live. Paramedics had dragged me back from the threshold of death.

But I would fight for Darian.

Sacrifice be damned, selfish or not, hopeless or not, I would fight for Darian.

I had no expectations of success, but I would try anyway, with all my meagre strength.

For Darian and for me, for my right to try, and his right to have me, and because I wanted him. I knew he would reject me and I knew it would hurt, but, even so, that nameless seed was still unfurling, unflinching and full-blossomed in the heart of some long-sealed garden.

21

TOMORROW

I stumbled around the back streets of Brentwood, heart pounding, squinting at Google Maps, trying to find Chloe's boutique. This was such a bad idea.

But then I found it. Bedazzled.

It was, indeed, bedazzling. My eyes recoiled. I pushed open the pink-painted door and stepped inside. More pink. Rack after rack of jewel-bright dresses. Gilded mirrors so ornate even the Victorians would have disdained them. Leopard-print throw pillows arranged on a pink satin chaise longue. And Chloe, in a charcoal grey pencil dress and a set of killer heels, glaring at me. She did not, however, seem surprised to see me.

She tipped up her chin like a woman preparing for battle. "I fink you've been totally aht of order."

"Bang out of order," I agreed.

Her eyebrows veed into a frown so tight it was like standing at the centre of a sniper's crosshair. "Are you being funny? Cos it ain't funny. It's aht of order."

I held up my hands in a gesture of abject surrender. "I know."

"What's wrong wif you? Why would you say summin like that to him?"

"Because I'm an arse."

"Yeah," she said fiercely. "Yeah, you are. I fought you wasn't. But you was."

I have so often claimed that I would rather risk hatred than endure pity, but it was only as I flinched from the fury in Chloe's eyes that I recognised yet another self-deception. Although I had earned it, her mistrust saddened me. There was no safety in being disliked. No solitary pride. Merely isolation, and the acknowledgement of everything selfishness and fear had wrought.

"Is...is he okay?"

"Course he is," she snapped. "Did you fink I was going let 'im sit arand crying after you mugged 'im off? It was—" She shook her head at the unfathomable awfulness of me. "—so aht of order, disrespecting Darian like that."

My heart gave a strange little squeeze. His name rippled through my mind, stirring a rush of memories: the curve of his smile, the flattened vowels that once offended my ears, the stutter of his breath as he came, the constellations of freckles across his shoulders.

"'E ain't been waiting for you or nuffin," she said sternly.

"Is he with someone?" I asked, unable to stop myself.

There was an excruciatingly long silence. Chloe's hands clenched into fists. "Oooh, I really wanna say yes. Cos it'd make you go away. But I ain't no liar so...no, he ain't. But don't go finking it's cos he couldn't be. Or that it's anyfing to do wif you. He's just been well busy wif work."

"I really need to tell him I didn't mean what I said." My voice warbled tragically. "I just want to apol—"

"You better not be sniffing arand trying to get back wif 'im," interrupted Chloe mercilessly, "cos you proper blew it." I glanced up and my expression must have betrayed me. "Omigod, you are. What a nerve!"

I sat down on the edge of the chaise longue and put my head in my hands. "I fucked up. But I know I want to be with him. More than anything."

She did not look impressed. "'Ow many monfs did it take you to work that aht?"

"It was...complicated."

"It wasn't complicated, honey."

I'd never heard someone use an endearment as an insult before. I could hardly meet her eyes. "Maybe it wasn't. I have no expectations that he'll forgive me, let alone want to try again, but I need to tell him."

Her foot tapped an angry rhythm on the floor. "Tell 'im what?"

"H-how I feel." Thankfully, she let that one go, so I rushed on. "And that I'm sorry and I didn't mean any of the things I said."

"Then why you say 'em, honey?"

A question I had asked myself repeatedly, obsessively, and still hadn't answered. Because I can't be trusted?

"We all say things we don't mean sometimes," I offered.

"Yes, we do," she agreed, nodding, and I had brief, ill-conceived hope that I might have won her round, "but it's fings like 'no, you look good as a brunette,' and 'no, you 'aven't got a big bum,' not fings like 'I'm only wif him cos he's cheaper than a prostitute.'"

"It was because I was scared, okay?" I pulled convulsively at my cuffs. "Because it was easier to pretend I didn't care than admit I did."

Chloe watched me squirm without much sympathy. "I fink that's pafetic. Well pafetic. I don't care what Robbie Williams finks abaht it."

"To be honest, I haven't asked him." I took a deep breath. "Will you please tell me where I can find Darian? Or give me his number. Or something? Anything?"

"If it was up to me," she said flatly, "I wouldn't."

"Well, it is kind of up to you," I pointed out.

"Well, no, it ain't. It's up to Darian. Cos if you wonnid to talk to 'im and I was like 'no way, cos you're a dickhead,' it'd be like in that movie where Leonardo DiCaprio is all...y'know—" She held up her hands and looked sadly at the ceiling, doing quite a good impression of a frozen, dead Leonardo DiCaprio sinking slowly into the depths of the ocean.

"What, *Titanic?*"

"Oh no, not that one. The uvver one." She thought about it for a moment. "Where he's trying to get it togevver wif this girl but she has to pretend to be dead or whateva and there's a message what says 'I'm not really dead, just faking,' but he don't get it and it's all bad."

"You mean," I asked carefully, "*Romeo and Juliet.*"

"Yeah, and don't look at me like that cos at school we done the one wif the witches. But the point is, I fink Darian shouldn't talk to you like ever again, but that's up to him, innit?"

"That's a very enlightened attitude."

"Yeah, it is." She nodded gravely. "And if you hurt 'im again, I'll cut your bollocks off."

My eyes fell on a pair of dress shears lying by the till. "Right."

"He's probably at home wif Nanny Dot."

"Of course. He lives with his grandmother. I should have guessed."

Dear God. Of all the men in the world, why did I want this one above all others? A glottal-stopping glitter pirate who still lived with his grandmother. In Essex. A joke, it had to be a cosmic joke. But it didn't feel like a joke. It felt like the realest thing I'd known for a long time. The clearest and the simplest. As though everything else was white noise.

Chloe scowled at me, and even through the Botox, it was ferocious. "Well, where else is 'e supposed to live?"

"I don't know. With friends? By himself, like a normal twenty-three-year-old?"

"Then who'd look after Nanny Dot? She 'ad a fall."

"His parents?" I shrugged.

Her eyes burned like twin fires. "'E don't know who 'is dad is and 'is mum left when 'e was two."

There was a silence so awful that a girl came in, presumably to buy one of the interchangeable, tiny dresses, took one look at us, and ran out again, wedges clattering on the wooden floor.

"I didn't know."

"It ain't a secret, honey."

There was another gruelling silence. Chloe's gaze was as unwavering as a spotlight. "You really hate me, don't you?"

She considered it. "I don't fink I hate you. I just don't fink you're a very nice person. And that ain't got nuffin to do wif being bipolar depressed."

"I know. And you're right."

"I fink you really let down Stephen Fry."

"I did. Also probably Robbie Williams." Her eyes narrowed, like insincerity-seeking laser beams. I quickly changed tack. "And I hurt Darian, I know. I'm not trying to make excuses—"

"You better not."

"I'm not. I have no excuses. Just a world of shame. But what I was going to say was that—" I paused, twisting my fingers painfully together, my nails catching at my skin. "—it's difficult, sometimes, for me to understand that I have the power to hurt someone. You see, it requires me to accept that somebody might like me in the first place."

She blinked, the coal black fronds of her lashes drifting up and down like palm leaves stirred by a desert storm. "I fought you was okay before you was a dick for no reason," she said gently. "And Darian finks you're some kinda super-genius sex god, so you must be doing summin ahwight somewhere."

"He...he what?"

"But," she pressed on, refusing to indulge me with more enchanting stories about what Darian used to think of me, "what are you saying all this to me for?"

"Well, you still haven't told me his address."

"Suppose I 'ave to." She picked up a pink, sparkly business card, turned it over, and scribbled on the back with a pink, fluffy pen.

I escaped a few minutes later, Chloe's final warning tolling in my ears: "You better not make me regret giving you that glardigan, honey." Safely out of sight of the shop window, I leaned against a wall, gasping a little, clutching the card in a sweating hand.

Now would be a really bad time to have a panic attack.

Unlike all the really good times to have a panic attack, which were myriad.

All I had to do was find Darian, try to make him understand why I'd done what I'd done, tell him I was sorry, listen to whatever he wanted to say to me (most likely "fuck you"), and leave again. And, somehow, in the middle of it all, find an opportunity to throw myself at his feet to prove that, in my hopeless, ramshackle way, I truly cared.

That did not require the courage of Ajax.

So, why was I about to collapse in the middle of Ropers Yard? I slipped the card into my breast pocket to keep it safe and tried to steady my breathing.

The truth was, Chloe had shamed me, not so much with harsh words, but by her actions. She'd given me Darian's contact details because she believed in his right to decide what he wanted. When had I ever done that? Even in Cambridge, I had put my pain above his and run away rather than face his anger or his hurt. I'd used him, and hidden myself from him, and finally betrayed him. Partially, yes, in the solipsism of depression, unable to see beyond my illness into a world in which other people were something more than hazy shadows cast across my sky. But mainly out of selfishness and fear, ingrained habits of self-protection turned in upon themselves like septic toenails.

The worst of it was, I was still doing it.

If I truly wanted to be with Darian, it had to be his choice, ☆ as much as it was mine. I couldn't keep manipulating him and deceiving him and trying to present myself as better than I was. I had to stand in front of him, in all my ugly, twisted selfhood, and tell him I wanted him. And hope, against everything I believed possible, that he could want me back.

That *did* require the courage of Ajax. And my heart was spinning like a Catherine wheel.

I simply couldn't imagine him saying yes. It had taken far too long, but I was, at last, capable of recognising that what I felt for Darian was real, not just a delusion born of madness or sex or loneliness or despair. He truly made me happy and, perhaps, I had the power to do the same for him. Not long ago, the idea that I could affect someone's life would have terrified me. Now I merely wanted to deserve that trust. Darian had treated me as though he'd had no fear of any pain I might cause him. Or, rather, that he believed I was worth it. And I had been too afraid, too lost, to see either his courage or his generosity.

What had he said? *Sadness is just a fing what 'appens.* Well, now it was my turn to open my heart and let him reject me, if that was what he wanted. I could bear a little pain for him, surely? For someone who—for a few shining moments—had helped me remember what it was like to feel human, happy, and hopeful.

I closed my eyes. Breathe, Ash, breathe.

And slowly, slowly, like watching toothpaste miraculously fold itself back into the tube, I pushed away the panic.

Then I walked towards High Street and hailed a taxi.

22

TEN MINUTES LATER

I was staring at the stained glass insert of Darian's grandmother's front door, trying to find both my courage and the sticking place. I didn't know how long I stood there. I probably looked like a very nervous door-to-door salesman. Or like I was casing the joint. Finally, in a rush of frantic energy that was closer to desperation than bravery, I knocked.

Darian opened the door within seconds. "Ahwight, babes?"

I'd been imagining this moment for months. Well, something like this moment, for in my wildest fantasies it hadn't taken place in a pensioner's semi-detached in Brentwood. Through sleepless nights and distracted days, I'd as good as lived every possible scenario: from the one where we fell immediately into a passionate embrace, to the one where he chased me down the garden path with a carving knife.

In none of them had Darian been wearing a Union Jack onesie. I had a vague memory of reading an article in *The Independent* about the sudden and inexplicable popularity of adult romper suits, but I'd never imagined I'd see someone actually wearing one. The Norwegians really did have a lot to answer for.

I stared at him. "You look like the British National Party's Easter Bunny."

He cast a proud glance downwards. "It's well safe, innit?"

"Not the word I was reaching for."

He smiled, a little uncertain, a little sad, and I realised I'd lost the right to be heedlessly insulting and watch him laugh it off because it would never have occurred to him to look for malice. I thought I knew self-loathing well enough that its barbs had long since lost their sting. But I was wrong. In my absurd visualisations, I'd always been so bound up in imagining Darian's reactions that I hadn't thought about my own. It hadn't even occurred to me I might just want to fall to pieces on his doorstep out of sheer sorrow and regret.

I stood there helpless and speechless until Darian took pity on me. "Didn't fink I was ever gonna see you again."

"Didn't Chloe tell you I was coming?"

He pointed at his swoony quiff. "This don't 'appen by magic, babes. My 'air would've been a right state if she 'adn't."

"Wait, you did your hair, but not the…" I pointed at the fashion homicide he was casually perpetrating.

"These fings take time, babes. And if a onesie's good enough for Cheryl Cole, it's good enough for me."

Either Darian was so superlatively beautiful that even a Union Jack onesie couldn't blight him, or I was so superlatively besotted that I found beauty even in his Union Jack onesie.

Or: I really was insane.

He took a slow, deliberate step back from the doorway, as if I were some kind of wild thing that would turn on him if he wasn't careful. "D'you wanna come in or summin?"

This had already gone so very awry. There was something a little jarring about his calm when I felt as jangled as a bag of cymbals. Why was he inviting me inside as if I were an old friend paying a casual visit? Shouldn't he have been yelling at me?

Slamming the door in my face?

"Do...do you mind?"

He shook his head. "Naw. Nan's out. Gone shopping wif the ghels."

He stood back to let me past. I was trying so hard to control my breathing, which had gone fast and shallow and terrified, that I somehow managed to trip over the very low, very obvious step. He caught my arm to steady me, warmth flowing from his hand. "Yorite?"

No. Not when his touch woke the memory of a thousand other touches. His hands on my skin. His body under mine. My mouth on his cock. Not when all I suddenly wanted to do was to fall down with him, right there on the paisley-patterned carpet, and never let go. "Yes."

We went down the hallway into a chintzy, grandmotherish living room. Or, at least, what I'd always imagined a grandmother-ish living room would look like. Cosy and cluttered, with over-stuffed sofa cushions and unnecessary end tables everywhere. Knickknacks and souvenirs were littered across every available surface, the tacky memoirs of English seaside towns, a porcelain plate propped proudly on a little stand, showing a badly painted map of Ibiza. On the mantelpiece sat a flourishing spider plant overspilling from a misshapen clay pot, clearly made by a child's loving hands and daubed with the legend *World* [sic] *Best Nan*. I tried to remember if I had ever presented something like that to my parents. Surely I must have? My mother would sometimes put my report cards on the fridge if I got enough As.

Tucked into the frame of the mirror over the fireplace were cards celebrating long-gone but still cherished occasions, and it was impossible to construct the wallpaper's pattern behind the pictures and photographs that covered it. It was like watching lifetimes pass before your eyes. There was Nanny Dot on her wedding day, hand in hand with a handsome young man in a soldier's uniform. There was a teenage Chloe, sunbathing in an extremely small bikini, looking like Humbert Humbert's dream come true. And Darian, of course. From smiling, pudgy childhood to a visibly unhappy adolescence to his grinning, glittering self.

I understood occasion photographs. There was a family photograph in our hallway. My mother brought us all together for a new one every five years. And I knew a framed copy of my graduation photo was hanging in one of the drawing rooms next to the one of my father shaking hands with Margaret Thatcher.

But these were photographs of nothing. A toddling Darian and a toddling Chloe standing, with slightly shocked expressions, in the snow. A tiny baby Darian cradled in Nanny Dot's arms. Darian in his school uniform, eating toast. Darian and Nanny Dot at the beach. Darian and Nanny Dot in the garden. Darian and Chloe, dressed to kill, sharing a bottle of champagne in the kitchen. Birthday after birthday after birthday. Christmas after Christmas after Christmas.

I was fascinated. So many meaningless moments. So treasured.

On one wall, surrounded by the smiles of other people, was a dark-haired woman with secrets in her eyes, her abstracted gaze seeking something only she could see beyond the frame of the photograph.

"Is that your mother?" I asked.

"Yeah. She left when I was little. I don't remember like anyfing abaht 'er."

"I'm sorry." Sorry for not listening. Sorry for not caring. Sorry for being too afraid to care. Sorry for being selfish. Sorry for being cruel. Sorry for being me. Sorry for not being one-tenth of the man you thought I was.

He shrugged. "Just one of 'em fings."

"Did you ever think of looking for her?"

"Course."

"What happened?"

He gave a strange sort of laugh. "Nuffin 'appened, babes. Life don't work like a storybook wif a proper ending."

"You couldn't find her?"

"Didn't look. We 'aven't gone anywhere, she knows 'ow to find us. I reckon if she wonnid to be 'ere, she'd be 'ere."

I didn't know what to say to him. "Well," I tried, "maybe she couldn't. For whatever reason." As comfort—or platitude—it might have been more effective if I'd actually been able to come up with a reason.

But he nodded. "That's what I like to fink. It's better than finking she just doesn't want me, janarwhatamean?"

I thought I'd long ago lost both the capacity and the desire to deal with the everyday pain of other people. There was nothing I could do that would make it better for him, but I wanted to stand at his side and let the world come, with all its minor setbacks and arbitrary cruelties. Maybe, in my frailty, I would flinch; maybe my strength would buckle; but maybe it didn't matter as long I was there.

And maybe it was all too late.

"I can't imagine anyone not wanting you, Darian."

His eyes met mine, clear as the sky, and he gave me a bitter little smile. "Course you can, babes." But before I could protest, he added, "D'you want anyfing. Like some tea or whateva?"

"No. Thank you."

We stood in the middle of the living room, suddenly looking at everything but each other.

"D'you wanna like sit down or summin?"

"I need to talk to you about what happened," I blurted out, finally managing to meet his eyes. "I need you to know I didn't mean any of the things I said, and I'm so sorry I said them."

Darian's gaze skittered away. "Aw, babes, that's ahwight. I mean, it was well 'arsh. But it's ahwight."

Chloe had been right. He was over me and had been for a long time. I tried to think of something to say, stuttered into helpless silence, and, this time, Darian did not help me. Locked outside his eyes, held at bay by his politeness, it felt like a cold and vast eternity. I tugged at my cuffs, mustering what remained of my dignity. "Oh, well, it's just, I wanted to—" It was all so completely hopeless. I was beached by his indifference. I had expected it. It was a fitting conclusion. But, God, it hurt. The true, pure sting of loss, untainted by depression, madness, or denial. "It's not even remotely all right." I swallowed what felt like a sodden lump of words and tears. "You don't have to be nice to me about it."

"Well, my nan always says it don't cost nuffin—"

"—to be polite," I finished.

"Yeah."

"Aren't you angry with me? You should be."

"Oh, I was, babes. I 'ad the 'ump like you wouldn't believe. But it don't matter now." He fiddled absently with the zip on his onesie.

And that was then I realised: he was lying to me. Something else I had apparently taught him.

"Darian." I tried to catch his eye, but he wouldn't turn his head, and I knew it for the rejection it was. "Darian, please. I know I behaved unforgivably, but you have to believe me when—"

"Mate, it wasn't a big deal." Finally he turned. His mouth was tight, and in the depths of his eyes, like a wisp of cloud, there was a piece of fresh pain I had put there. "Not 'til you made it one. I mean, I was well narked at first, but then I 'ad a fink abaht it, and I knew you didn't mean nuffin."

My mouth dropped open. Something brash and joyous filled my heart like fireworks. "You knew?"

"I'm not a total numpty. I could see what was going on. I

only came over cos they was being a bunch of bellends, and you looked like you was in a right state."

"Yes, but I still shouldn't have said what I said. I hate myself for it."

"Forget it." His voice had been brittle with assumed lightness, but now it turned sharp. "If you wanna feel bad, feel bad cos you dumped me in Cambridge wifout even saying 'fank you, 'ave a nice life.'" Darian scuffed his toe into the carpet. "I waited all night," he whispered, "but you nevva came."

My breath caught. I felt, suddenly, a little sick. "W-what?"

"It don't matter."

"Oh God." Of course he'd waited. Darian was the kindest person I'd ever met. Even after everything that had happened, he would still have given me the benefit of the doubt, which is more than I'd ever done for him. How had I convinced myself I was doing the right thing, running from him all across Cambridge, as though he were some monster of my own devising? I'd had my reasons, but it was like looking over my shoulder at depression: an irrational stranger's choices, driven only by the most incomprehensible shadows of the self. I reached for what seemed the simplest explanation. "I should have come after you, but I was too ashamed."

Darian only shrugged. "So I knew I'd 'ad it right the first time rand, and that everyfing you'd said was true."

I stared at him in dismay. It was too easy to imagine him waiting for me, a slender figure on the banks of the Cam, his shoes glinting like bits of star. And then what? A train back to

Brentwood in the early hours of the morning, the words he hadn't at first believed seeping into his heart like poison, tainting all the memories I'd clutched like precious things through these long, empty months? I'd ruined everything.

I opened my mouth to say something—anything—and burst into tears. It was messy and mortifying, and I'd had no idea I was still capable of it. Pressing both hands to my mouth in a futile effort to stifle my sobs, I spun away from him. But the more I tried to compose myself, the less I succeeded, and the worse it all became. "Oh God. Oh God. I'm so sorry." It came out a damp and hopeless garble.

My life had been little more than a parade of indignities. Mania. Institutionalisation. Drugs. ECT. Depressions so deep they had flayed my humanity to shreds and patches. The times I'd wanted to die. The times I'd tried. The doctor who sewed up my arms without anaesthetic to impress upon me the stupidity of what I had tried to do.

Yet they all paled to this: weeping my wretched heart out in front of a man who no longer wanted me.

Then Darian came up behind me and wrapped his arms tightly around my shaking body. It was familiar and perfect and unbearable, because I knew he would never do it again. For my sanity's sake, I should have pulled away, but I didn't. I leaned back against him, like a masochist onto a blade. I took a deep, shuddering breath. "You don't have to."

"Babes, I ain't gonna stand there like a lemon and watch you cry."

"I think"—my voice wavered—"I'm done now."

I wasn't done, not by a long shot. But Darian held me through it. And told me everything was *ahwight*, even though nothing was.

Finally, we were just holding each other, and I had no idea what it meant, or what was going to happen next.

Very gently, Darian drew away. I clutched for him but he shook his head. "I gotta." We faced each other again, across a distance that suddenly felt more like miles. Darian's eyes had that haunted look I'd seen earlier. "Listen, I know you feel proper bad abaht what 'appened. But you don't 'ave to cos it's...like 'appened. And it was nice you coming rand to say sorry, even though it took you like foreva, cos you didn't 'ave to do that eeva." He took a deep breath. "But I fink maybe you should go now."

Oh God. Oh fuck. Oh no.

I'd known he wouldn't want anything to do with me. I'd *known*. And, yet, somehow I'd come here anyway, led astray by a treacherous will-o'-the-wisp that had felt like hope. My heart did something private and melodramatic that I thought might be breaking. "But I haven't explained," I pleaded, as though I had any right to keep talking to him when he'd already told me he wanted me gone. "Or told you how much...how much you mean to me."

Darian had gone back to refusing to look at me. "Mate, I don't fink I care. You don't know what it's like for me, 'aving you 'ere, knowing exactly what you fink of me."

The words tumbled out, immediate and desperate. "You've got it wrong. I don't think like that. Please let me—"

"Ash"—God, my name sounded so strange on his lips. I would

have spun my soul into gold to hear him call me "babes" again—"I don't want you 'ere. Don't you get it? You're doing my 'ead in cos I know you fink I'm an idiot, and I fink you might be right cos I still care abaht you even after what you done."

I still care about you was all I needed to get me across the room as though my feet had sprouted wings, but Darian shied back like a startled colt, and I pulled up short. Touching him was something else I could no longer take for granted. I tried to explain instead, terrified it would not be enough. "I know I've treated you badly, and I know I have no right to ask anything more of you, but I'm here because I still care as well."

"*Still* care?" He blinked. "Mate, if you cared the first time arand, you gotta funny way of showing it, janarwhatamean?"

"I know. But...but if you'll let me, I'd like to show you now."

He gasped. "This is my nan's 'ouse."

"God, no, not like that. I meant, you know, with words."

"Oh right. Sorry. It's just the one fing I knew you was really proper into."

I winced. "I was into all of it. Yes, I loved fuc—" He gave me a stern look. "—having sex with you. But you cooked for me. And you talked to me. And you held me. And you made me feel everything was going to be all right, somehow, even when I was most afraid it wasn't."

His head drooped. "I dunno. Maybe. I dunno. Fing is, I don't fink you ever liked me the way I liked you." I opened my mouth to speak but he held up his hand, and I fell silent. "I should've known right from the start somefing was off, what wif someone like you liking someone like me." He chewed his lip. "Cos I know I'm like...ah, what's the word? Like what olives are like. Acquired taste. Cos I'm sort of a bit orange, and I fink I'm sometimes probably a bit shallow, and I spend like literally all of my money on clovves. But wif you, it was like, if this clever, sexy bloke can see summin in me worth 'aving, then maybe I'm ahwight."

"Darian, you're more than all right. You're—" I looked up wildly. "—amazin'."

"But," he finished, ignoring me, "all you ever saw was a bargain basement bang."

He was so right and so wrong. I'd certainly treated him like one. "No. I mean. At first. But, Darian, only at first. And maybe not even then. In Brighton, you were just supposed to be a stranger, but I kept seeing *you*, and then I wanted you, not the stranger."

He smiled then, but it was not a happy smile, and I missed his glittering pirate grin with an intensity that made my eyes burn with fresh tears. "Brighton, eh. I'd nevva met anyone like you. You was like so sad, I just wonnid to make you smile."

I reached out in desperation and took his hand. He didn't resist, but he didn't participate either. My fingers curled around his, begging for a response. "I've never met anyone like you either."

"Yeah, I've 'eard that one before."

"Darian, please, I don't know how many times I can tell you—"

"Well," he cut in sharply, "I dunno if you noticed, but I'm a bit thick so you might 'ave to say stuff slow and use small words."

What had I done? If I hadn't been clinging to Darian, I might have slumped to the floor with the sheer misery of it all. "I don't think you're stupid. I know I've made you think I do, but I don't, I don't, I never did, and you're breaking my fucking heart." I dashed fresh moisture from my eyes with the heel of my spare hand. "Will you stop it?"

Suddenly his fingers tightened around mine. "Aw babes, I'm sorry, don't cry."

"I'm not crying," I wept. "I'm just frustrated. I keep trying to tell you, but you won't listen, and you won't believe me."

He sighed. "I know I said I wasn't, but I'm a bit narked, okay? I can't help it. And, like, confused as well." His thumb moved absently over the back of my hand, as though he couldn't help but try to soothe me. "Cos it's been *monfs*. And you show up 'ere out of nowhere, wif no warning, no nuffin, to tell me...I still dunno what. That I've spent all this time getting over you for no reason cos it was all a big mistake?"

I crept forward another step, my body aligning to his, not quite touching but on a technicality only. "I-I know what I said at the wedding, and I know I treated you like you didn't matter." I swallowed, struggling with my truths, and staring instead at our entangled hands.

"Yeah?" Darian's voice was as gentle as the brush of his thumb against my skin.

"It wasn't...it wasn't that I didn't care." I bent my head and swiftly kissed the muddle of fingers, half expecting Darian would pull away, but he didn't. "I cared too much." My courage, usually the most faltering and unreliable of flames, flickered into sudden life, and I looked up. It was as though Darian had been waiting for me, his eyes so steady on mine and as infinitely blue as the promise of high windows. "I was terrified, okay? Because of how happy you made me, and how much you made me feel."

He nodded slowly. "Wish you'd just come after me, babes."

"So do I."

"Then why," Darian's voice rose, "the fuck didn't you?" Shock flashed across his face, most likely mirrored on my own, because it was the only time I'd ever heard him swear. Then he pulled himself out of my grasp and reeled away. "I was right there," he finished, not looking at me. "And then I was right 'ere." He took a few loud, slightly unsteady breaths.

How heedlessly and how deeply I had hurt him, too preoccupied, as ever, with my own pain and uncertainties. I wanted to go after him again, as if holding him physically could somehow bridge these other chasms, but I had already spent too long thinking only about what I wanted. I looked after him helplessly. "I'm sorry I hurt you."

He turned back slowly and then shrugged. "You really did, y'know."

"I know." I twisted my bereft fingers together. "I just wanted you so much that I thought I didn't deserve to have you."

"I'm not a Scooby Snack, mate." He frowned at me. "It ain't up to you whevver you get to 'ave me or not."

"I know. It was fucked-up and unfair." I tapped the side of my head. "Kind of mental, remember? But I know that doesn't make it any better." I met his gaze and tried not to flinch. "But now it's up to you, Darian."

"What is?"

Could I bear the rejection? Probably not, but I had come this far. For him. I could do this for him.

One right thing. Let me do one right thing.

He held me in the blue-grey horizon of his eyes, and I wasn't sure if I was drowning or flying, if I jumped or if I fell. "Whether you forgive. And"—oh God—"whether *you* get to have *me.*" Oh God. "Or not."

His expression barely changed, but there it was. Finally. Some curve of his lip or the brightness in his eyes, like the gleam of light at the heart of a pearl. My Darian, my glitter pirate. The man I wanted. The man who wanted me.

I rushed on. "I know I have no right to be here, I know I have no right to ask, but I just thought if I came and...stood in front of you, and explained, and tried not to fuck it all up too badly, you'd see that I...really like you, I've always really liked you, even when I've been awful, and, really, I'm just standing in front of you, asking you to—oh, shitting hell." Where the fuck had that come from? Even if I were the sort of man to make those sort of declarations, I'd like to hope I'd at least use my own words and not those of a cheesy romcom from the late nineties.

But Darian's face lit up like Christmas. "Aww, I love that film." He gazed at me expectantly. "Go on, then."

"Um. What? I've sort of finished."

"Babes, you 'aven't finished, and I've been waiting for this all my life."

I coughed. "You've been waiting all your life for a bipolar depressive to completely fuck up his relationship with you, and then take the best part of half a year to tell you he's sorry?"

"I could've done wifout that bit, fanks. But I do wanna know I wasn't just being stupid all that time for finking you was into me."

Oh God. I finally understood what he wanted. He wanted to actually hear the words. And, until he did, all my apologies and explanations weren't worth a damn to him. It was an absurd situation, as usual, but I shouldn't have been surprised to find myself in it. Pirates only really belonged in fairy tales anyway.

"Darian," I said, "Roland Barthes argued that a phrase as commonly used as the one I think we're discussing is essentially a meaningless signifier."

He blinked. "Right?"

"A linguistic feint, a formula stripped of ritual, neither a thing uttered nor an utterance itself. In short, as a statement, it's without value, and as a promise, it's without depth."

"Babes?"

"Yes?"

"I know you really like this Barfs geeza, but I'm telling you, as like a favour from me to you, this really ain't the time."

"But—"

"It don't have to be foreva or nuffin. It just 'as to be like possible, janarwhatamean?"

I twisted my fingers together, my nails pressing rictus grins into my flesh. "Why? Why does it even matter?"

Darian stepped back across the space between us. He reached out and gently caught up my hands, holding them between us as though in prayer. I certainly felt enough like a supplicant. His palms glided across my skin until they pushed back my cuffs and encircled my wrists, my twin scars.

There was no reason why it should have, but it calmed me, like the weight of his body covering mine. Mindless, I made a soft noise into the silence, and I heard Darian's breath catch in his throat. Somehow, all the distance was gone, our bodies pressing together on either side of my trapped hands. "Cos it does. It matters to me. If you really fink you feel somefing like that for me, even after everyfing what's 'appened, then I wanna hear it."

"Fine." I tried to sound grudging, but it was impossible. Darian believed me. He was close to me. He was touching me.

"But only if you mean it."

I closed my eyes, thinking of nothing but the warmth of his hands. The glitter on his nails danced in my darkness like dust motes. "How can I know if I mean it?"

"Cos you'll know."

"I do know," I whispered, "that you're the best thing that's ever happened to me." I opened my eyes again and there was Darian, waiting for me, through my evasions and hesitations, just as he'd waited one long night in Cambridge. Except, this time, I would not fail him. I would deserve him, somehow. "Whatever you decide, I need you to know that."

He nodded. "Ahwight."

His hands were so warm. I never wanted him to take them away, but there was nothing I could do to hold him there, except hope and trust he would stay. "And I need you to know that if you send me away, I'll go, and I'll be fine. I'll be sad, but I'll be fine. I'll live and I'll write and I'll miss you and think about you, and, truthfully, I'll probably wank over you, and I'll be depressed sometimes and mad sometimes, but you won't have to worry because I'll be fine. I never used to believe it, but I know it now."

He dipped his head to kiss my trembling fingers, and the scent of his hair gel rushed over me, so familiar I might have cried had I not done enough of it today to last me the rest of my life. "I know you will, babes."

"But I don't want to be alone anymore. I want to be with you, if you still want to be with me. If you can still find something worth wanting." I fought to sound normal but my every breath felt like a shudder. I could have stopped there, perhaps I should have, but I'd promised him everything. Even the ugliness. Even the truth. "Darian, I'm still mentally ill. I'll always be mentally ill. I have bad days and good days and very very bad days. Maybe you won't be able handle it—"

He silenced me with the lightest of kisses. "That's up to me, babes."

I shuddered on the sweetness of it, yet still afraid. "Okay."

"We can figure it aht."

"Okay."

His thumbs were tucked against my palms and I wrapped

my fingers over them, squeezing tightly, knowing at last how to say what I had to say. "I'm not here because I'm broken. I'm here because I'm whole. Difficult, potentially undeserving, but whole. And I don't need you, I just want you. I want you"—my voice had gone embarrassingly husky—"so fucking much. And—" Another breath, another breath. "—maybe I love you. Or could love you. Or might love you. Or may come to love you." There was a dizzy rushing in my brain, as though I was about to faint or have a nosebleed. "Or whatever."

"Aw, babes." Darian was grinning at me. "You're totes romantic."

I stared at him, stunned and horrified. "Oh God, it's true. I do. I actually love you. I really do." I laughed. Not entirely without hysteria. "I love you."

"Yeah." Darian nodded sagely. "I fought you did. Then I fought you didn't. Then I fought you *really* didn't. Then I fought you did again. It's all good, babes."

I leaned into him, because maybe I could do that now. It was awkward because he still had my hands, but I didn't care. He could keep them, forever if he wanted, as long as we could stay like this. Foolish thoughts, because everything changes, always, even—apparently—me.

"Is it?" I asked, suddenly too exhausted by tears and truths, too much emotion and frightening four-letter words to quite believe it might be. "Is it really all good?"

"Yeah. You know I fink you're amazin'."

"I'm sorry I'm such an utter wanker."

"Aww, babes, you're not really. You just pretend you are for some reason. I dunno why. Cos you're a bit weird sometimes, I fink."

I nodded. That was a fair assessment of my character. And more generous than anything I would have said or thought.

His hands slackened on my wrists and I looked up to see he was frowning again. I groaned. "Oh fuck, what do you want now? The moon on a stick?"

He still didn't smile, and fresh anxiety slipped down my spine like a silver blade. "D'you mean it, babes? Abaht wanting to be wif me. Abaht maybe possibly maybe maybe *maybe* being in love wif me? Everyfing you said before?"

Sheer, giddy relief expressed itself in exasperation. "Of course I fucking meant it. Do you think I just carved my heart into pieces for shits and giggles?"

"Calm dahn." Now he grinned, that beautiful, generous, absurdly glittering grin. "I was just checking. Cos, y'know, even though it's a totally meaningless linguistic fart—"

"Feint."

"Yeah, that. I fought you might maybe wanna know—"

"That's not necessary."

"—I might feel like being in love wif you too one day. Y'know, if you ever learn 'ow to use a cheese grater prop'ly."

"No deal."

But it was no use. The idea had taken root like a weed. Darian Taylor might one day feel like being in love with me. Like everything else in my life, it was nothing I would ever have thought

I wanted, but I would learn to cherish it. Maybe the day would come that depression would take him away from me—one way or another—but for now, it was enough. More than enough. More than I could have dreamed possible.

Darian was looking serious again. "So, lemme get this right. We're gonna make a go of it. You and me? Togevver? Even though I'm orange and you're mental?"

"Yes," I said. "Yes, please."

And I, once again, threw myself enthusiastically into the embrace of a man in a Union Jack onesie. Darian's arms enfolded me, sweeping me into his warmth, and I pressed my face into the safe darkness of his shoulder. "I can't promise it'll be simple. I can't promise there's any future in it, and I certainly can't promise I'll watch *Strictly Come Dancing* with you—" He gave a horrified gasp. "—but I will try. I know I don't deserve it, but please let me try."

"Yeah." I heard the familiar smile in his voice. "Ahwight."

23
NOW

He catches my face between his hands, his painted fingernails twinkling like stars, and when he kisses me it feels a bit like fear and tastes a bit like tears, but it's as bright and sweet as sherbet, and I decide to call it joy.

BONUS MATERIAL

Enjoy both beloved and brand new behind-the-scenes material as Alexis Hall takes you on a tour of the world of *Glitterland*, including:

Darian's Nanny Dot's Cottage Pie
"Aftermath"
"Shadowland"
"The Glass Menagerie"
Author Annotations

DARIAN'S NANNY DOT'S COTTAGE PIE

For the inside:

  1 tablespoon olive oil

  1 big massive onion

  2 carrots

  2 bits of celery

  3 garlics (bits, not whole garlics, donut)

  1 pack of mince

  Half a measuring jug of beef stock

  Red wine

  1–2 tablespoons of something tomatoey (puree for poshos,
      but you can use ketchup)

  Splash of Worcestershire sauce

  Splash of tabasco

  Mixed herbs what you can get in a jar in the supermarket

  Like one of them bay leafs

  Salt 'n' pepper

For the mash:

  Pound of potatoes (King Edwards or Maris Piper, not weird sorts)

Knob of butter (that's not being rude, it's just 'ow you say it)

Splash of milk

Lots of CHEESE (poshos can use gruyere but for the rest of
us some proper mature cheddar is well nice)

Parmesan (again, optional for them what want to make it all
posh)

Pinch of nutmeg

What to do:

1. Put the oven to 180 (that's C not F)
2. Chop the shit out of everything
3. Heat the oil in a frying pan, and dump in the onion,
   celery, and carrot
4. Then add the garlics
5. Let everything get nice and brown
6. Throw in mince [PRO TIP: if the mince is being soggy
   and getting everyfing greasy you can add some FLOWER
   FLOUR to stop it]
7. Add all the uvver stuff in what seems the right amahnts
8. Add salt 'n' pepper
9. Put summin over the pan and leave for 10–20 minutes or
   until everyfing is nice and it ain't a soup
10. Stick in oven dish (TAKE OUT THE BAY LEAF DO NOT
    EAT)
11. Boil the potatoes and mash them up wif the milk, the
    cheese (what you've grated earlier, you did grate it earlier,
    right?), the butter, and the nutmeg

12. Put the mash on top of the uvver stuff in the oven dish

13. Do the salt 'n' pepper

14. Make it look well good by smoothing it out wif a knife or whatever

15. Bake in the oven for like 'alf an hour until it's all gold and smells amazin'

16. Eat wif bipolar boyfriend or uvver loved one.

AFTERMATH

Darian insisted we stay for a cup of tea with Nanny Dot. I insisted we return to London for immediate debauchery.

We stayed for tea with Nanny Dot.

And Darian held my hand over the table, his silver-tipped fingers curled warm and unflinching around mine, like the promise of uncountable tomorrows.

I tried to be polite, but my thoughts were a scatter of disconnected words, my heart a swirl of cherry blossoms caught upon the breeze. The world spun wildly around its new axis: each fresh moment of our touching.

At last, we said our goodbyes and left together. Together.

It still did not feel quite possible, a dream beyond dreaming, a thing too precious and too fragile. And the train station, with its stream of strangers and its cold, metal geometries, was, quite suddenly, a monster. Rattling teeth and chattering claws, looming walls and receding spaces.

"Yorite, babes?"

Darian's voice came to me quiet through the chaos, and I remembered how to breathe.

I shuddered. Nodded. Smoothed my cuffs over the heels of my hands.

Nothing but Basildon at rush hour. Nothing to fear.

A commuter pushed into me as he barrelled towards the exit. I had already regained my balance, but Darian reached out his hand, and I let him steady me anyway, simply for the pleasure of knowing he was there. I looked up, into his eyes and into the smile I knew was waiting.

"Faggots!" A cry, both gleeful and accusatory, rising from the depths of the station like some primordial kraken.

Darian cringed, the light fading in his eyes, though he did not pull away.

I put my hand over his and gave his fingers a brief, defiant squeeze. Then we walked into the station.

Together.

"It's bang aht of order," muttered Darian as we slipped through the barriers. "In this day and age. It's like...disgraceful."

Disgraceful. I gave a splutter of laughter.

"It ain't funny, babes."

"No, I know. But is that the best you can do?"

"Fink you can do better?"

"Um, intolerable? Unacceptable?"

"Mate, that's what you say when you go for a spray tan and it comes aht all streaky."

"All right, all right. Despicable? Reprehensible?"

His grin gleamed, sweet and sudden as a shaft of sunlight. "Reprehensible. Lie-kit. Aw, you're so clever. babes."

Sherbet-bright happiness surged through me again, just as fresh and dizzying as when Darian had kissed me in his grandmother's living room, though this time it brought with it a swift, sharp pain. "Oh God, I never thought I'd hear you say that again."

"Babes." His shoulder nudged gently against mine. "It's ahwight."

I nodded and tried not to be afraid. "It will be." And, as the train screeched into the station, I put my lips to his ear. "I really need you to fuck me."

He went a little red under his tan and wriggled with some mixture of eagerness and embarrassment. "And I fought I'd never hear you say that again."

I stayed pressed up close to him—not caring what anyone thought or said, not caring about anything but Darian and being with Darian. "Did you miss it?"

"I missed you, babes, being you, wif all your bossy, sexy cleverness."

"Oh God." I clutched at his arm and, at that moment, we both stopped pretending and fell into something that could only have been an embrace, entirely unheeded amidst the flow of people. "Please, take me home."

In the hallway outside my flat, he tugged me away from the door, spun me round, and shoved me—entirely unprotesting—against it, and kissed me with exquisite, annihilating tenderness. It was almost more than I could bear, to have so much, when I had come so close to having nothing. Darian, my glitter pirate, the brightest heart of my greyest years. I closed my eyes, as Icarus must once have done, and was glad to burn.

Darian's hands entangled with mine as his mouth seduced me and his body pinned me. I had missed the way he smelled, cologne and chemicals and hair gel, and the way he tasted, Darian, purely Darian, clean as water, the way he touched me, gentle when I needed gentle, rough when I needed rough, the familiarity of his body, his long thighs and narrow hips, the silken strength of him, all his myriad beauties and all his unguarded mercies.

A breathless moan spilled from my mouth into his, and I felt its echo in the quickening of his heart against mine.

"D'you fink," he whispered, "maybe we should like...go inside?"

I tilted my hips, my cock nudging clumsily against his. "You started it."

"Keep that up, mate, and you're gonna finish it."

It took both of us, in the end, to open the door, our shaking hands tumbled together, half-helping, half-hindering. Two steps over the threshold, I peeled Darian out of his leather jacket and dragged his T-shirt off with such determination I heard one of the seams tear.

"Oi, babes, you know how I feel abaht clovves. Don't go trashing 'em."

"Then"—I yanked at his belt—"get naked more quickly."

One of his boots clunked onto the floor. "See, this is why onesies are proper nice."

"I refuse to be seen out in public with a man wearing an adult romper suit."

Darian slithered against me as he pushed his jeans over his hips. "Love me, love the onesie."

I slid my hands up his chest, his skin alabaster smooth and flawless beneath my palms, like something from a fairy tale. I had fully intended to deliver a cutting retort about loving the onesie being beyond the power of a rational man but, somehow, entirely different words slipped softly between my traitorous lips. "I do love you."

His breath swirled warmly against my cheek. "Don't fink I'm evva gonna get tired of hearing that."

"Well, you did warn me you were incredibly shallow."

He wrapped his arms around me and pulled me close, his lips grazing my brow, then the edge of my jaw. I shivered slightly, though I couldn't have been cold, enfolded as I was by a naked Darian.

"Wait a minute," he said, sweeping his hands across my still-covered body. "'Ow come it's always me what 'as to get 'is kit off?"

"You distracted me."

I went to slip the jacket from my shoulders, but Darian reached out and stopped me. "I wanna do it."

"Get on with it then."

He laughed. I'd missed that too. His ridiculous, fearless laugh. "You're so romantic."

He took my hand and pulled me into the bedroom. He flicked on the light and then halted abruptly.

"Omigod, what 'appened?"

"Pardon?" I followed his horrified gaze. "Oh right. That."

Nearly every item of clothing I owned was piled on the floor or strewn across the bed. My monochrome rainbow: navy blue, charcoal, pearl grey, black.

I cleared my throat. "I...I wasn't sure what to wear...I mean, I didn't want to look like I was, um, trying too hard, but I didn't want you to think I'd made no effort at all either so...I...well." I tugged at my cuffs and tried to smile. "Also if you said no, I was going to come home and drown myself in them."

"And I fought I 'ad a lotta stuff." He sounded somewhere between awed and appalled.

I stared at my feet. "I...buy things when I'm miserable."

"Aw, babes, so do I. Nuffin wrong wif a bit of retail therapy."

"Yes, but I'm miserable a lot."

He turned back, brought my hand to his mouth, and kissed it lightly. "You must've been proper scared coming to see me."

I lifted my head and met his eyes. They were greyish in this light, with the promise of blue glimmering in their depths. "It was the most terrifying thing I've ever done. I was so afraid you wouldn't...want me."

He drew me close. "Course I want you. For a clever bloke, you can be a right donut sometimes." He leaned in and kissed the tip of my nose, something which ought to have made me feel completely ridiculous. And, frankly, did. But, for some reason, I didn't care. "It's well special, being wif you."

"Oh yes, I'm sure it's ducky. People queue up to date clinically anxious lunatics who take six months to—"

"Babes, you gotta let that go. It's 'appened. Done wif. Ova."

I took an unsteady breath, but it didn't help. Shame and regret were caught like fishing wire in my throat. "I'm trying. It's just...hard to believe sometimes."

"What is?"

"What you said." He gave me a look. God. Darian, my Darian, and his need to always hear the words, even when I lacked the courage to utter them. But if that was what it took, I would crawl through the dust of my heart to give him what he wanted. "About it being special. Being with me."

There. My petty fears, so insurmountable sometimes, skittered about our feet like cockroaches. Mortified, I closed my eyes. And Darian kissed me softly over them, like he could teach me how to see.

"Don't be a numpty," he whispered. "There lots of special fings. Like, the sex. 'Aving you being, y'know, like you are...it's like I'm some kind of god, janarwhatamean?"

I twisted my fingers against his. "I love fucking you."

"Yeah, I worked that out." I opened my eyes again to find him smiling wickedly at me. "Not totally thick. But it's uvver stuff as well. Like maybe you fink I'm beautiful whevver I make a mayja effort or not."

"I wanted you even in that bloody onesie, didn't I?"

He nodded. "Yeah. It's nice, babes, it's well nice, being wanted whateva. And, look, you've got us 'aving anuvver deep convo wif me standing arand wif my bits hanging out."

"Sorry." But the whole situation was so ridiculous—and so very typical—that I felt my lips twitching upwards.

Darian swooped in and kissed me hard, like he was trying to pin the smile to my mouth. "And I like doing that. Lie-kit a lot."

"Kissing me? Believe me, that's an impulse you're always welcome to indulge."

"Well, yeah, but I meant making you smile. Cos you don't do it much so it's like...yeah, achievement. Well special."

"Oh Darian. I don't deserve—"

"Babes, don't take this the wrong way, but shuh up. It's all good."

I seized another kiss, swift and sweet from the corner of his lips. "All my smiles, you can have all my smiles, whenever I can find them."

"See," he said, as though it was the simplest, most obvious thing in the world. "Nobody's ever made me feel like you do."

I wasn't quite ready to believe it. But, perhaps, one day.

"Anyway." He gave me a sly look from under his lashes. "I fought there was a plan."

I swallowed, slipped my hand from his, and flung wide my arms. "I'm all yours...*babes.*"

He grinned his glitter-pirate grin and stepped after me. "Been wanting to do this for like evva." Very carefully, he arranged me to his satisfaction, drawing my arms down to my sides and forcing me into a pose I suspect he misguidedly believed to be relaxed, before he slipped my jacket off. He paused, looking for somewhere to put it.

"Oh, don't worry about it. Everything's already a mess."

"Gotta take proper care of your clovves."

"Right now, you have to take care of your—" My voice faltered. "—bipolar boyfriend."

He instantly dropped my jacket onto the floor, and I sent a mental apology to Messrs. Gieves & Hawkes. But I could not have imagined a better cause.

"Aww, that sahnds well nice."

"Being mentally ill?"

"Boyfriend, donut."

Darian closed the distance between us again, the heat of his body spilling over me in offering and invitation. He turned up my collar and began to loosen the knot in my tie. His fingers were careful, as though they were touching my skin, not a piece of cold silk. The faintest of creases formed between his brows as he devoted himself to his chosen task.

"God, you're gorgeous," I choked out helplessly.

He glanced up with a grin and a "Fanks," and tossed the tie over the jacket. Waistcoat went next. And now I was freshly aroused and trembling, my breaths echoing harshly through the silent room. I felt tenderly and relentlessly flayed, made precious by his attention, beautiful beneath his eyes, old scars and new skin, and hopes I had long thought lost.

Darian cradled one of my hands and slid the cufflinks free from the sleeve of my shirt. "Y'know, it was like the first fing I fought of when I saw you in Brighton."

I gave him a somewhat dazed look and tried to make my voice work. "What?"

"Doing this. Taking all your clovves off. You was like so prim, janarwhatamean, and proper buttoned up."

"And you...you seemed like such a nice young man." His fingers skittered over my exposed wrist, and I had to stop and steady my breathing. "I had no notion you were entertaining such lascivious intentions."

The other cufflink popped free, and I muffled a moan. "You 'ave no idea, babes. I'm like Britney, me."

"In what regard?"

His eyes gleamed. "Not that innocent."

I spluttered, secretly—or not so secretly, from Darian's gleeful cackle—amused.

His hands moved to my shirt, undoing the buttons one by one, while I watched, enraptured once again by the star-bright silver at the tips of his fingers.

"It's well nice," he went on, "like being wif a proper gent."

I fixed my eyes upon the far wall. "It's how I know I'm not in hospital. It reminds me I'm...not...ill."

He put his mouth between my collarbones and kissed his way down the line of skin he had uncovered, leaving behind little pieces of heat like treasure pots waiting at the end of a rainbow. And, suddenly, no days seemed to matter but this one. I clutched at his shoulder to stop myself falling.

"God, Darian, fuck me, please fuck me."

He bestowed another of his deep, warm kisses on some otherwise unremarkable bit of flesh. "In a bit."

I jerked against him. "For fuck's sake."

He laughed, stood back up, untucked my shirt, and drew it slowly down my arms, briefly holding them trapped within the fabric. I sealed my lips over a sound that might have been perilously close to a whimper. Darian pressed his mouth to mine, his thumbs arcing over my nipples, until I gasped and writhed and entirely forgot it was within my power to get free of my own shirt. Darian's erection, pressed between our bodies, was as hot as his mouth.

"Please. For fuck's sake. Please." I had no idea what I was asking for. "Y-yeah."

Darian tugged the shirt clumsily away and shoved me backwards onto the bed. I landed, uncaring, on a pile of absurdly expensive suits, kicking away my shoes, as Darian dragged off my trousers and boxers. He scrambled between my legs and—

"Omigod, babes."

"What? What's the matter?" I pushed onto my elbows.

His hand closed around my wrist and turned over my forearm. "Omigod, babes." And then I remembered.

There was a very long silence, made cacophonous in my ears by the thundering of my heart.

"There's some bloke's name written on your arm," said Darian, at last.

I passed my tongue across my dry lips. "Well, we was proper in love. Together for like a month."

"Omigod, babes." His shaking fingers traced the letters of his name. "This is well classy. I can't believe...cos you was like... omigod, babes."

"Sometimes," I whispered, "I think it's nice to have things on the outside as well as on the inside."

"But...but...like...what if I'd been like *no*?"

I couldn't meet his eyes. "I didn't do it to win you back. I did it so I'd always have that reminder of...of what you meant to me. So I'd always know it was real."

"Why didn't you say summin?"

"I said lots of things."

"Yeah, but you could've like...I dunno, if I'd known, I'd've been, right let's go, janarwhatamean?"

I gaped up at him. And, as ever, he caught me somehow with his beauty, and I could not look away. "Seriously?"

"Nah. I needed to hear all that stuff what you said, and I reckon you needed to say it."

I nodded, and, just then, the admission didn't feel like weakness. Not with Darian watching me like that, with his eyes so full of light and so much warmth.

Then, he grinned, and the tightness in my chest eased. "It's still the second nicest fing anyone has evva done for me."

"The second nicest? What's the first?"

He kissed my arm, right over the worst of the scarring, where his name began. "Well, there was this boy who was like just a boy and he stood in front of me, asking me to love 'im."

I pulled away and covered my face with my hands. "Don't fucking remind me."

He laughed and rolled me over, catching for my wrists. His thumb caressed the tattoo, and I almost thought I felt it shiver, as though in answer to his touch. "I fink you're one of 'em secret romantics after all, babes."

"I am not!" I sat up in outrage and he pushed me back down.

"I'm gonna be so nice to you, babes."

"I think it's the least you can do, after saying such vile things."

He ran his tongue over my arm, over the tattoo, and over the rough, ruined skin, my scars and stitches. It was an intimacy I would have permitted no one else, but this was Darian. He could not make it better, he could not make it beautiful, but he left a trail of damp warmth and a shimmer of physical pleasure across all those memories of pain.

I shuddered, surrendered, and dared to let him make me feel.

When he glanced up again, there was a glint in his eyes. "I wanna see it, babes."

"Yes, well, it's right there. Not going anywhere. The mad woman who did it told me she would personally end me if I lasered away her art."

"No, I mean I wanna be wif you and...*see* it."

I blinked. "Oh, right." For some reason the idea flustered me and pleased me at the same time. I'd done it for me, as much as for him, but I liked—no—I loved that he liked it. "Well, never let it be said I am not an obliging lover. Do you want me to lie here with my arms outstretched like Jesus Christ while you fuck me?"

Darian frowned thoughtfully. "Not sure I'd be into that, babes." Then his attention settled on the ornate curlicues of my bedstead. "Gotta better idea." He untangled himself and yanked open the drawers of my bedside table. "You're so kinky," he said happily.

"What a gentleman chooses to keep in his bedside drawers is his own business."

But Darian was enthusiastically rummaging. Finally he swung back round with a pair of—oh, fuck no—fluffy leopard print handcuffs hanging from his index finger.

"Safeword!"

He looked surprised. "Really? I fought you'd be well up for it."

"Oh, I am," I said far too quickly. "Just not with those. They were purchased as a joke, I'll have you know."

"Like your peacock pants?"

"Yes."

"But you still wore 'em, babes."

"Very much not the point. Besides," I added with impressive nonchalance, "those things open with a catch you can reach even when wearing them, which rather defeats the purpose, don't you think?"

"Dunno, mate, but you seem to know what you're talking abaht."

I could not entirely repress a shiver. "I just feel that if one is to be...restrained...then one should feel...properly restrained."

Darian's eyes flicked to my cock, which had taken the opportunity to express a degree of enthusiasm for the concept with a distinct and eager twitch. "Come on." He crooked a finger. "Hands up."

My dignity required at least a token of resistance. "Darian, please don't make me do this, not with those. I mean it. Seriously, I won't—"

"Hands." His voice cut over mine, not precisely sharp, but exquisitely certain. I gave him my hands.

He crossed them at the wrists, twisted the central chain of the cuffs around one of the iron spirals of my bed, and then snapped them into place. I couldn't help myself: I moaned. And almost forgot I had a point to make. "This is ridiculous," I said, as sternly as I could, which wasn't very because my breathing was quick and shallow. "Look, what's the point of a pair of handcuffs when you can..." I groped for the catch, only to discover I was positioned in such a way that I had no hope of reaching it. "Oh God." I tugged. Then twisted. Metal chittered mockingly. I was about to flip myself over, as it would likely loosen the chain, when Darian straddled me.

"Ngh," I said. "Ahwight, babes?"

I was so very all right. "How...how did you know to do that?"

He beamed. "I told you. Britney."

"Oh God."

I pulled again at the handcuffs. I was truly trapped. My heart performed an excited little quickstep.

"You look amazin'." Darian loomed over me, his eyes and fingers caressing the tattoo. And then he kissed me, pushing his tongue deep into my mouth, so that I could only lie there, shudder in my bonds, and take whatever he gave. I strained against him, wanting more, wanting everything. Metal sang against metal. His moans swallowed mine. His breath was my breath. And my heart beat *Darian, Darian, Darian.*

At last he drew back.

"Ash," he murmured, stroking the arch of my cheekbones,

the bridge of my nose, the tip of my chin and then down my trembling throat. "Babes."

"D-Darian." It was about the only response I was capable of giving him. "I love you." Or there was that one, wretchedly trite though it was.

His fingers skimmed my taut, exposed forearms, with their mismatched scars and the one piece of beauty I had found a way to put there. And then his mouth was hot against my body, the sweet-sticky scent of his hair curling over my senses like its own familiar kiss. I closed my eyes and let pleasure claim me.

Let Darian claim me.

Helpless, at my own instigation, I could not remember ever feeling quite so safe, quite so real, my body neither a prison nor an escape, and my mind, my shattered, self-destroying mind, temporarily quiescent.

All I had to do was feel, and it was the deepest, most perfect bliss.

Darian's gift, one among many.

By the time he put his mouth upon my cock, I was a creature only of moments, remade in each new touch, each new kiss. I arched off the bed with a hoarse cry, digging my nails hard into my palms to prevent utter disgrace.

My eyes flew open.

"Darian, Darian, I can't. I'll—"

He stopped at once. A flush gleamed from beneath his tan and his hair was in disarray, the gel partially sweated out. His hands soothed over mine, until my fingers eased and unlocked.

"It's...it's been a while," I gasped, squirming under him.

Darian drew in an equally uncertain breath. "Not sure I can wait eeva, to be honest wif you, babes."

I glared at him somewhat hazily. "Just fuck me, okay?"

He grinned. "So bossy." And reached into my bedside table, groping around for condoms and lube.

"And don't...tease me." I was already more than half-delirious, and I didn't care, for once fearless in my wanting.

Then came the sound of tearing foil, and the soft damp glide of slickening fingers moving against each other in the sudden silence.

"Fuck, Darian, please, I need—"

He pressed inside me with assurance, stretching and preparing, and not enough. Not enough.

I twisted, pushing against him, begging with my body. And this did not feel like weakness either. It felt like greed, like joy, like truth. Not the scattered ashes of my self, but something as real, and solid, as a lump of coal; a dull black jewel with a secret fire.

"Darian, I lo—"

His cock shoved into me roughly, but not painfully, tearing a needy cry of mingled relief and impatience from my throat. I pulled against the cuffs, feeling them rub against my skin, even with protective fluff, but liking the restriction, the faint hint of pain and the sense of being doubly held, both by Darian and the cuffs he had—deplorably—chosen.

I threw my legs around his flanks and pulled him hard against me, until he was fully sheathed. He fell forward over me, smooth hot skin, sweat-slickened, and muffled a soft, lovely noise into my neck.

"Aw, babes, feels like...homecoming or summin."

"Fucking kiss me."

He laughed and obliged, bracing himself on his elbows as he moved within me, shallow, rocking thrusts that made me gasp against him and arch frantically to meet them.

"And—" I tore my mouth from his. "—fuck me properly, for fuck's sake."

He rose up onto his knees, sliding a little deeper. My head fell back against the pillows, between my bound hands, and I groaned in shameless wanting.

"It don't," he panted, "cost nuffin to be polite."

He drew my legs onto his shoulders, stripping my last shred of control. "Oh fuck, oh God, Darian, please."

"Y-yeah."

Neither of us put in an impressive performance, but it didn't matter. He fucked me hard, his hands gentle and his eyes shining, locked on mine and on the tattoo on my forearm. And I came apart in a handful of brightly splintering moments, for once untainted by knowledge of the shadows that gathered on the other side. It was a pure, fathomless pleasure, as rightfully mine as any other, not merely the tatters of a thing other people called happiness, snatched like a thief in the dark. I lost myself and did not fear the finding, for I knew Darian was there, with me, holding me and waiting for me when the light faded.

I pushed open my eyes and he grinned lazily down at me. "Love watching you."

Then he buried himself deep enough to send a shock of response through my exhausted body and came with something that sounded almost like a growl, his head thrown back, my name an incoherent prayer falling from his lips. I gazed at him through a sated blur, wondering how I could ever have doubted his beauty. It was just another illusion, of course, but just then I found it difficult to doubt anything. Even myself.

He eased himself out of me and reached up to release the cuffs. I reclaimed my wrists, wincing slightly at the stiffness in my arms, blood and freedom rushing back with a prickle of pain.

But it was all right. Nothing I could not bear. At least, for now, when I had this too, the promise and the possibility of Darian.

"Oh no." He sat up, damp and tousled, looking anxious. "What am I like? Left the wet wipes."

"There's tissues in the drawer."

"Yeah, but bet they ain't Olay, babes."

"Your cock is spoiled."

We cleaned up.

"Gotta be nice to yourself, babes. It's like...important."

I shoved a pile of suits onto the floor and pulled Darian into my arms. He tucked his head under my chin, curling close against me. His heart steadied against mine.

"All right, all right," I said, as ungraciously as I could while feeling so ridiculously fucking happy. "We can go out tomorrow and get some brand-name wet wipes."

"D'you mean it?" I couldn't remember ever having inspired delight so easily.

"Whatever you want. Whatever makes you happy."

"That'd be well nice." I felt the sharp-tipped flutter of his lashes against my skin. "And I'm gonna need a decent hairdryer if I'm gonna be, y'know, arand lots. And, seriously babes, moisturiser. You 'aven't got like...*any*. What's wif that?"

I hid a smile in my hand and then sobered again. God, he would probably want to go to Boots, or Debenhams, or Harrods for all I knew. I tried to imagine it, those vast, chaotic labyrinths, filled with people and unpredictabilities. And Darian scampering about, glittering, gleeful, beautiful, and mine. Yes, it would probably bore the shit out of me, and yes, it was a panic attack waiting to happen, but I wanted to be there. For him. With him.

Maybe the anxious beating of my heart betrayed me.

"It don't matter if it ain't tomorrow. Just, y'know, when you feel like it."

I thought about tomorrow. Tomorrow with all its unknown challenges. Getting out of bed. Leaving the house. Having conversations. Being alive.

"I c-can't promise."

Darian gave an immense, catlike yawn. "S'okay."

"But I can..." I swallowed. "I can try."

We were quiet awhile. Darian's fingers sought out the tattoo and wandered idly up and down my forearm.

"You know," he whispered, "I fink you're like amazin'. Fank you for being wif me."

I gave him a foolish little squeeze, wordless, grateful, in love, and a little afraid.

Tomorrow was waiting. And the day after. And the day after. And then the day after that. Only so many reprieves until my next depression.

But that was tomorrow, tomorrow, and tomorrow. There were a lot of nows before then, and this was one of them. I looked down at Darian, who had drifted effortlessly into blissful, heedless sleep, just as he had that first time in Brighton.

And, in the privacy of that fragile, fleeting moment, I found myself smiling, just a little.

From the Author

This is a bonus story written specially for this edition of Glitterland. *Readers have often asked me exactly what happened between Niall and Max while Ash was with Darian at Max's stag party. Well, you asked. The answer is this:*

SHADOWLAND

"Is Ash all right?" are literally the first words out of Max's mouth when he sees me.

So I smile as if the reply I'm about to make is a joke. "How should I know? I'm not his keeper anymore."

Except of course I am. He wouldn't have been here tonight if not for me. For that matter, he wouldn't be here at all. It's surreal, the fact I've saved somebody's life. I keep waiting to feel like a hero. But if I was a hero, I wouldn't wonder so much about a quantum universe where I don't go back. I wouldn't wonder if that doesn't make it easier for everyone. I wouldn't wonder if I'm happy there.

"I think I saw him leave with someone..." Max is scanning the crowd, distracted, still thinking of Ash. Then he remembers I exist. "You know that's not what I meant. He talks to you."

"He talks to you."

"Not like he used to."

Am I ever going to have another conversation with Max that isn't about Ash? Is he ever going to look at me and see me? Has he ever? "At university?"

He nods. And just like that, memories are tugging at the shutters in my mind. Pressing their palms against the dusty glass. I see Ash as he used to be, pretentious even at eighteen, with his tongue dripping words like a trophy wife her diamonds. I hated him—most people did—and envied him and longed to be near him. Or to be him. Back then, it was hard to tell the difference.

He was the first person I ever came out to, after my mother. And he laughed. Laughed at my hesitations, my barely-swallowed shame. Called me a sweet, provincial lad. And, laughing still, went down on me. I had always imagined kissing. A willow tree. Moonlight. I don't know. Not this pornographic panoply in a gold-struck backstreet. And afterwards I remember thinking: is this it, is this the great sin? Have I damned my soul, my mother's soul, for this?

But there are other memories too. Breakfasts in hall. And walking home with the dawn chorus. And afternoons when Ash would lie on his back on my bed, with his feet against the wall, talking. Shoes and ships and sealing wax and cabbages and kings. I can't recall what he spoke of, only that I listened, and his words beat their wings inside me like caged birds and—

This is so fucking typical of Ash. Even my present, these few snatched minutes with Max, he finds a way to twist, to taint, to occupy and claim.

"I don't think he trusts me anymore," Max is saying.

And I have to lock my jaw so I don't tell him I don't care about Ash. That I'm sick of talking about Ash. "Do you want to go for a walk?" I ask instead.

His eyes widen, catching an infinity of colour in their pristine depths. "What? Now?"

"We can come back." I smile as if I'm whimsical and nostalgic and caught up in the moment. Instead of ugly and desperate and unremittingly unloved. "Let's go down to the beach. For old times' sake."

"Um..." Max hesitates. He so obviously doesn't want to be alone with me. If I had any pride left—if I hadn't forfeited the pieces of it like deodands—I'd have backed off. Left us both a little grace.

"Please?"

A silence between us that slicks the surface of music. "Well, all right," he says. "But not for long? This is supposed to be my stag night. I can't just disappear."

Outside the silence is deeper still, hollowed out by too many unsaid things, and too many said ones. We edge 'round, push through revellers. One of them tries to give Max his phone number. He declines with a smile and the flicker of his ringed finger. And suddenly a stranger's eyes are upon me too, full of questions.

I slide my hand possessively into the crook of Max's arm. I mean, why not? In some universe, it's true. Max is slightly tense beside me, but he doesn't pull away. Because that's the thing about Max, his greatest weakness and mine: he's so *fucking* kind. He knows what I'm doing—that I'm pathetic enough that I need some stranger I'll never see again to believe I'm the one Max is wearing a ring for—but he still plays along.

It embarrasses him, my stupid game, but he won't embarrass me. Not even in front of a man I'll never see again and shouldn't care about. A man who won't think about this for longer than thirty seconds, who probably won't even remember it in the morning. And yet it's still the closest I'm ever going to get to what some part of me still believes should be mine: the life with Max that Ash stole from me twice over. Once just by being Ash. And then by introducing Max to Amy, which I know isn't technically his fault, but I can convince myself it is. Besides, it's easier to blame Ash than to think too hard about the fact that Max never really wanted me. And, for that matter, neither did Ash. He just gave up in my vicinity and I let him.

It's not far to the beach. We walk in silence. Max still hasn't shaken off my hold or told me to let go. He's probably thinking we look companionable or that if he insists he might hurt my feelings. Which he would because I'm not asking for so very much. Some of his time, a walk, a touch. In that other universe, of course, he's here with someone else. Ash? Maybe he's congratulating Max. Wishing him—us—happiness. But, no. In every world I can imagine, Ash is Ash, and broken, and he'd never be kind. He'd consider it banal. The truth is, I'm not kind either. Kindness is the privilege of people like Max, who have everything easy.

Pebbles crackle beneath our feet as we make our way towards the silver seam of the tideline. I can see the shadows of other couples, but it still feels like the beach is ours and ours alone. Behind us, Brighton is noise and light and sex. But here the shadows are soft and the stones glisten beneath the moon. The pier casts its reflection in gold against the mirror of the sea and my hand is warm because Max is warm. Over the years, I've collected so many secrets from his skin. His too-big toes. The reassuring solidity of his thighs. The fact that the undersides of his forearms are smooth as milk, but the tops are stippled by hair so pale you can only feel it, and when you rub your fingers across it the unexpected roughness is like a cat's tongue.

Max, as ever, is the first to break the moment. "We shouldn't stay too long."

"I know." I say it placidly, though my heart roils with *can't you even give me this.* "But we don't have to leave yet. Do you remember when we'd come down here on a Friday or a Saturday and dance all night? Then stagger out here to watch the sunrise together."

I'm not sure but I think he rolls his eyes. Some of my best memories—times when I was happy or, if not happy, at least hopeful—and they were nothing to Max. "We were eighteen. Nowadays I'm more of a *sneak one more episode of Peaky Blinders before bed and sleep right through sunrise* kind of man."

"Wow," I drawl, Ash-like, "you sound a thrill-a-minute."

"Well"—he gently extricates his arm from mine—"isn't it lucky you aren't expected to marry me?"

My eyes fly to his, stricken. Because I'm not lucky, I'm fucking desolated. "That's not... I just meant...you seem to be really embracing the heteronormative tedium."

"Oh God..." Fervour, and a touch of self-directed amusement, turns Max's voice into a caress. "I *love* tedium. If you ask me, tedium is the most beautiful thing in the world."

I know better than to speak ill of Amy. The optics of it are bad. But I can't resist a little dig. "That's quite the compliment to your fiancée."

"No," Max insists, "it is. I'm not saying I don't value all the other things—passion, excitement, sex on the kitchen table." He's been flinging his arms about to demonstrate passion, excitement, sex on the kitchen table, like some deranged impresario. But then he stills, hugging himself against a chill only he can feel. "It's just it feels like such...such a gift, you know? Having this person who has seen you tired and ground down and dull, who has been there when you've come home moody and exhausted and unsexy, who's had an early night with you *instead* of sex on the kitchen table, or thrown aside a plan to go somewhere or do something so you can spend a day in pyjamas, sometimes not even bothering to talk to each other. Amy's seen all that and shared it with me, and she wants me anyway, finds me attractive and fun and worthy of being with anyway." He laughs, the sound so full of tenderness it makes me nauseous with jealousy. "That's the most romantic thing anyone has ever done for me. The most loving." And then he turns to me. "Don't you think?"

"I wouldn't know," I tell him. With Ash, it was fifty-fifty whether he'd greet me at the door, wild-eyed, his words an endless torrent, the house in carnage around him, or I'd find him in bed, where he'd been all day, a human stone, barely capable of opening his eyes.

Max throws an arm across my shoulder like we're friends. "You will. Has Ash texted yet?"

"What?"

"He left with a total stranger in the middle of my stag night."

"Sorry, you have met Ash, haven't you? That's exactly the sort of thing he does."

"Only"—Max's eyes are wide with naïve concern—"because he's not good at taking care of himself."

"Oh, he knows exactly how to take care of himself."

"Niall." Now there's something chiding in Max's tone. Like I've been derelict in my duties. "He could be in trouble."

"With the Sparkly Epaulette Serial Killer of Brighton? He's probably just blowing him in an alley."

"Niall," says Max again.

I shrug out from under his arm—desperately wanting to be touched, and unable to bear it. "Ash was a slut long before he lost his mind. If anything, his behaviour tonight should be reassuring."

Max's eyes are pearls in the moonlight. Judgemental pearls. "Will you text him? Please?"

"Why don't you fucking text him?"

"Because he'll ignore me."

As if he hasn't been ignoring me for years. "Fine."

I pull out my phone with ill-grace and send Ash the barest minimum message. And we stand there, on that shining beach, as the waves crawl lazily back and forth across the shingle, and wait. And wait.

"See," I say at last. "He's too busy fucking to give a fuck."

"Or he's—"

"Max." I turn his name into a blade to sever his words. The ribbons of caring he wreathes around everyone else. "If Ash dies, it'll be at his own hand. We know that for a fact. We literally know that."

"Oh God." Max covers his face with his hands. I'm shocked to see that his fingers are trembling. "I don't even want to think about it...about what would have happened if you hadn't been there."

I *hadn't* been there. That was the whole fucking point. It was why he'd done it. Because I wasn't there to stop him. "Well, I do have to think about it," I snapped. "I have to think about it every fucking day."

"Niall."

This time, when he says my name, it's full of softness. It's everything I need from him. And all I can think is, *at last, at last*, as he draws me into his perfect arms and holds me tight. His hair tickles my brow. His heart lies against mine like they belong together. I breathe in the familiar, beloved scent of him: salt from the sea, sweat from the club, the warm amber notes of his cologne, and the edge of sweetness that could be vanilla or just his skin.

"We came so close to losing him," he murmurs.

That's when I realise this isn't for me at all. It's for Ash. It's always for Ash. And this is supposed to be some kind of mutual consolation. "You're fucking obsessed with him," I hear myself say.

Max blinks against my neck. I feel the catch of his eyelashes. A trace of his tears. "He's our friend."

"Maybe you should marry him instead of Amy."

I'm needling him. I don't know why. What I expect to gain from this naked bitterness. But Max, of course, takes me seriously. "I love Amy. And Ash doesn't love me."

"He's not capable of love. He only capable of sex and self-harm."

"You know that's not true."

I do, mostly I do. Or I used to, before the years stripped us all as bare as trees in winter. "Can we..." I ask, "can we not talk about Ash. Just for a bit. You're getting married. And we're...we're here too."

"You're right." Max gives a decisive sniff, brushing his wrist across his eyes before he smiles down at me.

And I can't help myself, a shiver of pure sweetness runs through me, makes me gleam like the sea wrack at our feet. It's the first time I can remember feeling something like happy in— well. Since the last time Max smiled at me, I suppose. With Ash, I'm the taller. With Max, it's the other way round, and there's something vertiginously romantic about it. A sense that he could sweep me away like a fairy tale. Not that he ever has. (Or will?) Instead, the old, helpless hurt rises inside me. If we're a fairy tale, it's *The Snow Queen*, except it's Max who drove himself into my heart and splintered there.

For a moment, I think he's going to touch my face. But he just draws back and pats my shoulder. "My marriage isn't going to change anything," he says.

"It changes everything."

His jaw tightens—almost as if he's irritated with me. Which he has no right to be. "What's it going to change? We'll still be friends. Because that's what we are, Niall. We're friends."

He passes it down like a jail sentence.

My nails are biting into my palms. I push them harder, wanting marks, the taste of pain hot and sour at the back of my throat. "You know how I feel."

"I know how you used to feel." He glances my way again, his gaze resolute. "But it was a long time ago."

"For fuck's sake, it never changed. I love you." In that moment, it sounds like anger. "I've always loved you. I always will."

Max gives this sigh, as if my love is an inconvenience. A burden. "Maybe. Love is...it's a lot of different things. Whatever you feel for me, it's not how you feel about someone you're meant to be with."

"Jesus, will you listen to yourself?"

"It's the truth," he says simply.

I genuinely can't tell if I hate him. "Of course I want to be with you. It's all I've ever wanted." Sometimes it's the only thing I want.

He shakes his head. "You don't know me."

"How can you say that? We've been friends for a decade." I narrow my eyes. I'd like to say I'm not calculating how to get under his skin. But I am. "I've literally been inside you."

It works. Max makes a self-conscious noise, the sort of half-abashed laugh that usually means he's blushing. He's oddly tender about sex, the way I used to be once. "I didn't sleep with you to give you a weapon to wield over me."

"I'm just reminding you," I lie.

"I don't need reminding. I can remember it for myself."

"Do you, though?" I can't tell if I'm pleading or being sarcastic and I'm not sure Max can either.

The worst of it is, my own memories have faded a little. I've held them too closely. I'm a sinner in Tartarus, trying to gather water in my bare hands, feeling it slipping inevitably away, no matter how fiercely, how urgently, I try to grasp it. And now whenever I think about it—Max in my arms, his breath upon my neck—all I have left are questions: did he have an appendix scar, or was it a trick of the light; did he say what I thought he said; what was the exact timbre of his voice raised in passion; how did he feel, really? Or does everyone, when you get right down to it, feel the same? Heat and skin and bodies together, and emptiness after.

"Yes," Max is saying. "I remember everyone I've had sex with. I don't see why it can't be respectful and meaningful, even if you're not in a relationship."

I don't want to hear this. I don't want to hear any of it. I take a few steps away from him, letting the cold sea air wrap itself around me. "You know what I think...?"

"No." There's a touch of wryness in the word. "And I have the oddest conviction I'd be better off not knowing."

"I think you're a coward."

Max isn't the sort of man who gets angry easily. "Do you?"

"Well, you have the choice, don't you? So, you chose the path of least resistance. A safe, easy, conventional relationship with a woman."

For a long time, Max says nothing. Fragments of strangers' laughter drifts towards us, caught upon the breeze like lace. Then, very quietly, "The woman is called Amy."

I make an impatient gesture. "I'm aware. I'm just making a point."

"Well, I don't like the point you're making but I absolutely refuse to spend my stag night giving you—someone who should goddamn know better—bisexuality 101."

It's the most perverse of impulses: whatever it is that makes me, in a fucked up moment, determined to incite his anger, and then hate myself the second I do. I wish the tide would come in and wash me away with the broken shells and the mermaid's purses. I belong on the ocean's floor with the most hideous of bioluminescent fish. "You never gave me a chance."

"You see something in me that isn't there. Some reflection of who you should be or what you think you should have. Something I can't give you, anyway." Max's gaze drifts absently over the waves. "We both deserve more than that."

I'd roll my eyes, but he isn't looking at me. Instead, I drench myself in venom. "Oh, save it for your therapist."

"I have," Max says mildly, "and I do." He's still furious with me. "Though, for the record," he goes on, "if you think Amy's my *safe choice*, you're seriously out of your mind. Falling in love with her, building a future with her, trusting her with everything I am—I've never felt so vulnerable in my life."

"All right." I make a gesture of what I hope comes across as reasonable conciliation. I might as well be begging for mercy.

Max is not feeling merciful. "You and I, we fucked. Amy is inside me every minute of every day."

"All right," I say again.

And then my body goes and strips me of whatever dignity I have left because I start to cry. Not the first tears I've shed for Max, but the first I've shed in front of him. And if he truly believes what he told me—that love is abject and unglamorous— then he's never had more proof of my love than he does now. Because the price of learning to weep furtively is that sometimes you can't. Like you've been building up a sorrow debt that will later shatter you, covering everyone around you in the blood-streaked shrapnel of every hurt you told yourself didn't matter.

Max runs a distraught hand through his hair. "Fuck. Niall, I... fuck, I'm sorry."

I shake my head, not quite sure what I'm trying to communicate.

"I'm so sorry." He pulls me, partially resisting, back into his embrace. "I shouldn't have said any of that. It's just...when it's about Amy—actually, no. I won't try and make excuses. I've been beastly. Forgive me?"

It's a while before I can speak. I'm nothing but a bundle of yearning, mortification and misery, sobbing against Max's shoulder. It's typical of Max that he's unperturbed by this. Or rather, he's clearly upset that I'm upset, but the emotional tsunami itself he manages as if it is somehow not appalling. As if I have not ruined his stag night. Ruined everything.

Eventually, I gather enough of myself together that I'm able to look up at him. With an apologetic half-smile, Max brushes the moisture from beneath one of my eyes. I have no idea what to say to him. Whether I should apologise or try to explain or—

"Kiss me," I beg-blurt-demand.

Max blinks. Then leans in and presses his lips to my forehead.

"Properly. Like you used to." Even *I'm* wondering what the fuck is wrong with me. I've never been less kissable.

"I'm engaged."

"Amy won't care. She doesn't even believe in monogamy."

"*I* believe in monogamy."

I slide a hand behind his neck, my fingers in his hair, my palm to his nape, drawing him closer. "Please. I can't let this be our last memory before—"

He cuts me off with a sharp sound. "I'm getting married, not getting buried. And you'll see me at the—"

My lips are on his. A clumsy pleading rush of sex and pain and *why don't you love me.*

He could push me away. I'm clinging but I've no leverage. All he has to do is turn his head, step aside, and it's over. I'll be a discarded heap on the shingle and he'll be free.

Instead, though, as hesitantly as a bride, he kisses me back. So slow and sweet, I nearly start crying again. It's like something from another world, as insubstantial as the moonlight upon my lips.

"I really do care about you, Niall," he tells me after. "And I really am sorry for what I said and for...for everything."

I give him a little push. "You even kiss me like you're making excuses."

"That's not what I'm doing."

"It's what you've always done."

His eyes widen. In this light they're silver, as blank as mirrors. "I've always been very clear with you."

"Of course you have." I hardly recognise my own voice, salt-raw from the sea and my tears. "But you've still let me pine after you for years."

He recoils, too shocked to even deny it. "What? How? You moved on. You were with Ash."

"But it was you I wanted. It's only ever been you."

"Please don't say that." Both his hands are in his hair. "It's too fucked up."

His dismay makes me laugh—not because I'm enjoying it, but at least I can feel it. It's more mine than a tender, star-studded kiss could ever be. "Ash doesn't have the monopoly on fucked up, you know."

Max is silent, the seconds flicking by. "I don't understand how you could do that to him. He'd just come out of hospital. He was vulnerable and—"

"And what?" I snarl. "I took advantage of him by taking care of him?"

"You don't think he deserves an opportunity to be loved for who he is? By someone who isn't using him for..." He breaks off. "God knows. To prove their own virtue?"

It's nothing I haven't, in my darkest moments, thought for myself. But it's different when Max says it aloud. As if when Aslan ripped the skin and scales from dragon-Eustace's back they'd found only more dragon beneath, selfish and greedy and irredeemable.

"Did you really think," Max is asking, "I'd see you with Ash and...what? Immediately conclude I wanted you for myself?"

Maybe? But I somehow manage to sneer at him, "Oh, you're such a good fucking person, Max. The only one of us who ever sees things clearly. Like you don't have this weird little crush on Ash."

He draws in a sharp breath. "That was a long time ago as well."

"Why didn't you fuck him? It's not difficult. He's not exactly discriminating."

"I suppose," Max says slowly, "I thought he needed a friend more. But nowadays he won't even let me be that."

I close the gap between us, leaning up the length of his body, putting my lips to his. "You're no better than I am. And maybe being with Amy lets you pretend you are but that's the future. You might as well be fucked up with me now."

"I'm not doing this with you." He hasn't moved though. His breath curls against my mouth like smoke.

"Because you don't love me?"

He nods. "I love Amy."

"But you hate me sometimes, don't you?"

He nods again.

"Then give me that."

And, this time, when we kiss it's wholly mine. He kisses me like he's trying to take something from me, and leaves my mouth slick and swollen, copper-hot. I'm hurt and exhilarated and punished and sick all at the same time. It's nothing I want, and everything I need, and the only thing I can have.

Our bodies are serpentine, entwined and struggling, as we fall beneath the shadows of the pier. I almost trip over the base of one of the supports and Max pushes me hard against it. The shape—wide, then narrowing—makes it awkward. I'm pinned and teetering, rust and salt grinding beneath my shoulders.

Max's teeth are at my throat. The waves that sweep over my feet are viciously cold. Above us, the underside of the pier is a criss-cross of iron through which the light breaks in sharp porcelain slivers. It falls haphazard onto the shadow-roughened sea and is quickly lost.

"Niall, we should—"

I drag my shirt over my head and let it drop. The wind scrapes its claws down my arms. Max's kisses bloom like bitter roses, each ache exquisite, the only part of me that feels alive. That feels anything.

I want to be fucked like this. If I can't have Max—and, honestly, I never could—I'll be something he regrets. Something he hates himself for and twists himself up with longing for. Something he can't take with him into his perfect, happy marriage.

I'll be the worst of him. And he'll never forget me.

My phone rings.

And when it rings a second time, Max stops. Stares at me almost like he doesn't recognise me. "That could be Ash."

I'm about to tell him later...that I don't care...that he should kiss me, touch me, make me hurt.

But Max pushes his fingers into my pocket, slides my phone frec, answers it and holds it out to me.

Ash's voice—tinny with distance, breaking with fear: "I don't know where I am."

"Ash?" I don't know what I'm saying. "What do you mean? Where are you?"

"I just said. I don't know. I...I've been stupid. I need to get home."

Max is turning away from me. I fling out a hand, trying to stop him. "Can't you call a cab?"

"Yes...no... I don't know." Ash sounds on the verge of a panic attack. "I don't know. I don't know the number. What if it doesn't come? I don't know."

Max, I mouth. *Please.*

He shakes his head.

"Can you come and get me?" For someone who claims to hate begging, Ash certainly does a lot of it, in bed and out.

The golden light of the pier spills over Max as he steps from beneath it. He looks like a prince released from a curse.

"Oh God, Ash, can't you—"

Max is halfway up the beach now. He doesn't even look back.

He just leaves me, as he always leaves me, to drown in everything I can't have. Will never have. Could never have had.

"No, no"—Ash is babbling at me—"I can't. Please, I need to go home."

"Okay, okay," I say, too weary to muster even a semblance of reassurance. "I'm coming."

It was inevitable, really, that I'd end my evening picking up the pieces of Ash.

The pieces of me I'll leave on Brighton beach with the rest of detritus.

From the Author

Ever since the publication of the first edition of Glitterland, *readers have been speculating about what the Rik Glass novels actually look like. I've always hesitated because sometimes I think fictional works of fiction are best when they're left to the imagination. But in my imagination, at least, the Rik Glass books—written, as they were, by a man who hates himself and at least pretends to hate writing them—look like this:*

THE GLASS MENAGERIE

A Rik Glass Novel
By A. A. Winters

CHAPTER 1

There were two things Rik Glass hated: crime and lions. And now those two things he hated had teamed up to throw him a party at a club he hated full of guests he also hated.

He hated when that happened.

Of course the party wasn't a party, it was a murder. And the guests weren't guests, they were a dead body. And the club wasn't a club, it was the lion cage at London Zoo.

His secretary—his new secretary: poor Lisa just hadn't seen that mincing machine coming—had put the call through at quarter to eight that morning.

"Hey Rik," she'd said, "there's a new case. The head zoo-keeper at London Zoo wants you to go and check out a dead body in their lion cage."

"Goddammit," Rik had said. "I hate lions. But crime never sleeps in this city, so I guess I don't get to sleep either."

"Why do you hate lions?" the new secretary had asked, but

Rik hadn't answered. How could he answer? What could he say? It was just an old wound that itched inside him. A memory he'd tried to bury and never quite could.

So he'd gone out, headed to the zoo and found the zookeeper and let himself be shown the cage where it had all happened. The most recent murder, and the one that still haunted him after all these years.

"Who's the stiff?" he asked. Not that stiff was really the right word—whoever the poor bastard had been, they'd been torn to ribbons. Long, thin, floppy ribbons that were scattered around the cage like decorations at a kid's birthday.

"I was hoping you'd tell me," said the zookeeper.

"You'll be lucky if he can tell you anything," said a voice from behind them. Rik knew who it was before he even turned around: DI Amanda Burnham—ex partner, ex lover, all-time rival. "This is a case for the real cops."

Rik glared at her angrily. "I am a real cop. You know that internal affairs fitted me up."

"I know you made too many enemies at city hall," said Amanda. "And that you don't know how to play by the rules. You should walk away from this one, Rik. It'll be bad for you."

That sounded like she knew something he didn't. "What do you know that I don't?" he asked.

"I'm saying you should back off. Back off for your own good." She gazed up at him with those blue eyes he used to love so much. "Besides, I thought you hated lions."

That was the last straw. "I do hate lions. But goddammit,

Amanda, you know I've never quit a case and I'm not going to start now."

They glowered at each other for a moment. Rik Glass said nothing. And maybe Amanda was right, maybe he should leave this one to the "real" cops, the ones who hadn't been through hell, who didn't wake up in the night with demons chewing on their livers. But that wasn't his style—it never had been. "Open the cage," he told the zookeeper.

"But, the lions," the zookeeper said.

"I said open the cage."

He opened the cage, and Rik Glass went inside. The lions lay all around him like oversized golden throw pillows as he made his way over to the biggest chunk of corpse. He was risking being eaten, but maybe deep down that was what he wanted. Maybe he was just looking for a chance to live that day over, to go back and make it so that *she* survived instead of him.

Not that he ever could.

The body was a mess, and now that he was closer he could see how shredded it had really been. The limbs were gone, the torso ripped open and the face...now that was strange.

Rik Glass was just leaning over the body when he heard a growl behind him. Turning, he saw a lion prowling towards him with malice in its gleaming eyes.

"I hate lions," he murmured to himself.

Locking eyes with the beast, he backed away slowly. The trick was not to show fear: lions were lazy, cowardly animals and they'd only attack you if they had no easier option. At least that was the theory—he'd never put it to the test.

And then the lion sprang.

Rik Glass put up his fists—he'd always been a fighter and he'd always known he'd go down fighting—but he never had to use them. The lion's body dropped, unconscious, just a foot away from where he was standing.

Turning back to the door, he saw Amanda lowering a tranquilizer gun. "I'm sick of pulling your ass out the fire, Rik."

"My ass is just fine," said Rik. "But you need to get in here. There's something you should see."

Watching the other lions carefully, Amanda entered the cage. "What is it?" she asked.

Rik went back to the body. Of course there was a sleeping lion right next to it now, but he'd seen worse things at crime scenes.

"What is it?" Amanda asked again as she came over.

"This man wasn't killed by a lion," said Rik Glass. "This man was shot."

AUTHOR ANNOTATIONS

Look for the star symbol as you flip through the book to discover what Alexis Hall was thinking while writing *Glitterland*.

Chapter One

1. *Paragraph begins with:* My heart is beating so fast.

    Alexis: In an early draft, this was past tense. But I moved it to present because, well, panic attacks (or a prelude to a panic attack) always happen in present tense, don't they?

2. *Paragraph begins with:* Later I would see how pathetic it was.

    Alexis: I don't have anything useful to say to this except 'Oh Ash.' Ash was a complicated protagonist to write because he's profoundly unsympathetic in many ways: I think my, perhaps controversial approach to dealing with this, was having him hate himself most of all.

3. *Paragraph begins with:* I sat down on a wall to wait.

> **Alexis:** You can tell this was written a while ago because heroes who smoke are an increasing rarity. Can't exactly image Ash vaping on the street corner, though.

4. *Paragraph begins with:* I'd never meant to hurt to Niall.

> **Alexis:** Well, this is a mood. But it's one I get. Feeling obligated to someone, especially if you believe yourself incapable of any sort of reciprocation, can be really toxic.

5. *Paragraph begins with:* It had made a certain amount of sense.

> **Alexis:** This is obviously Ash's POV so it's hard to know if he's being uncharitable to Niall through his own cloud of self-loathing and resentment. I like to think Niall probably didn't feel that way when they first got together. He probably does now though.

6. *Paragraph begins with:* I tried to smile.

> **Alexis:** When I wrote this, I was similar in age to the characters and I think maybe I, too, was grappling to some degree with the complexities of reconciling who you were, and how you lived, as a university student with where life takes you over the next decade. I think part of what makes the Ash/Max/Niall dynamic so messed up at this point in time is that they haven't fully grappled with this themselves.

7. *Paragraph begins with:* "So when you went completely batshit."

    Alexis: Institutionalized was 'sectioned' in the original draft (as in sectioned under the mental health act) but apparently Americans would have been very confused. I'm honestly not keen on 'institionalised' here because it's not something we say so much in the UK but, y'know, compromises for an international audience.

8. *Paragraph begins with:* "Because I feel guilty all the fucking time."

    Alexis: Speaking of unsympathetic characters, Niall is not exactly covering himself in glory in these opening chapters. But I kind of wanted to make space for the idea that living with someone with severe mental health issues is genuinely difficult in its own way.

9. *Paragraph begins with:* In the past, we are drinking tea.

    Alexis: Oh look, another tense shift, because I'm just... like...so arty. Seriously, though, I wanted to explore the idea that the only bits of Ash's life that feel real and present to him are, ironically, the past and his mental illness. Though, of course, this changes very explicitly by the end of the book.

Chapter Two

1. *Paragraph begins with:* It was a Friday night.

    Alexis: I have a kind of private joke that there's probably a once per book limit on using either synaesthetic or chiaroscuro. But this is Ash so naturally he whacks down both at once.

2. *Paragraph begins with:* They were playing the sort of deep.

> **Alexis:** This is one of many TS Elliot allusions in the book. I'd invite you to try and catch 'em all like Pokemon but I'm not even sure I could.

3. *Paragraph begins with:* All the counselling in the world.

> **Alexis:** This is so over-wrought but one of the advantages of writing a character like Ash is the freedom to express things as he would. Essentially this a stylistically unreasonable description of the unreasonable thing that depression is.

4. *Paragraph begins with:* I pulled out my phone.

> **Alexis:** I've always said I never saw an over-used device I didn't want to use more, but there is so much light/ shadow imagery in this book I'm *almost* embarrassed.

5. *Paragraph begins with:* He was a ridiculous creature.

> **Alexis:** This is a little nod to Brideshead Revisited, another rather overwrought novel about a self-destructive gay man who went to Oxford.

6. *Paragraph begins with:* "Fuck you."

Alexis: I've kind of always had a bit of a thing for writing romantic scenes where neither character fully understands the stakes: I mean, poor Darian thinks he's getting a fling with a posh hot bloke, and Ash is just a desperate lonely mess throwing himself into sex because he thinks it's the only thing he can have. If he knew what was going on, Darian would feel so guilty about the teasing.

Chapter Three

1. *Paragraph begins with:* Apparently my latest book had been well received.

   Alexis: I always feel a bit self-conscious about writing writers, on account of...y'know. Being a writer. So I generally write writers who are, to some degree... okay, I hesitate to use the term 'hack'. But they're pretty often people who perform writing in a devalued context. Although, when it came to Ash, I was actually thinking of Georgette Heyer, who was always super disparaging of her own work which makes me sad because her books are so fun. But there is something kind of complicated about the idea that you should or could be doing one type of writing rather than the one that you're either good at, well paid for or like. In an ideal world, all these things should unite.

2. *Paragraph begins with:* "Gropebuttock."

> **Alexis:** I am at least 67% there's a street in London called Gropebuttock Street but I might just be making it up. Or have dreamed it. Or something.

3. *Paragraph begins with:* I wandered the flat.

> **Alexis:** There should actually be an app for this. Something that undoes all the stuff you do in the midst of a mental health crisis.

Chapter Four

1. *Paragraph begins with:* I met Amy, as arranged, at The Three Crowns.

> **Alexis:** This scene has been mildly, very mildly extended, from the one in the originally published edition. I was asked to trim some of the bants, but I put it back for both flow and character, and also to lend a bit more clarity to what went on at the stag night between Niall and Max, how Max feels about it, and how Amy does.

2. *Paragraph begins with:* "God, no."

> **Alexis:** One of the few elements of my writing I'm happy to say is drawn directly from life.

3. *Paragraph begins with:* There was no way I was ever going.

Alexis: Okay, now I'm actually worried I answer writing questions like this.

4. *Paragraph begins with:* "Don't fink 'e's in."

Alexis: With this line I wanted to hint that Darian does actually think about things, for all that he doesn't express himself in a way Ash deems acceptable. Ash by contrast can drop a fancy quote or babble on about cultural consciousness but he consistently evades anything that would require him to think too much about the world or his place in it. To put it another way, it is Ash who sees through a glass darkly and Darian who knows himself OH DO YOU SEE.

Chapter Five

1. *Paragraph begins with:* He laughed, messing up the rhythm.

Alexis: I think it might have been in reference to this scene that I have always signed my books in purple ink.

2. *Paragraph begins with:* Whatever the internal mechanism.

Alexis: One of the reasons I like writing sex scenes in intense first person is you can fuck the language as well as the characters.

Chapter Six

1. *Paragraph begins with:* I pointed at the jar of Branston Pickle.

    Alexis: I'm not sure where I fall on the Branston Pickle: Food Or Condiment debate. I think anything one can hypothetically eat straight from jar (not that I would ever do a thing like that) is probably a food.

2. *Paragraph begins with:* He fell on top of me, howling with laughter.

    Alexis: Sex with awkwardness and laughter is some of my favourite sex to write about.

Chapter Eight

1. *Paragraph begins with:* "Ash, hi!"

    Alexis: I sometimes wonder whether in the horrendous love dodecahedron that was Ash, Niall and Max's university love life, Max had a bit of a crush on Ash to which Ash remained and remains stubbornly oblivious.

2. *Paragraph begins with:* "That's reassuring, ta."

    Alexis: I think "enjoys detective stories but never sees the twist" tells you everything you need to know about Max.

3. *Paragraph begins with:* "It has to be an impressive salad."

    Alexis: Ash's compulsive need to impress Darian—to impress people in general—is very much his worst character trait I think. It leads to his worst decisions. But it's also a self-protecting impulse.

Chapter Nine

1. *Paragraph begins with:* He laughed.

    Alexis: Cosign.

2. *Paragraph begins with:* "Yes, but what about the future?"

    Alexis: We don't learn a lot about Ash's parents in the book, but I've always secretly thought they were judgy. Judgy while also being performatively supportive.

3. *Paragraph begins with:* I was jealous of the camera.

    Alexis: If we're playing Hunt the Barthes, he also wrote a book (well a very short book) called Camera Lucida, which was an exploration of photography (specifically how photography acts upon on the spectator) and kind of a memorial to his late mother.

4. *Paragraph begins with:* "Lots of fings, babes."

    Alexis: Ash does do a lot of lying in this book, a bit to himself, occasionally to the reader, but mostly to Darian.

5. *Paragraph begins with:* Or try to.

    Alexis: Ash falling in love, the tl;dr

6. *Paragraph begins with:* I sighed to demonstrate.

    Alexis: I've always been fascinated by the secret language of cryptic crosswords. Unlike Ash, however, I don't do them often enough to be fluent.

7. *Paragraph begins with:* "How much cheese do you want grated?"

    Alexis: A man after my own heart. 'All of it' is the only amount of cheese that matters.

8. *Paragraph begins with:* Truthfully, it didn't go.

    Alexis: On the nose, Hall. Very on the nose.

9. *Paragraph begins with:* So I dug out my dusty—very dusty—Scrabble set.

    Alexis: Food and games: the foundation of most Alexis Hall romance arcs.

Chapter Ten

1. *Paragraph begins with:* I could not quite contain a spurt of laughter.

Alexis: This used to be a real thing. I hope it is still—but, who knows, post-pandemic.

Chapter Twelve

1. *Paragraph begins with:* "It's well reem."
   Alexis: Wow, this takes me back to the 2000s.

2. *Paragraph begins with:* "You leave it to me, ghel."
   Alexis: I'm really happy himbos are a thing now. Because everyone loves a himbo.

3. *Paragraph begins with:* I shed my bespoke suit.
   Alexis: Tesco's carrier bags seem to have a distinguished history in my work.

4. *Paragraph begins with:* I stuck my arms through the sleeves.
   Alexis: I definitely saw something like this somewhere which is what inspired it, but I've never been able to find it again. So, err, the moral of this story is: if you ever see a glardigan, buy it immediately.

5. *Paragraph begins with:* "Yeah, yeah," said Darian.
   Alexis: I feel I should note my other works contain more positive duck representation.

Chapter Fourteen

1. *Paragraph begins with:* "I don't want your love."
   Alexis: Jeez Ash. It's like you and Niall are having a who-can-behave-worse-to-the-other competition.

Chapter Fifteen

1. *Paragraph begins with:* "I dunno 'ow she's managed."
   Alexis: I love Paul Delvaux but this is honestly a pretty fair description of Sleeping Venus.

2. *Paragraph begins with:* I dropped to my knees.
   Alexis: Normally I would try to avoid a run of sentences all structured the same way (in this case "I verbed") but it felt important to this moment that Ash was linguistically present. That he is doing, choosing, giving. Finally.

3. *Paragraph begins with:* I pushed him back and crawled over him.
   Alexis: I think this might also be the first appearance of a bedside drawer with revealing contents.

4. *Paragraph begins with:* "Y'know, the wavey fings."
   Alexis: This is a small tribute to Len Goodman who used to be the head judge on Strictly before Shirley

Ballas took over. He always used to say seven with the emphasis on the VEN rather than the sev.

Chapter Sixteen

1. *Paragraph begins with:* "Yes, death is so very ugly."
   Alexis: This scene is really hard for me to read, like, a decade later. God knows how I managed to write it.

2. *Paragraph begins with:* Oh, how I wished it were true.
   Alexis: This quote comes from A Lover's Discourse: "Language is a skin: I rub my language against the other. It is as if I had words instead of fingers, or fingers at the tip of my words. My language trembles with desire". Though, of course, Ash and Darian have been rubbing their languages against each other for the whole book.

Chapter Eighteen

1. *Paragraph begins with:* "Is there any way I could convince you."
   Alexis: To think I would later write a whole book about this ;)

Chapter Nineteen

1. *Paragraph begins with:* "Bah. It's just like a smaller version of Oxford."
   Alexis: No lies detected.

2. *Paragraph begins with:* "Precisely," I said.

> **Alexis:** ASH. I have written some excruciating scenes in my time—Ardy going to dinner with Nathaniel and Caspian, the Blackwood family garden party—but this might still be the worst.

3. *Paragraph begins with:* "Wow." He looked thoughtful.

> **Alexis:** An on-going theme of my work, I fear. Wonder why.

Chapter Twenty

1. *Paragraph begins with:* One day, after meeting Max for coffee.

> **Alexis:** I am somewhat sad to think that if time has not taken these, the pandemic probably has.

2. *Paragraph begins with:* "I like a man who knows his fabric."

> **Alexis:** Deliberate foreshadowing or pure serendipity? Who knows. (It was the second).

3. *Paragraph begins with:* Sleepless, staring at the ill-shapen lump of the glardigan.

> **Alexis:** I tend to have ambivalent feelings about romances where the main characters are separated on page for extended periods but sometimes it's necessary. And I felt it was necessary for Ash specifically, both to push the boundaries of his own

world a little to better encompass the people who love him, and to come to terms with the trueness of his own feelings: love and loss for Darian, and vulnerability and selfishness, all independent of mental illness.

Chapter Twenty-one

1. *Paragraph begins with:* If I truly wanted to be with Darian.
   Alexis: Honestly, I think this is not Ash-specific. I think it's a universal relationship thing. And I think it's the hardest thing in the fucking world.

Chapter Twenty-two

1. *Paragraph begins with:* He smiled, a little uncertain.
   Alexis: I think this remains one of the hardest scenes I've ever had to write. Because the book is so intensely first-person, it was too easy to get embedded in what Ash needed and not think about what Darian needed. But I like to think I got there in the end.

2. *Paragraph begins with:* Knickknacks and souvenirs.
   Alexis: Only Ash would sic erat scriptum a child's handmade mug.

3. *Paragraph begins with:* I was fascinated.

> **Alexis:** Again, there isn't much about Ash's family in the book, but I think you can tell a lot from his reaction to Darian's.

ABOUT THE AUTHOR

Alexis Hall writes books in the southeast of England, where he lives entirely on a diet of tea and Jaffa Cakes. You can find him at quicunquevult.com, on Twitter @quicunquevult, on Instagram at instagram.com/quicunquevult and on Facebook at facebook.com /quicunquevult.

Also by Alexis Hall

London Calling
Boyfriend Material
Husband Material